The Vanishing Girls

Callie Browning

Also Available

Paradise Scandal Series

The Girl with the Hazel Eyes

Copyright

The Vanishing Girls

ISBN: 978-976-8306-01-2

FIRST EDITION

Follow Callie Browning

@BajanCallie:

Instagram

Twitter

Facebook

Scan to unlock the latest behind-the-scenes photos and details.

www.calliebrowning.com

Dedication

Sections of this book make reference to the lives of the incredible women who have influenced me. I stand on the shoulders of giants and for that I am eternally grateful. Thanks to my incredible family for their patience.

CONTENTS

Trigger warnings

Violence against women.

Misogynistic language.

Blood.

Chapter 1
The Light in the Dark

WANTED:
Office Assistant for growing business in Bridgetown.
Must be comfortable around blood & entrails.
Must own a car.
Able to work flexible hours.
Apply in person to 444 Buckworth Street, Bridgetown.

Holden looked at the ad again and wondered where he had gone wrong. Not a single applicant who turned up had fit the criteria. One thought Holden was a butcher; she didn't mind quartering loins of pork but drew the line at cutting up humans. Another lady insisted she could manage flexible hours as long as she could come after 9 a.m. and leave at 2 p.m. since she had school-aged children but no car. Holden ran his finger over the crinkled newspaper and re-read each word four times. Finally, satisfied that the fault didn't lay with him, he wiped his ink-smudged hands on his crisp white handkerchief.

He reclined in his rickety chair, his back to the world as he sighed at the ceiling. Behind him, a large window covered by sun-bleached industrial blinds overlooked Buckworth Street. It was one of the busiest roads in the city, lined with all manner of reputable businesses like supermarkets, welders, and accountants. But at dusk, when flickering street lamps cast a polka-dotted line of light along the sidewalks, the street reduced itself to seedier trades. The steady cha-ching of cash registers turned into the steady click-click of high heels as ladies of the night bustled past, followed by the shameful shuffling of their clients' shoes. These ladies gathered at a grimy alcove next to the pharmacy just up the road. Holden had heard of their existence but had never encountered them.

Restless, he wandered to the room at the back of the building where he kept the corpses. He stared at the space, his mind awhirl with thoughts as the smell of formaldehyde made him wrinkle his nose. Despite being only thirty years old, his life already felt hard-lived. His desperation was so pronounced that he feared it would ooze from his very pores. All of the action happened at the front of the building where the bills were piling up, but the situation at the back was a stark contrast because the work wasn't. The mahogany clock on the wall chimed seven times, each peal a hollow sound that echoed off the white tiled floor. Surely no good could come from worrying about things he couldn't fix at this hour. He fastened the door and returned to his desk.

Holden packed his attaché case with files and took his time turning off the lights. He was securing the last window at the front of the building when he heard a quick rap on the door. Peering between the vertical blinds, Holden saw nothing. He shrugged and picked up his case. No sooner than he stepped outside, he heard a voice.

"I thought you'd never open this door," said the person silhouetted by the streetlight behind her. She was shorter than he was, and shapely, with a crown of poofy hair atop her head.

Startled, he squinted at the silhouette. "Who are you?"

"Eileen. I'm applying for the job you advertised," she said, stepping into the light. Her dark skirt was short, and her blouse was fashionable, even if it was too low-cut to be entirely respectable. Surely, she too had not read the description correctly.

Holden rolled his eyes. “Ma’am, are you sure you’re at the right place?”

Eileen grinned and quirked an eyebrow at him. “Blood, guts, my own car, flexible hours? If that’s the opening, then yes, I’m at the right place.”

She flicked the photocopied ad that was stuck to the door and eyed him warily. “Maybe I should talk to your boss instead.”

Holden bristled, his pressure rising at the inference. “I *am* the boss.”

“Hmm…you can’t blame me for thinking otherwise,” she said, tapping her lips. “You’re trying to intimidate instead of interview, which runs counter to the whole ‘you’re in charge’ thing.”

He clenched his jaw. “This job wouldn’t be a good fit. You’re too…” he waved his hands vaguely, unsure how to say “unsuitable” without sounding arrogant.

He caught the subtle shift of her posture, the steely resolution that took hold and told him that she was sturdier than he thought. “I’m a hard worker, I’m honest and you could do a lot worse than me."

She was right. Clearly, she was the only one who understood what was required. Holden wanted to turn her away, but so far he couldn’t think of a reason to do so other than she was far and away the most beautiful of all the applicants. His reservations about good-looking assistants came from his father, who always told him to hire men or women who weren't too easy on the eyes. "Son, there are two things a businessman doesn't need: debt and distractions. The latter leads to the former, so hire accordingly."

"Miss, it's a bit late, and I don't know if this position would be right for you."

She raised an eyebrow. "Once you don't pay me with marbles, it's right for me."

Holden frowned, his irritation growing. "You won't take to such a gruesome profession as this."

"And what profession would that be?"

Holden straightened his shoulders; he knew now was the time to hammer home the reality. "Cutting up dead people, injecting them with chemicals and overseeing their burials."

Eileen shrugged. "Sounds like how I spent last weekend. When can I start?"

Holden squinted at her; he wasn't sure if she was joking or depraved. Her smile, even in the dim light, was mischievous. Holden thought back on the long day he had. The countless interviews that led nowhere. The stack of bills. The worrisome call from the bank.

He pressed his fingers to his temple. Undoubtedly, hiring Eileen wouldn't be the worst thing he ever did. He sighed and stretched out his hand toward her. She grinned and shook his in return.

* * *

THE NEXT DAY, Eileen drove onto the gravel lot behind the building and parked next to the detached garage that housed the hearse. In the bright light of the morning, there was no hiding that the funeral parlour could benefit from some paint and repairs. It was a sorry little affair tucked under the canopy of an old mahogany tree on the fringes of Bridgetown. Hemmed in by a bakery on the west and a hair salon on the east, shifting winds wafted the smell of jam puffs and chemical relaxers across the parlour's car park.

A steady stream of cars drove by as Eileen sniffed the mingling scents and savoured the morning's rays on her face. It was almost June and that was the only time of day when the sun didn't have the concentrated warmth of a malfunctioning appliance. Overhead, the funeral home's sign creaked eerily in the slipstream of a passing lorry, adding to the uneasy feeling that gnawed away at Eileen's gut. "Working at a mortuary is better than being unemployed," she whispered as she pulled her handbag higher on her shoulder. But even that stab at positivity couldn't whisk away the fear that settled inside her.

Eileen had lied. She was anything *but* at ease around blood and entrails. Working at a funeral parlour wasn't her childhood dream job, but it was 1985; any job was a dream job as long as you were getting paid. The global downturn of 1979 had trickled to the island's shores and left an unemployment rate in the high double-digits. Every job, especially low-skilled posts, was highly coveted. Which meant that holding on to fear was not an option.

Eileen walked up to the door of the faded peach building and stepped inside, marvelling at the fact that no-one had thought to change the wall colour as long as she'd known the building to be there.

What she didn't know was that the founder, Holden Davis Senior, was a savvy businessman who adhered to the teachings of P.T. Barnum with zealous fervour. In the 1950s,

Holden Senior painted the building a vivid shade of peach which was unheard of at the time. When a sign was erected declaring the fruit-coloured fiasco to be Davis and Son's Funeral Parlour, there was public curiosity, but during a press interview, Holden Senior quoted Barnum and said, "No one ever made a difference by being like everyone else." Newspapers ran front-page stories and editorials for weeks declaring the building to be a "blasphemous eye-sore" and a "sure sign of moral decay".

That was all it took. Between the central location just a hop and skip away from the bus stand, the garish colour and low pricing, the poor and huddled masses came en masse for their burial arrangements. Somehow Holden Senior had created a strategy heretofore unseen in the funeral world: the volume pricing model. Business boomed, and he went to his grave certain that his offspring would carry on his legacy.

Now, just a few years after his death, times had shifted, and the funeral parlour wasn't as relevant as it had been.

* * *

THE BELL JANGLED and Holden looked up to see Eileen open the front door with a bright smile on her face as she said, "Good morning!"

"Good morning," he stood up and abandoned his tea, feeling as though the small room had gotten that much tinier once she had entered it. The front office was an open-plan space with two desks, two chairs and a small filing cabinet partially hidden behind a room divider. He saw her stare at the piles of paper on the cabinet, heard her wordless question as to why the desk was so dusty.

Holden cleared his throat and gestured to the workspace opposite his. "You can set your things down here. Well," he clasped his hands and stepped from behind his desk. "I wasn't able to elucidate on this last night given our brief meeting, but this is a family-owned business which prides itself on delivering high quality at low prices. The staff is small. There's Clifford Chase, who drives the hearse and does some of the preparation; his son, David, helps out part-time with collections. Otherwise, it's just me." He steepled his fingers. "Holden Davis Junior," he said as though it was an afterthought.

"I need someone to drive me to meetings and grief visits, answer the phone, do the filing and generally keep this place from crumbling around my ears."

The placid smile on her face unnerved him. "Does that sound like something you can do?"

"Yup."

"Good." He straightened the lapels on his charcoal suit. "Be aware that death waits for no-one, not even us. Funerals can be competitive so whoever gets to the scene first has the best chance of getting the client, so you must be able to ferry me around at a moment's notice. Do you understand?"

"I do."

"Fine," Holden cleared his throat. "Now, there's the matter of wages." He extracted a folded piece of paper from his breast pocket and offered it to Eileen. "I'm not sure what your previous package looked like…"

Eileen held back a smile. Many black women in the 1980s didn't have packages unless they were wrapped in brown paper and smelled like lamb. Wages were just enough that they didn't have to choose between feeding themselves and a beloved cat.

"...but I believe this to be fair. And I'll reimburse you for travel."

She pursed her lips. "It won't make me a Rockefeller, but it's fair," she replied before she took it and tucked it into her bra.

Holden raised an eyebrow, thought better of replying and gestured to the stacks behind her. "Start with the filing; then we'll get to the other things. I'm stepping out now, but I'll be back soon."

She stacked the papers into a pile before pulling a small brush and cloth out of her handbag to dust the typewriter and wipe the desk. Holden furrowed his brow, wondering why she carried her own cleaning supplies but said nothing.

He had opened the door to leave when he heard her say, "Last night you made it seem like I'd be embalming corpses by the dozen. Or was that to frighten me?" He stopped in his tracks as he gauged her question. She had looked up, but her hand kept a steady rhythm as she cleaned. Her eyes were alight with mirth.

Holden pursed his lips. "Well...corpses are in no hurry, so we needn't rush. These stuffy papers are bothering my sinuses." The bell on the door jingled as Holden pulled it closed, keeping time with his footsteps as he stomped off.

* * *

"GOD, HE'S UPTIGHT," she muttered. Her new employer was broad-shouldered and clean-cut, his tailored suits not yet shiny from years of being overstarched like some elderly business men she'd come across before. He had dark brown skin, striking features and beautiful teeth. Eileen suspected he'd be handsome if he'd smile and pull the stick out of his ass once in a while. She sighed as she properly took in her surroundings for the first time.

The office and its contents were old fashioned and had the washed-out pallor of a black and white film that had been colourized. Holden's desk was clinically neat; only a black leather book and two pens rested on the polished wood. "Looks about right," she observed. Eileen's desk wasn't so fortunate. A wall of receipts and letters stared back at her from every square inch of the desktop. Eileen realized with a sinking stomach that Holden didn't plan to train her. She was a woman, after all, so he assumed she understood office procedures. The truth was that she had started cleaning to buy time.

She turned to the grey filing cabinet next to the desk and pulled open the drawers. Her forehead crumpled. There were two files: Bills and Funerals. The shabby folders had faded from butter yellow to a grimy off-white and were stuffed to the gills with unsorted receipts and invoices. Clearly, her predecessors didn't understand office procedures either. She sighed and sat down to work.

By the time lunch rolled around, she had labelled twenty-seven manila folders and filed away half of a stack of paper, hoping that she was doing it right. As she worked, she kept hearing the muffled sound of furniture being moved around in the room behind her. Figuring that no harm could come from giving herself a tour of the place, Eileen pushed herself away from the desk. Behind Holden's station was a yellow door where the kitchenette/lunchroom resided. Closer to her desk were two doors; a frosted glass one with gold lettering declaring it to be the Prep Room and a varnished oak door on the right. She thought it wise to leave the Prep Room for another day; she wasn't sure what surprises she'd find in there. She pushed the door to the right.

The large square space was cold and ringed with stacks of wooden folding chairs that leaned against the chestnut wainscoting. A man who resembled a daddy-long-legs was humming *We've Only Just Begun* as he polished the panelled walls with something in a yellow jar that smelled like citrus. He looked like a dark-skinned hippie with his tie-dyed shirt and zealously patterned pants.

"Good morning. I'm Eileen. Are you Clifford?"

He spun around, flecks of polish flying from the rag onto the wainscoting. "Ah, yes, yes. De boss man tell me a new girl starting." He wiped his hands down the front of his pants as he studied her for a moment; the orange streaks blended into the pattern seamlessly. You prettier than the last two though," Clifford said, as though it was important she knew that.

Eileen blushed and laughed. "Thank you. You're very kind."

He scratched his face, leaving a shiny stain beneath his handlebar moustache. "I did a little concerned, to be honest. I even tell he to get glasses because I thought he couldn't see that they didn't doing a good job either." He squinted at Eileen as though trying to find competence etched in the lines of her face. He nodded, satisfied. "You more serious than them."

Eileen grinned, her eyes afire with amusement. Clifford had a knack for saying things in a way that wasn't offensive, each sentence sounding like an observation that only just crossed his mind. She liked him.

She extended a hand to Clifford. "Nice to meet you." She glanced at the jar by his feet. "That smells nice."

He beamed, his face alight with pride. "Yeah, I does make it myself. I learn this at my grandfather knee, Lord rest his soul. Davis Senior put he in the ground and I polish up the casket myself with this same oil right here."

He cocked his head to the side before saying soberly, "Good luck with de new job, sweet girl. This life ain't for everybody." Behind the closed door, the rotary phone rang with a muffled jangle like it was underwater.

Clifford screwed the cap on the jar and raised an eyebrow at her. "That phone like de Grim Reaper he-self. I suggest you answer it."

Eileen spun around and rushed to her desk. She lifted the black rotary phone's receiver, her pen poised over a notepad as Clifford came into the room behind her while wiping his hands on a clean cloth. He was impassive as he watched the colour drain from her face. He waited until she'd hung up and asked, "Where am I headed?"

Eileen stared back at him, her fingers and face numb with shock. "Huxley."

Chapter 2
Unsweetened

The month of May might have been rolling to a close, but the harvest season was in full swing. Every factory buzzed with activity as Bedford trucks rolled in, their cargo beds stuffed with fat stalks of sugar cane. Managers paced in front of chalkboards filled with quotas and yields that haunted them at night. A sick engineer or broken down truck brought out cold sweats and ulcer pills. But sometimes, these mundane obstacles paled in comparison to life's more grisly problems.

Such was the case when a short, slim manager with a balding pate, named Herman Walkes, pulled out what was left of his hair after he got the disturbing news. Walkes slammed a red helmet onto his head, stormed across the yard and into the factory. He marched past the massive roller where the aroma of pressed cane juice wafted into the air, past the boilers, and into the engine room where the scent of molasses gave way to the stench of engine grease. Behind the heavy iron door, a small crowd gathered next to the controls. They looked up in unison as Walkes threw up his hands and huffed, "What the ass happen now?"

Gibson, the line supervisor, stepped forward. He clutched his clipboard and said, "Well... I loaded the cane on the belt and everything start moving down the line. I ain't see nothing funny 'til John shout that something catch up in the number three press and tell me to stop it. I hit the override the same time." Sweat beaded on Gibson's top lip, and he shuffled his feet as he glanced at the press from the corner of his eye. "Then I see something on the belt."

Walkes squinted at Gibson. He'd barely heard him over the puffing and squealing of the machinery, but the story made no sense. His irritation grew as Gibson spoke again.

"So I call you because you is the man in charge."

"Gibson, stop talking all over your face. Show me the problem!"

The tall, stocky man pointed at the belt leading to the cane crusher's heavy iron teeth. There, intertwined among the tangle of canes, was a woman's bent leg under the hem of a yellow dress.

Walkes stepped gingerly toward the body, the engine's clanking and wheezing fading around him as though he'd fallen headlong into an alternate reality. A light breeze swept through the vent shaft and across the conveyor belt, fluttering the woman's dress and making his heart skip a beat. After a few seconds, sure that the young lady would never move again, he fainted.

* * *

By the time Walkes came to, his head throbbing from the generous bump on his noggin, production at Huxley Sugar Factory had been ground to a halt and the police had been summoned. Every piece of machinery was silenced, their motors put to rest as the plant was declared a crime scene and investigations began. Walkes gave his statement to an officer, conveniently leaving out the time he'd spent sprawled on the floor. He shouted every word of his account, his mind unable to reconcile the fact that Huxley was quiet for the first cane season in over thirty years.

Police milled about in the yard, questioning workers as investigators with gloved hands collected anything that might be connected to the woman's discovery. Photojournalists wiggled camera lenses between rusty chain links, searching out the best angles to capture the unfolding saga on film and guarantee healthy newspaper sales the next day.

The funeral home's unmarked van arrived and removed the body around noon. Just down the road in a freshly cut field, uniformed officers combed through rotting heaps of cane trash for clues, a more daunting task than searching for a needle in a haystack.

It was the second body discovered in a cane field that year, both of them young women who had gone missing shortly before their bodies had turned up. The first victim, Anna Brown, had disappeared one sunny Thursday morning after she'd waved goodbye to her neighbour and said she would return later that day. But it was not to be. The neighbour promptly went into labour and delivered a bouncing baby boy the next morning. She didn't notice that Anna hadn't returned until days later when the phone in the apartment above kept ringing and waking her newborn.

That murder had perplexed the public for days before being swallowed up by the news cycle. Anna had been relegated to the annals of history until the discovery at Huxley. Now Anna's name was being dusted off, and new life breathed into her murder case. Word spread like wildfire that another body had been found, renewing the public's thinly veiled zeal for mystery and intrigue.

Eileen had expected Clifford to return with a sad face and drooped shoulders when he came back around closing time, but his lope was as measured as it was when he left. Clifford seemed to sense Eileen's nerves; he smiled at her, but his face sobered when he looked across at Holden. Clifford flicked his eyes to the right and went into the viewing room. Holden took the hint and followed, closing the door softly behind him.

Eileen eased her chair as near to the door as she could, a manila folder and hole punch on her lap as a plausible excuse in the event she was caught eavesdropping.

"Before I forget, your boy was there today," chuckled Clifford.

"Oh, was he now? I imagine he's not too pleased that we got the body and he didn't."

"It's a *bloody* shame, ain't it?" Clifford said mockingly. "I think what really annoyed him was that Derricks sent Wilson with me so I could get to the morgue faster. You know how that kinda thing gets his dander up."

"The commissioner sent an outrider? Why?"

"Told me not to say anything, but I gonna tell you; Derricks scheduled a press conference tonight on de seven o'clock TV news."

Holden's words were low and urgent. Eileen held her breath and pressed her ear against the door, straining to hear his voice as he asked, "Clifford, what are you telling me?"

Clifford's disgust was evident as he said, "Boss, something ain't right."

"Meaning?"

“Meaning that I was doing this for long enough to know when to get worried and right now I worried because…”

The phone rang, startling Eileen and making her curse as she rolled her chair to the desk to snatch the receiver. She gave the person directions to the funeral home as quickly as she could, rolling her eyes every time he misspelt ‘Buckworth Street’. By the time she’d hung up, Holden and Clifford were coming out of the room and neither of them said much as they closed the building for the day. Eileen sighed. She’d have to watch the evening news to learn more.

At the supermarket, women bent their heads together and complained bitterly about insecure men who preferred to take the lives of innocent females instead of improving themselves. The gas attendant who filled Eileen’s tank talked animatedly to her co-worker, both of them exchanging snippets of conversation and shocked gasps. The roar of traffic at the nearby intersection drowned out much of what they said, but she caught the words “sugar factory” and knew that word had begun to spread. On an island with just over a quarter of a million people, bad news spread quicker than cheap margarine.

But nowhere was the furor of the gossip more robust than in the rum shops. As Eileen drove down the unpaved road toward her apartment building, she couldn’t miss the crowd that spilt out of the doors as everyone exchanged rumours over glasses of rum and coke.

Eileen let herself into her apartment and raced to turn the TV's knob. The ending of the news intro flashed across the screen and she heaved a sigh. She was just in time. She stood in front of the television set, her dusty shoes still on her feet and her eyes glued to the screen. The television anchor outlined the grim details of the discovery as a montage of images appeared: the sugar factory's exterior, a photo of a smiling young woman, and her grief-stricken relatives huddled outside Huxley's gate. The newscaster's disembodied voice identified the young woman as Lydia James before the screen switched to live footage of Hugh Derricks, the new police commissioner. Derricks shuffled his papers as he greeted viewers and then cleared his throat and fixed his gaze on the prepared statement in front of him.

"Today at nine o'clock members of the Police Force were summoned to Huxley Sugar Factory to investigate the discovery of a deceased female. She has been identified as seventeen-year-old Lydia James of Number Eight, Wicklow Gardens. Given the evidence, we are treating this as an unnatural death."

He went on, "The Police Force has reason to believe that this death is connected to that of twenty-two-year-old Anna Brown who was discovered in January in Marrilow Fields and Nora Edwards of Morris Hall who was found at the Golden Greens Golf Course last year. Although the victims are not known to each other, it is believed that these murders are being perpetrated by a single individual.

Across the country, from plush living rooms in the heights and terraces to tight tenantry homes in rural lanes, fathers bolted doors and mothers slammed sash windows as telephones rang. Sadness turned to confusion and every Barbadian's blood ran cold.

For the first time in the island's history, a serial killer was on the loose.

Chapter 3
The Slasher

A country's vitals can be taken with its news headlines and Barbados' pulse was palpitating at an unprecedented rate. 'Serial Killer Strikes!' screamed the next morning's headline. 'Cane Slasher!' read another in thick black letters, a reference to the slash and burn method used to kill off crops. The media painted the killer as a sinister loner who lurked among darkened fields and preyed on random women. As the day progressed, the moniker was shortened to 'Slasher'. It stuck.

Rumours and supposition only served to double down on the country's panic. People sat vigil by rotary phones and rushed off callers to keep the lines free. When the phones did ring, their loved ones safe for one more day, they'd speculate again who was murdering young women and why.

Was it really a serial killer?

"Them things don't happen in little Barbados. God is a Bajan."

Or a sick coincidence?

"Girl...I ain't know. But it got to be..."

They had to believe the latter. That those dead women were wicked and had wronged some jealous lover or angry neighbour and the police weren't doing their job. Some separated themselves, glorifying the imagined piousness that helped them sleep — albeit uneasily — at night. The possibility that a madman was on the loose, picking off women at random filled them with terror. And yet…

The unexplained murders of three young women with no connection to each other were impossible to explain otherwise. The country became divided: men lived life as usual while women went on self-imposed dusk-to-dawn curfews even though the Slasher's victims had gone missing in broad daylight. Nora Edwards had gone to meet her outside man, Anna Brown went missing after she went to town and Lydia was on her way home from school. The coincidences stopped there.

At the funeral home, the news affected everyone differently. Clifford read the newspaper, his lips pursed in disgust as he flipped the pages. Eventually, he slammed it on Eileen's desk and said he was going to the shop for a beer. Eileen followed suit, saying she would take lunch early and slipped away to the small kitchenette with her food well before eleven o'clock. Holden sat at his desk, balancing his books, oblivious to his staff's worries and didn't respond when either of them left.

When Holden finally extracted himself from his ledgers, he found Eileen asleep at the lunch table with her arm thrown over her head and her mouth hanging open.

He glanced at the clock on the ivy-patterned wallpaper above the small fridge and then at Eileen. Her soup was untouched in the small glass dish in front of her, the steam having turned into droplets that clung sadly to the glass cover and dripped back onto the food.

He started a pot of tea, making more noise than necessary as he went, but still, she slept. The kettle whistled loudly and Eileen didn't budge. Holden sighed. He wasn't good at this type of thing, he realized as he shook his head irritably. *Should I get Clifford to wake her?* Clifford had no qualms about breaching any sort of boundaries. The only problem was that Holden didn't know when Clifford would return. Finally, when Eileen was officially twenty minutes late, he cleared his throat and tapped her shoulder. "Ahem. Pardon me," he said.

With one bleary eye, she stared at him for a moment before she apologized and tried to stifle a yawn as she trudged off to her desk. Holden's irritation grew. It was too soon for her to be sleeping on the job. He sighed. The last set of interviewees didn't give him much hope that he'd be able to replace Eileen anytime soon, but he wondered grudgingly if the lady with no car and three children would be willing to meet him halfway.

* * *

IN MANY WAYS, Eileen's new job reminded her of when she was nine years old and had jumped in front of a raging pit-bull so it wouldn't bite her friend; it seemed like an epic adventure in theory but was a foolhardy exercise in reality.

Her typing was atrocious. She stabbed the keys with two fingers in a way that Clifford said made her look more like a rabid switchboard operator than a secretary. On the third day, Holden frowned when he dictated a letter and realized Eileen couldn't take shorthand but declared her quite fast without it. She had feared he would prattle on but to his credit, Holden was as clear and decisive with his speech as he was with everything else.

Clifford watched from the other side of the room, smirking as he flicked a toothpick up and down in his mouth. After Holden left for lunch, Clifford asked, "You ain't went to no sort of secretarial school, did you?"

"No," Eileen said as she dotted out her fifth error with correction fluid. She pushed the typewriter carriage to the left and slowly clacked out a new sentence.

"And you don't plan to tell the boss you can't type nor nothing so?"

"I'm doing fine without it."

Clifford looked around and shrugged in agreement. In less than a week, Eileen had cleared away three months of filing and cleaned the office until it was spotless. Letters went out on time and phone messages were accurately delivered. She looked up from the typewriter and caught his eye. "But you knew that. You just like shooting the piss at me."

Clifford grinned. "It's true. If you didn't poke those keys like hot coals, I didn't gonna guess that you is a greenhorn."

Eileen laughed and then frowned when she noticed three extra spaces in her sentence.

By Thursday, Eileen's confidence was sky-high because she would be attending the first funeral she had helped to organize. But later that day, she found out that she had overlooked a crucial detail. And she would be up to her neck in trouble when it came to light.

That evening, Eileen drove through the big white gates of Southbury Cemetery and scanned the graveyard for the dark green tent Clifford had mentioned. The cemetery was filled with uneven rectangular humps and overgrown by grass and weeds that stretched from one end of the cemetery to the other. A few graves were marked with rough-hewn wooden crosses that only matched the ambition of well-kept graves in Anglican churchyards with lacklustre results. Just beyond the small white chapel in the distance, she saw the tent. Sandwiched between an open plot and a pathway bordered by blue flowers, the sides of the tent flapped like wings in the evening breeze. Holden and Clifford stood at the back of the tent, dressed to the nines in their dapper coattails. She smiled and handed Clifford the two wreaths that had arrived late that afternoon.

The bereaved huddled together and sang in warbled tones as the casket was lowered, their pitch rising in tremulous waves as a scatter of dirt and stones hit the walnut veneer. An old woman, bent at the waist and clutching a cane, hobbled up behind Holden and Eileen as the gravediggers worked in the late afternoon sun. The woman looked around for a moment, watching the family fussing and hugging each other before she asked in a strong voice, "What wunna doing?"

The deceased's daughter sniffed and said, "Miss Johnson, we ain't know you came to Daddy's funeral."

Miss Johnson shuffled her false teeth, her mouth puckering with sarcasm as she replied, "Good thing I come too, 'cause wunna bury Herbert in the wrong spot."

Whispers turned into gasps and confused exclamations as everyone looked at Miss Johnson. The daughter's mouth hung open as her brother stepped forward in an immaculate black suit and said, "You always getting in people's business. What you talking about now?"

Miss Johnson shrugged, a smug smile on her face as she said, "Lucky for you that I decided to get in yours today." She drew back her cane and knocked his shins with a loud whack before turning to point at the other end of the cemetery. "I went to every village funeral since 1963 and your father was to bury with your grandfather close to the cemetery gate; I ain't know why you putting him up here by the chapel."

The crowd's murmuring stopped as everyone looked curiously at everyone else. The son rubbed his shins and looked at Holden, pain overwhelming his grief as he asked, "So whose grave is this?"

Holden plastered on a smile and said, "I'll double-check my files, please excuse me for a moment." Under his breath, he muttered, "Eileen, to the hearse."

"Kinda reminds me of when Batman tells Robin 'to the Bat Cave'," Eileen said with a weak chuckle. Her laughter sounded like it was running low on batteries and Holden stalked toward the hearse, clearly not amused by her attempt at levity. Eileen wished she would keel over then and there into the grave with Herbert. Clifford followed, an easy grin on his face as he watched Holden scan through a manila folder while Eileen wrung her hands. Holden's eyes swung left to right across the page and a sheen of sweat spread across his brow as alarm grew on his face.

Holden slapped the file on his thigh. "We were supposed to bury him in N94; this is M94," he fumed. Clifford shook his head in amusement. Holden glared at Eileen again but said nothing as he squared his shoulders and went back to the family. His tone was apologetic as he promised to relocate the body to the correct spot within twenty-four hours. Behind him, Eileen noticed the grave diggers working at a frantic pace, each of them glancing over their shoulders at her as they plunked soil into the hole. Eileen bit her lip and whispered to Clifford, "If they're moving the body, why are they still putting in the dirt?"

Clifford raised an eyebrow at her and laughed. "Them fellas don't get pay for half a grave, so they making sure the job done. Can't blame them for that." He quirked the toothpick at the side of his mouth. "Plus, you don't think the boss paying to dig three holes, nuh?"

"Three?"

Clifford jutted his chin at the men patting the mound of soil they had finished shovelling at warp speed. "Dig to put him in, dig to take him out and dig to put him in the right one."

"Oh…" Eileen's face fell. "I didn't study that."

Clifford's smile was benign. "That's alright. We gonna help you this first time."

"F-first time?" Eileen stuttered.

"The boss likes to make sure that staff know not to do these things twice." He clapped her on the shoulder. "We going bring the shovels and pick you up tonight." He said, glancing up at the gloomy sky and then down at her high heels. "Wear boots; it's gonna rain."

* * *

Eileen's arms and shoulders ached on Friday morning. She could barely move her limbs enough to tuck the newspaper under her desk and leaf through the classifieds to find a job that didn't involve her slinging mud in the dark. Most of the openings for women required a secretarial certificate or advanced sewing skills. There was only one that she was qualified for: a simple black and white listing for a maid with a phone number printed beneath it. Eileen was about to clip it out when she noticed that the obituaries — which Holden read religiously every day — were on the other side of the ad. She sighed and tucked it away, making a mental note to do it later that day.

The rest of the morning dragged on. Letters were sent, calls were answered and bills were paid. By the time parliament's clock tower bonged twelve times, Eileen was so exhausted that she couldn't lift her arms to eat the rice and stew she had brought. It turned out to be a blessing in disguise.

Unbeknownst to Eileen, Holden always found it best to throw new assistants in at the deep end during the first week. It helped him to avoid unnecessary paperwork with the unemployment office if they couldn't withstand the pressure. He summoned Eileen to the back of the building and handed her a folded bundle with a coat and gloves and instructed her to put it on. Then he took his time wheeling Lydia James across the prep room's white tile floor.

Eileen watched him, all the while feeling like she was drowning in the voluminous prep coat that brushed her gloved knuckles and grazed her ankles. Her pulse hammered in her throat as she stood next to the wide stainless steel sink. In her imagination, the young woman smelled sweet like bagasse and molasses after being found in a sugar factory. The reality wasn't so pleasant. The metallic scent of alcohol rose in the air when Holden pulled back the white sheet. Eileen gagged.

Holden pretended not to notice as he described the embalming process in graphic detail before cautioning Eileen to let him know if she felt faint or nauseous. She folded her lips together and nodded.

"Now," he said, slapping his gloved hands together. "This is the moment of reckoning; help me move the young lady so we can begin."

Together they transferred her to the embalming table, a white marble slab with a sunken ring carved into its perimeter. The room was frigid, but sweat broke out on Eileen's forehead as her back bent with the weight in her hands. Holden dangled a fat yellow sponge in front of her and pointed to bottles of shampoo and bath liquid on the shelf, before he reached over and turned on a faucet. Water streamed down from a broad shower head that hung from the ceiling onto Lydia. Eileen had never noticed it before, a strange omission for her eyes to make given the circumstances. Despite Lydia smelling so sterile, Eileen realized some things weren't washed off from Lydia's visit to the pathologist. There was dirt under the young woman's nails and a dusting of pollen came out of her ears when Eileen rinsed her off.

"Bless you," Holden said when Eileen sneezed.

As she washed Lydia from tip to toe, Eileen's teeth left four sharp indentations in her lower lip that would linger for days. Her eyes actively skipped over the sewn up gash on Lydia's neck and the coarse black thread that pinched the pink flesh beneath the Y-shaped cut on her torso. Eileen squeezed a blob of shampoo into her palm and asked Holden, "Why did they cut her hair?"

"Hmm?" he replied absently as he scribbled notes in a folder. "Oh, they take samples of hair and blood for tests."

Eileen touched her gloved fingertip to a small bald patch at the base of Lydia's scalp. Something about that patch, no bigger than a knob of butter, rattled Eileen. Without it, Lydia's Afro was incomplete, reducing the young woman to nothing more than a pile of evidence for a police investigation.

"Who does the make-up?"

"Clifford mostly. He's artsier than I am."

"Can I do it?" The words came out of Eileen's mouth before she could stop herself. Her desire to give up on this job had been replaced with an emotion she couldn't express. One man had robbed this young girl of her life. Another had left her with scars. A woman should be the one to make her beautiful one last time.

Holden's hand hovered over the folder as he studied her for a long moment. "Are you sure?"

She swallowed. "Yes."

He nodded once and went back to his notes, surreptitiously watching Eileen as she gritted her teeth and finished her task. By the time the soap bubbles ran down the drain, Eileen exhaled and smiled, proud of herself for having made it through the ordeal.

"Excellent job," Holden said as he inspected her work. "Next, we embalm."

In minutes, Eileen's pride turned to an entirely different feeling while she held a washcloth doused in peppermint oil beneath her nose, afraid to move it lest the smells overwhelmed her. Perhaps she had been too flippant when she had brushed off Holden's concern about her not being able to stomach the job, but she'd been desperate. With rent and bills to pay, she couldn't afford to be picky. The fact that Holden hadn't delved too deeply into her background was also advantageous. Now, as Holden prepared the remains of Lydia James, Eileen questioned every aspect of her life, wondering how she'd ended up inside an ice-cold room at 5 p.m. with a man whose sole intention was pumping the blood out of a body and filling it with chemicals.

Eileen's stomach churned. She was glad that she hadn't eaten lunch; the digested remnants would have made an appearance right there and then. She claimed she had to go to the bathroom, blaming it on the large glass of lemonade she'd had earlier as she rushed out. Holden said nothing, but the smile that tugged at his lips let Eileen know the jig was up. She scrambled up the corridor toward the lavatory, her stomach spasming until she lunged inside and splashed tap water on her face. Trembling, she sank down on the closed toilet with her head in her hands.

Cold seeped under the door, wrapping itself around Eileen's exposed ankles and snaking up her body until she shivered. Shame ate away at her as she considered her options. She had been ready to quit until she decided she wanted to help Lydia. On the surface, there wasn't much that separated her from Lydia; she could see herself in the young woman's smooth face, her bitten nails and the inoculation scar on her left arm. Plus, that smirk on Holden's face was infuriating. Eileen sighed. Not only was she was stubborn, but she also hated being wrong, two qualities that had gotten her in trouble many times before. She had to see it through, but there was no way she could do so locked inside a bathroom. She took a deep breath, stood up and left the bathroom.

"I've got a lot of respect for you," Holden said as soon as she returned. He rested a syringe on the table and looked up at her as he cocked his head to one side and said, "I'm not the easiest person to work for and this certainly isn't the most pleasant job in the world, but you haven't complained once."

Eileen hadn't expected that. She supposed it was as close to a compliment as she would get from Holden. Her heart swelled. Maybe it wouldn't be so bad after all.

* * *

THE NEXT DAY, at a quaint whitewashed church not too far from where she'd been born, Lydia was laid to rest. Her parents rubbed her twin brother's back as he slumped down in the pew after vomiting just outside the door. Eileen was sitting in the hearse and had seen when he dashed outside. Luke didn't resemble his sister much. He took after his father and Eileen imagined that Lydia looked like her mother did when she was seventeen. She had watched as his body heaved and shuddered, trying to rid itself of grief, but only managing to expel air and acid. As Luke went back inside the church, Holden strode out to the car, sat in the driver's seat and balanced the programme on his lap. "Not coming in?"

Eileen glanced at Holden's programme. On the front was a smiling photo of Lydia, her life story told in the tiny dash between the two dates beneath her name.

Eileen shook her head. "It's too sad. Not sure I can handle it."

His eyes betrayed wisdom beyond his years as he said, "Some funerals are like that. But some are joyful. I buried an old lady last month who lived to a hundred and I couldn't help but feel grateful to be around the good energy in that church. Everyone was glad to have known her, glad that she had a long life."

Eileen's eyes grew damp. "Yes, but no-one is glad now. Lydia wasn't given a chance at a long life."

He bowed his head. "I know now that I buried the second victim too. I pray Lydia is the last."

The wind picked up, swooping through the churchyard and bringing with it a groaning wail that filled the air with such misery that Eileen's heart clenched in her chest. There was no doubt in Eileen's mind that it was Lydia's mother.

Holden checked his watch. "They'll come out after this hymn." He glanced at Eileen and said in a low tone, "In some ways, this job gets easier. You'll see."

With that, he got out of the hearse and headed up the pathway just in time to direct the pallbearers down the aisle. A sea of people in black swayed and sang as it made its way out of the church, grief bowing them at the waist. As they walked, the dust beneath their feet swirled in the wind, stirring up a musty graveside smell that drifted into the hearse as they sang 'It Is Well With My Soul'.

In later years, Eileen would reflect that Lydia's funeral was a turning point. Something shifted inside her as she watched Luke step onto that hillside. The tear stains on his face glistened in the waning sunlight as he helped carry his sister's coffin. His suit was a size too big for him, his youth exposed in the double-cuffed hems that weighed down his boyish limbs. He clamped his jaw as his slippery palms gripped the brass handles, making his way to the hill's crest, then leaned over and deposited his portion of his sister's weight on the long straps stretched taut across her grave. He loosened the strap closest to his feet and eased Lydia gently down, down, down. And then, when she was finally at the bottom of the dark hole, he plopped down next to it and cried.

Chapter 4
The Other Brother

The spate of serial murders had fueled rum-soaked arguments for days, but shortly after Lydia's funeral, the newspaper delivered a fresh scandal that, while deathly, was far less dangerous.

Two years earlier, when Grenadian Prime Minister, Maurice Bishop and his closest cabinet ministers were dispatched in a gruesome coup, it triggered a political upheaval that forced the island's medical school to seek a temporary home in sunny Barbados, meaning the not-so-sunny arrival of the requisite cadavers for studies. Rumours that the corpses were connected to mafia money created the kind of juicy scandal that provided enough fodder for the media and calypsonians to keep them busy for months.

The only person who didn't have a problem with the medical school was Holden, simply because Davis and Sons Funeral Home had just won the lucrative contract of ferrying the cadavers from the port to the school. Despite the promise of added business, he reminded Eileen of Ebenezer Scrooge the way his disgruntled sighs punctuated the manic tapping of calculator buttons that Wednesday morning.

Eileen was peering through the blinds when Clifford roiled in from outside, his gangly movements like those of a gun-slinging spider on his way to the saloon for a hit of sarsaparilla. He toted his homemade yard broom made of coconut frond spines and bound with an old mackerel can.

"Boss, I need oranges."

Holden's shoulders slumped as he turned squinted eyes on the older man. "Clifford, explain why I spend more on fruit than formaldehyde. I'm an undertaker, not a hawker selling fruits in Eagle Hall market."

Clifford's head hung to one side. "Boss, you know it for de polish."

Holden huffed. "Clifford, polish sells for a few dollars at the supermarket. For God's sake, just buy some."

"See… dat is the Babylonian system. All this convenience gonna kill we. This is the eighties, but I bet that in 2020 when the world got self-driving cars and that kinda thing, we going find out that all of these chemicals was destroying we livers." He banged the ceiling impatiently with the yard broom and swatted the white dust that floated down around him like a reluctant snow storm. "It is the least you could do since you ain't listening to me about this asbestos. I see how them does make it overseas. Keep breathing in this and the nasty Babylonian polish and you going be in the prep room just now with them duppies."

Holden scrubbed his face but said nothing as he dug into his pocket and handed Clifford two twenty-dollar bills.

Eileen pressed her hand to her mouth to restrain a laugh as Clifford sidled away complaining that up to now the government still hadn't thought to issue fifty dollar notes, yet another sign of their "colonialist antics".

Holden side-eyed Eileen before he pursed his mouth and sucked air between his teeth. "Clifford drives me insane with his flower child folly, but he works hard and the polish smells good."

Eileen tried to help herself, but couldn't. She burst out laughing. For the first time, Holden's face broke into a genuine smile. The worry lines on his face faded and his eyes lit up as he grinned at her. His shoulders relaxed and for the first time, she felt at ease around him.

"I want to ask a question and I hope it doesn't sound rude."

He nodded.

"How did you manage to hire Clifford?"

"I didn't. I inherited him along with the business. I like to imagine that he wandered in here when the place first opened and my father took a shine to him."

Eileen bit her cheek. Informal interviews were obviously a hallowed tradition at Davis and Sons.

"When did your father start the business?"

"Since the fifties, even before independence. My father was a man of vision, always planning for growth. A few years ago, he commissioned a state-of-the-art building with massive refrigeration capacity and a large parking bay. He said it would be the largest, most modern facility in the Caribbean. That's how he managed to get the contract for the crown's collections: capital cases, pick-ups from government-owned hospitals and that kind of thing."

Eileen looked around the cramped space at Buckworth Street with its faded peach walls, old-fashioned wainscoting and the rotting lean-to at the back and wondered what went wrong. Holden seemed to read her mind. "It's in St. James." His face soured. "My brother runs it." Eileen wasn't sure, but she could have sworn she also heard him mutter "into the ground."

Comprehension dawned on Eileen's face. "Oh, yeah. The name of the business is Davis *and* Sons. You have a brother."

Holden's good mood evaporated as he grunted. "My younger brother, Paul. You'll meet him soon enough."

Something about the way Holden responded told Eileen it was best to go to lunch and not ask any more questions. A few minutes later, Clifford joined her on the picnic bench at the back of the building and said, "The boss don't like talking about Paul too much."

"You heard that?" Eileen asked, mouth agape.

"Yup, I went to de vendor round the corner so I didn't gone too long."

Eileen stirred her soup and shrugged guiltily. "He seemed really annoyed when I asked about his brother."

"Old man Davis had one business and two sons. That's where the problem usually starts," said Clifford with a wry grimace. He explained that despite having two locations, the business was legally considered as one entity. Paul didn't hurt his head with mundane concerns such as haggling for government contracts. He left that to Holden but still profited from it since he was legally entitled to half of the collections. Instead, Paul focused on the extras: large viewings with hors d'oeuvres and a horse-drawn carriage festooned with flowers which he drove while wearing a top hat and coattails. When the money for those rare events ran out, Paul would literally steal bodies from under his brother's nose so he could claim the funeral payments.

"Young Davis changed these locks twice already because Paul came down here after hours." Clifford chuckled as he regaled Eileen with Paul's schemes. She had to admit the stories were funny when Clifford told them, but she could see how Holden's stoic nature would war with Paul's free-wheeling tricks. She had sized Holden up the first morning, and though he seemed pulled together, he had the scuffed edges of a man whose mind bore the burden of constant loneliness. 'Strong' and 'capable' were the first two words she would use to describe him. 'Empty' would be the third. Now at least, some of it made sense.

* * *

"EILEEN, WHAT'S YOUR LAST NAME?"

She glanced up from the typewriter. "Why?"

"I'm labelling pay packs."

She shrugged. "You pay in cash and I'm the only Eileen here."

Holden squinted at her. Good gracious, she was difficult. "Eileen, I like consistency. Just tell me your surname."

"It's the eighties; pop culture has paved the way for strong, independent women to be recognized by only one name. It's Eileen...like Cher or Madonna."

Holden could feel his pressure rising; Eileen couldn't type and she'd drive him to drink. *What a great boss I am,* he thought irritably as he scratched her name on the envelope and tossed it on her desk.

He was just about to head into the back to close up for the weekend when the bell on the door tinkled and Hugh Derricks walked in. The police commissioner greeted everyone and asked, "Is Clifford here?"

"Check the viewing room."

"You could come too, young Davis."

Holden shook his head in exasperation. His father, Clifford and Derricks had gotten together monthly to drink for almost twenty years. Since his father had died, the visits had become infrequent and now he suspected that Derricks only came because he expected Holden to provide the brandy.

Holden directed him into the viewing room. Clifford hailed the commissioner and quickly set up a small plastic table and three chairs before pouring each of them a generous helping of liquor.

"Wha' happen?" Clifford asked the commissioner a few minutes after they'd sipped from their glasses.

"The prime minister has me under a lot of pressure. A serial killer during my first month on the job?" Derricks' slouched shoulders barely lifted when he sighed. "You've seen the dump sites; a cane ground is probably the worst place to look for evidence. To compound the situation, these girls didn't go to the same schools or work at the same job. Hell, I'm not sure they ever met."

Holden didn't envy Derricks one bit. Police commissioners in any country had a daunting job, but it was no mean fun to be called incompetent before you cashed your first pay cheque.

"Are you sure it's not a copycat killer?" Holden asked.

"That's possible," answered Derricks with some reluctance. "But the modus operandi is the same and we didn't release how they were killed to the public. Dog-bite-it, the only reason I can talk about this is because you've both seen the bodies." He downed the rest of his drink and refilled his glass. "They all had that cut on their necks."

Holden's hand paused in mid-air as he peered at the commissioner, racking his brain for details about the victims he had prepared for their funerals. He remembered the stitches in the shape of a ninety-degree angle on their necks.

"It's true, both had their jugulars slashed," Clifford said.

"All three," corrected Derricks. "Paul collected the first girl so you wouldn't know about her, but all of them had the same cut."

Derricks sipped his drink and caught Holden's eye. "This killer can't get so lucky three times in a row, he's obviously a doctor or someone who knows how to find the jugular in the first place."

Holden wasn't so sure. "And making L-shaped cuts? I studied anatomy and proper technique dictates that incisions be as straight as possible."

Clifford agreed. "Only somebody sloppy or nervous would operate like that." He tilted his chair until it balanced on its back legs. "Derricks, if I was you, I woulda get one of them psychics from overseas that does solve crimes to come and tell you who the killer is. Hire one of them white women with the shawls and bangles that does clink on them wrists like cowbells."

Derricks glared at him, obviously mystified by Clifford's nonsensical beliefs. "And let the PM get rid of me to make the cowbell psychic the commissioner?" He gulped the rest of his brandy and slammed the glass on the table. "I'm going back to Central. Have a good day."

Clifford raised a shoulder and picked up the brandy bottle. "I thought it was a noteworthy suggestion."

The two men sat in silence, mulling over what Derricks had said for a few minutes before Holden glanced at his watch. It was almost 6 p.m., well past the usual closing time. "Let's lock up."

Clifford stayed in the viewing room to put away the chairs and table, while Holden took the glasses to the lunchroom. To his annoyance, Holden found Eileen fast asleep for the second time since she'd been working there. *How on earth could one person sleep so much at work*, Holden wondered as he soaped the glasses. Through the kitchenette door, the phone rang. Holden kept washing, assuming Clifford would answer it, but by the fourth ring, it was clear that Clifford had already snuck out the back. "Knowing him, he probably ran off to draw up under Dorothy again," Holden muttered as he rinsed his hands and ran into the office. But it was to no avail. By the time he snatched up the receiver, he only heard the drone of dial tone.

He was beyond irritated as he marched back to the kitchenette and shook Eileen awake. "I'm closing up," he grumbled as she stretched and yawned.

It was times like these when Holden felt his already tenuous grasp on the business slipping. He often felt alone, adrift in a sea of responsibility that no-one else understood. Every day felt like a test of his patience and endurance, one with shifting goal-posts whose only constant was that time was always against him.

Holden stormed through the office, slamming windows and turning keys in locks so roughly that each click echoed through the building. When the phone rang again, Holden managed to answer it in time. His pulse raced as he crossed the office floor in two long lopes to stick his head through the door and say, "Let's go. Collection in Bridgetown."

At the crime scene, a constable diverted traffic over one of the city's main bridges and directed Eileen to park behind a crowd gathered under a neon sign advertising Lucky Slots and Beer. The onlookers' faces glowed as though powered by nuclear energy beneath the sign's harsh artificial light. Holden peered through a gap in the crowd, trying to get a better glimpse of the scene unfolding on the dark street. Up ahead, two assistants from Paul's parlour carried away the covered body of the elderly man who had collapsed and died of a heart attack.

A tinted black Camaro cruised past them and the driver honked the horn. Holden stewed silently in the passenger seat of Eileen's car. Holden could just imagine the smug look on his brother's face. It was the same look Paul had flashed him twenty years ago when he'd left two fat slugs in Holden's school shoes. Holden had jammed his feet into the shoes, jumped off the top step and ran to the front gate before he felt something like warm jello oozing through his socks. He'd heard a roar of laughter and looked back to see Paul, tears rolling down his face as he slapped his thigh. Holden was lashed for not looking into his shoes before he put them on and destroying his socks. Paul was scolded for playing a trick on his brother. Holden had always been perplexed by how granular his own punishments were while Paul's were wrought out of deference for patient child-rearing. Now, Holden seethed with anger the same way he had that day.

Eileen shifted the car into gear and said, "We'll get the next one, don't worry."

Her statement didn't placate him enough. "How can we when you're always asleep?" he snapped. "We got here late because I had to wake you up again."

"I'm sorry," she said sheepishly. "I was tired."

He'd never asked about her personal life, but one possibility of why she slept so often made him irrationally upset. Was she pregnant? She'd never mentioned a husband, but that didn't mean she didn't have one. Why wasn't she like other assistants who complained about their bunions, diabetic mothers and lazy boyfriends?

"You're tired all the time and it's disrupting my work. Are you pregnant or something? And why won't you tell me your last name?"

Eileen's eyes narrowed as she folded her arms across her chest and stared at him with a tight smile. "I sleep during the day because I'm afraid all the time and staying up at night is the only thing that comforts me while a serial killer is on the loose."

Her thinly veiled sarcasm dripped with impatience. Holden squirmed in his seat.

"Every noise is a rapist coming to take the only thing the world says that I owe it. Or a thief coming to seize the few coppers in my possession because the truth is that you only pay me enough to make me a middle man between you and the bill collectors. The day *you* walk the road and have to clutch your purse *and* your private parts is the day you'll stop asking me why I can't sleep at night."

Holden felt he should be upset that an employee spoke to him this way. Yet, he only felt embarrassed. Her words made him think of the first Slasher victim he'd collected: defensive wounds, angry bruises and a river of dried blood on her neck. Even in death, the young woman looked scared, her empty eyes frozen open when he'd arrived at the scene. Holden wanted to apologize to Eileen, but she turned up the radio so loudly that he'd have to shout for her to hear him. He could tell she was upset from the way she gripped the steering wheel and clenched her jaw as she drove.

She pulled into his driveway ten minutes later and stared through her window while she waited for him to get out. He lowered the radio's volume and clasped his hands for a moment, mulling over how to phrase what was on his mind. "You know…I didn't think about it like that. I'm sorry for not considering how the average woman feels in this situation. But…," he paused and looked at her, "…I'm not heartless. Just because I didn't understand doesn't mean I *can't* understand. If you have problems, you can tell me. I'll help in any way I can."

Her shoulders sank as though she'd had the fire sucked out of her. She glanced at Holden and said, "I'm sorry too. I'm tired, but I shouldn't be so rude to you." She shook her head self-consciously. "And I will try to talk to you more."

He wanted to say something else but decided that they had made enough progress for the night. He simply tilted his head and replied, "Get home safely." He climbed out, closed the door gently and watched Eileen drive to the other end of the semi-circular driveway and turn left to head home.

The night air was crisp and cool, but Holden's mind was troubled. Eileen had been forthright about her fear, but not much else. He had asked about her last name twice. The first time she'd used humour to deflect his question. The second time she'd neatly glossed over it by discussing what she considered to be the crux of their conflict. Holden scratched his chin as he unlocked the door. There was no denying it: she was hiding something.

Chapter 5
Inside a Killer's Mind

Dry grass, ripe ackees and the sight of tractors hauling cane to sugar factories were the hallmarks of a Barbadian June that gave the phrase 'long summer days' a whole new meaning. During rush hours, long caravans of vehicles would trail the bright red tractors on the two-lane highways, leaving the cars' occupants with little else to do except chitchat on their extended journey. It was during these car rides that Eileen had grown accustomed to Holden's good-natured grumbling, finding his observations both comical and profound. He was a deep thinker, capable of simultaneously invigorating her mind and making her laugh until she collapsed in tears. He appeared to relish amusing her and took to talking more than he did in the presence of other people. Her initial reservations about the job slipped away and soon her interactions with both Clifford and Holden improved.

On one particularly hot day, as they passed the scorched banks of the Constitution River on their left and Queen's Park on their right, Holden grumbled, "Look at this ten-story eyesore. It breaks up the skyline like a concrete exclamation mark."

Eileen grinned. The concrete exclamation mark Holden referred to was the new central bank. It was just around the corner from the funeral home and had been a topic of public contention for months since it would be Barbados' tallest building once completed. It was hard to miss, visible even from parishes in the middle of the island like St. George and St.

Thomas. Traditionalists felt it compromised the rustic appeal that lured visitors to the island. Progressives felt tourists wouldn't come to an island lacking the necessary infrastructure to support a burgeoning economy.

Holden spent his life in a constant limbo of embracing the old and reluctantly fending off the new, which left him squarely on the outskirts of the debate — he didn't mind progress, but took umbrage when it blocked his view.

"More and more, this place is reminding me of London. Big buildings, traffic...oh goodness, the traffic. I wish I had a private underground tunnel so I could drive anywhere I wanted."

Eileen snickered, "I didn't know you could drive."

"I have a license. I simply choose not to drive."

"How come?"

He exhaled deeply, his chest dropping like a sunken soufflé. "I had a bad accident two years ago. I was fine, but I was trapped in the car with my father's body for hours until help came."

Eileen bit her lip. She had assumed he was cheap or had some neurotic reason for being a businessman without a car. Now she felt horrible for prying. "I'm sorry for your loss."

Holden's eyes glossed over for a moment, unseeing and distant as though the memories had taken shape before his eyes. "I think if he had struggled before he died, it would have been different. But being inside that car — calling out to him over and over as he grew cold — was excruciating."

The thought of it made Eileen nauseous as she reversed her rusty blue Toyota Crown into the car park behind the washed-out funeral parlour. She wondered why she had bothered being nosy.

Eileen escaped to the lunchroom, hoping her embarrassment would cool off before she faced Holden again. The newspapers were open on the table, covered in Clifford's biscuit crumbs. The police hadn't made any breaks in the Cane Slasher case and for the most part, the murders had gradually sunk beneath the front pages. That day, one of the dailies ran a lengthy article on page nine headlined "Profile of a Killer". As Eileen read the story in the muted brightness of the small kitchenette, goosebumps covered her arms as she realized with searing clarity that she had the wrong idea all along. The psychiatrist who penned the piece believed the culprit to be one man who had evaded capture for months because he was cunning and meticulous. The article noted that the women who vanished were between seventeen and twenty-three years old, which hinted that the Slasher had good social standing that would endear women. The isolated dump sites supported this theory because the killer probably had access to a car, a luxury available to less than a fifth of the population. The good doctor warned that a lapse in murders wasn't indicative of the killer's rehabilitation, but rather a sign that he was planning, waiting to slake his blood lust once more. She warned women to be extra vigilant in the coming months as the Slasher would surely strike again.

Eileen's heart beat faster at the idea that the murderer was masquerading as every woman's dream, flaunting attributes that would prove deadly if he got them alone. She had assumed it would be easy to spot a serial killer; now she wasn't so sure.

Her mind flashed back to her childhood and the ominous warnings she'd heard when coming home late.

"Walk fast."

"Avoid shortcuts."

"Always tell somebody where you're going and let them know when you get in."

Her childhood had been a talisman against fear, and she'd had automatically rebelled against the advice. She'd found these redundant tips to be a double standard; none of the neighbourhood boys suffered through pre-outing lectures. All she got when she pointed out the unfairness were deep frowns and frustrated responses: "They're boys, they don't have to worry."

Boys, Eileen remembered thinking bitterly. She didn't see the difference. When Timothy Rudder had braked his bicycle suddenly with Eileen sitting on the handlebar, both of them had flown off and scraped their knees. Same blood, same pain. But different rules: Timothy was petted and comforted with the standard, "Boys will be boys." At Eileen's house, she was told, "Stop — getting — mix — up — with — little — boy — things", each word punctuated with a stinging lash across her legs.

But this killer who went around snuffing out the lives of young women was the first proper example Eileen had of why boys were different. Women lived in constant fear of being assaulted, robbed and murdered for no reason other than just existing. How do two sets of people, sharing the same planet, breathing the same air, get such different realities to navigate? She envied Holden's habit of walking home late at night. There were times she was afraid to even run down the apartment stairs and jump behind the wheel of her car to leave home, far less walk through her poorly lit village.

The faint jingle of the telephone in the office snapped Eileen out of her thoughts. Death was calling again.

* * *

HOLDEN BUSTLED INTO THE LUNCHROOM ten minutes later, pulling on his jacket. "Eileen, we're going to Shorey Lakes."

"Who died?" she asked as she folded the newspaper.

"My mother's cousin's husband. Clifford left already." Holden blew out an impatient breath. "What are you doing?"

"Just gimme a minute." She dug around under the kitchen sink and emerged with the Baygon tin before she pushed her sunglasses on her face like a movie star. "Let's go."

"Eileen, it isn't for me to bring up the delicate issue of stealing supplies, but why do you take insecticide with you every single time you leave?"

She tipped her sunglasses at him as they walked out the door. "Why is it a delicate issue? You're the boss and if I'm stealing, I'm stealing."

Holden grimaced as she opened the car's hood. "Maybe upon our return we could have a little chat about impropriety."

"Impropriety?" Eileen asked, as she unscrewed a hose and pulled a plastic garnish off the engine. She cocked her head to the side and uncovered the can. "Frankly, I see this as a company perk. You said you'd reimburse travel expenses and this helps with the upkeep of my vehicle."

She pressed the dusty garnish into his hands. He looked at his soiled fingers and said in surprise, "Upkeep?"

“Yeah. Cover your nose.”

He didn’t have enough time to remove his pocket square before a thick cloud of insecticide issued from the nozzle into the car’s engine and filled the air. It stank to high heavens, and it was all Holden could do not to choke. He coughed and sputtered, and by the time he stopped, Eileen had put everything back to normal.

“The starting motor doesn’t work properly. Baygon gives it a little kick.” She winked at him. “Normally, I do it before you get outside, but you moved too fast today. Get in.”

Holden sniffed himself and sighed. He smelled like the exterminator with the heavy tongue who sweated too much and called him “Hoddeh”.

The engine wheezed and sputtered, rocking back and forth like a sick horse on race day. With a loud bang, the car shot forward across the gravel parking lot and straight into the busy street.

Holden held onto the door handle for dear life, clutching his pocket square to his chest as he muttered two curse words.

“Oh shoot, I sprayed too much,” Eileen laughed as the car tumbled across the road and mounted the sidewalk as traffic swerved to avoid them.

“Why don’t you get a new car?” Holden spluttered angrily as the car bumped its way off the sidewalk and back onto the asphalt as vehicles around them screeched and honked.

“Oh, please. You’re vexed ‘cause I’m stealing Baygon. How would you get on if I asked for a raise?”

Holden hated it when she was right.

* * *

WITHIN TWENTY MINUTES, they'd left the narrow streets of Bridgetown, driving past churches and rum shops before turning down a steep incline set among the east coast's renowned red clay hills.

On the way down the incline, Holden realized that Eileen's brakes were less reliable than he had thought. His bowels almost helped him confirm that giving her a raise would be a worthwhile investment, but the road soon levelled out, saving his dignity from certain peril. He pressed his handkerchief against his forehead, dabbing away the sweat that dripped into his eyes. The drive was the perfect metaphor for his perception of Eileen: wild and unexpected and certainly never dull.

Up ahead, a wooden sign with cracked black letters pointed them to the small picturesque seaside village of Shorey Lakes. Chattel houses opened their back doors to a view of the Atlantic, their hinges weeping rust-coloured tears from years of exposure to salt-tinged breezes. Instead of cars in driveways, overturned Moses boats with weather-beaten hulls rested on sandy banks beneath lanky coconut trees that swayed to and fro.

Eileen turned between two houses onto a road which was little more than a sandy track split in two by scraggy crabgrass. She pulled to a stop next to a freshly painted boxed cart filled with husked coconuts. Up ahead, he saw three cars parked beneath the shade of an almond tree, including a sleek 1982 Chevrolet Camaro. He cursed under his breath. "Paul."

Holden looked across at Eileen. Her face was impassive, but the look in her eyes didn't escape his notice. He chewed the inside of his lip, blaming himself for tainting her view of Paul.

Sand crunched beneath his feet as he walked to the chattel house with the open front door. Holden was about to step inside when he bumped into an elderly man and two tall, hulking figures.

"Oh, dear," said the old man as he peered owlishly up at Holden. "Young Davis, I should have known you'd be here."

Holden smiled and gestured to the slim gentleman. "This is Dr Thorpe. He's the government pathologist. He pronounces the time of death whenever a person dies outside of a medical facility. Dr Thorpe, this is my new assistant, Eileen."

"Lovely to meet you, young lady." He shook her hand loosely and said, "I mustn't tarry; I'm trying to get to town for my pudding and souse before they sell out."

"Uh...today isn't Saturday, Dr Thorpe."

"It isn't?" He pushed his glasses up on his nose as he stared at Holden. "Oh yes...too much work and too little time, you see. Well, I'm going home then." And with that, he bustled down the little lane hitching his pants as he went.

Out of the corner of his eye, Holden noticed Eileen checking her watch. It wasn't even noon yet and Dr Thorpe was already clocking out for the day. Typical.
"He's...nice."

"Yes," Holden grinned. "He's a little eccentric, but very nice. He was doing this since I was a little boy, so you can imagine just how long he's been around. He's retiring next month, so you may not see him again after today."

Holden turned to the paunchy man and robust woman and said, "And these are Dorothy and Lloyd Greaves, owners of Happy Home Funeral Parlour. This is Eileen."

Holden held back a grin as Eileen stared at the siblings; he knew the questions that would come later. Dorothy clasped Eileen's hand briefly before she turned to Holden. Even without high-heels, Dorothy was as tall as both of the men. She leaned in and asked in a husky whisper, "Is Clifford with you?"

Holden gave a slight shake of his head. "He already came and went."

Dorothy pouted. Lloyd's mouth soured as he tapped his foot and looked at his watch. "These country gizzards are broke and we're late," he grunted.

Holden raised an eyebrow. "They're my relatives."

Lloyd didn't seem to care. Without saying another word, he walked to a dark car, slipped behind the wheel and started the engine.

Dorothy sighed, her gentle disposition rattled by her brother's rudeness. "You know how he is." She wiped a smear of pink lipstick off Holden's cheek and smacked him playfully on his chest. "Tell Clifford to call me. I hope to see you again soon, Eileen," the older lady said as she put her handbag in the crook of her arm and carried her sturdy frame to the car.

"Are they twins?" whispered Eileen as she watched Lloyd steered the car onto the main road.

"No, they've just got their father's genes. You can always pick out a Greaves from a mile away." Holden pulled back the curtain and ushered her inside. "After you."

The Rediffusion box hummed in the background as a small crowd gathered in the living room. Paul stood in the centre of the room pouring shots of brandy for everyone. His resemblance to Holden was undeniable, with the exception that he was slim for no good reason, making him look like a tall, dark egret. Holden eyed the crystal decanter with a lavish 'P' etched into a crest on the bottle's neck and grumbled beneath his breath.

Out of the corner of his eye, he saw Eileen lift a shoulder and say, "You've got to admit it's a nice touch. Liquoring up people to seal a deal is just good business."

Paul's eyes narrowed when he saw Holden looking at the decanter, but he took care to smile broadly as he said, "Oh dearest me, Holden came to offer his sympathies. Sit down, brother, and join us in a drink to send off Cousin Earl."

Holden plastered on a smile identical to Paul's and said, "Oh, I shouldn't." He turned to the family sitting on the chair. "But just know that I feel poorly about Uncle Earl's passing."

Paul smiled tightly. "He's our cousin; he married Beryl who's Mummy's first cousin."

Holden stared back. "And we call her aunty since she's Mummy's age, so obviously, we call him our uncle."

"Cousin."

"Uncle."

"Jesus, two of you are worse than Cain and Abel," Eileen muttered as she rolled her eyes.

Holden clenched his fist and was about to tell Paul just what he could do with his crystal decanter when he felt a gentle hand on his arm. Eileen stepped forward and addressed the family members who sat in a line on the three-seater chair. "We came to pay our condolences and see if there's anything we can do to help."

Holden sucked in a breath realizing how unprofessional it was for his assistant to have to quell the bickering with his brother. He had to take charge of the situation.

"We're here for you, Laverne," Holden said to the plump young woman sandwiched between two old ladies. He leaned forward and hugged her. She sniffed and waved her handkerchief at the brothers. "It is the sugar, you know. He didn't listen. Doctor said to cut out the sweetbread and the turnovers, but he would still eat them things."

The brothers nodded in unison.

"After the foot was cut off, every morning he used to sit by the window and wait until I was gone to send the little boys to the shop to get him a rum and a Coke."

Laverne wiped her nose and laughed at the memory. She turned her teary face to Eileen. "What kind of help you could give?"

"Tell us what you need."

Laverne studied Paul and Holden for a moment before her eyes opened and her mouth hung open like a trap door. "Oh, yes...two of wunna is undertakers." Fresh tears ran down her face and she raised her palm skyward. "Thank you, Jesus! Mummy was right: the Lord don't come, but he does send. Two of wunna gonna bury Earl."

The brothers glanced at each other and Eileen's eyebrows knit together in concern.

"Well... not together, you see. Holden has his own funeral home and I have mine. Mine is fancier and has more hearses and better fridges, but it's up to you to choose," Paul pointed out.

"That is a matter of opinion, but I think it should come down to whom Earl had a better relationship with," retorted Holden.

Their cousin bit her lip as she considered what they said. "That is true."

"I saw Earl up to last week," offered Holden, hopefully.

"Yes, but did he see you?"

"Just because the man was cross-eyed didn't mean he was blind, Paul."

"You do this every time. Always think you're the smartest."

"It's *smarter* and, yes, I am."

Laverne stood up, taken aback by their argument while she was trying to grieve. "Look, this don't make any sense. We want the best for my brother." She turned to Paul. "You say you got the best fridges and hearses, so you can deal with him."

Paul tossed a smug grin at Holden and said, "Laverne, we're going to give Earl the send-off of the century. Best flowers, coffin...everything."

The two old ladies sitting in the chair broke down in tears again as Laverne threw herself on Paul and hugged him. "You is a angel. Knowing we ain't got no money and coming all the way up here to let we know you goin' pay for the funeral all by you'self."

Paul's grin disappeared. "Pardon?"

"Yes! I tell my mother that we need help burying Earl, and she called wunna, but I didn't realize that you were going to pay for the whole thing."

Paul coughed uneasily. "Uh, that's not the message I got."

Holden clapped him on the shoulder. "Paul, you're a regular stand-up guy and Earl deserves the best. I'll send a nice wreath as my contribution." He smiled at Paul. "It's the least I can do."

* * *

THE DRIVE BACK to the parlour wasn't as jubilant as Eileen expected. She thought Holden would gloat since he hadn't been saddled with Earl's funeral as Paul had been. But as the sun dipped, filling Eileen's battered car with warm golden light, Holden mused quietly.

"What's wrong?" she asked as they turned off the bumpy lane and onto a long country road lined with banana trees.

Holden smiled sadly. "Paul and I have been fighting since he was born and now I wonder if we'll ever stop."

Eileen bit her bottom lip but said nothing.

"Laverne said she wants the best for her brother and I'm trying to remember if Paul and I ever genuinely felt that for each other. The fact that I have to question it is sad."

Holden looked at her. "I don't want a full church and empty sentiments when I die. I've spent too many years in cold rooms with the dead and at some point, I'd like to enjoy the company of the living." He sighed. "But sometimes… that feels like too much to ask."

Chapter 6
Life on a Desert Island

The whistling frogs had clocked out and the roosters were crowing when Eileen's phone rang the next morning. Though the sky was still the colour of acid-washed jeans, she shook off sleep and quickly dressed for work. She stuffed a pack of Sodabix in her bag as she ran down the apartment stairs, being careful to move quietly so she wouldn't wake the mother and baby who lived downstairs. The two-story building was the tallest structure in Hampstead Village, a modest district crisscrossed with winding tracks buttressed by palings and barely wide enough for a person to walk through. Even at that early hour of the morning, she noticed subtle signs that the village was coming to life. Outdoor eaves sheltered bulbs that illuminated backyard bathrooms as some villagers eased into corrugated metal enclosures, tremulously testing the water with gritted teeth. Others rubbed sleep from their eyes as they ambled across congoleum-covered floors to open brightly painted jalousie windows and put battered kettles on stoves.

The blue Toyota was in its usual spot in the recess under the staircase. Since the police had announced the Cane Slasher's presence, she had taken to locking the car every time she left it unattended. Now she muttered under her breath and looked over her shoulder at the overgrown field next to the apartment as she fumbled with the keys. She scrambled into the car and turned the ignition. As she drove and chewed a biscuit, she listened to the news with interest. The government pegged the next year as one for growth in several sectors; she prayed it materialized so she could find a job with better pay and better hours.

Just before she turned onto the main road, she saw two people at the bus stop. Despite not knowing them, but she knew bus fare could suck the life out of a low-income wage. That was enough to make her roll down the rickety window and ask, "Y'all going to town?"

They nodded and hurried to the car. Eileen leaned over and pulled the passenger door handle since it couldn't open from the outside.

"Morning," both of them chirruped to Eileen with a slight twang that squeezed the life out of the 'or' in the word. The man who introduced himself as Chris got in the front seat and the woman waddled around to the driver's side of the car and sat behind Eileen.

In the rearview mirror, Eileen saw the heavy-breasted woman with the quick eyes and unruly mouth purse her lips. The woman took in the exposed springs that jutted out from the back of the front passenger seat and the long metal rods that dangled from the door's cavity. Next to her, the broken window inched its down into the door every time Eileen drove over a bump in the road. The woman's brow furrowed and she clutched her fake leather bag to her bosom as she met Eileen's eyes in the mirror.

"I's Debra. You's the girl that just move into the apartment by the tamarind trees?"

Eileen could tell from the way Debra asked that she already knew, but Eileen still replied, "Yes."

The woman nodded in a self-satisfied way and leaned into the seat with a huff. Eileen's left eye twitched; she suspected that Debra had a running commentary on every and anything, adding flourish and supposition to every retelling. Debra seemed intent on confirming the theory when she said, "Well, I ain't know if you know, but that apartment blighted."

"Uh…that's unfortunate, but thanks for telling me."

"Ain't nothing 'unfortunate' about it. Lock your doors and mind your business. That's what I do and I already live longer than my grandmother."

Eileen bit her lip. Debra didn't *seem* like someone who minded her business. Her eyes challenged Eileen in the mirror. It was obvious that she was eager to reveal more details about the apartment's blight, but refused to give them up without a half-hearted struggle.

After what Eileen suspected was an agonizing moment for Debra, the woman changed tack. "I'm surprised that a high brown-skinned girl like you move into that apartment though. Your family ain't got money?"

Chris' shoulders hunched as he tried to fold in on himself while he kept his eyes on the road ahead and Eileen's eyebrows almost touched her hairline. "I don't have any family, so there's no family money to have," she said, trying to laugh off the woman's intrusion.

"Hmph." Debra seemed dubious about Eileen's claim; she probably thought Eileen was a rogue daughter who ran off to slum it with the common folks as a way to punish her parents.

Eileen asked quickly, "Which bus station are you heading to? Lower Green or Fairchild Street?"

"Chris does go to Lower Green. I work at the supermarket on Buckworth Street."

Eileen's breath caught in her chest. The mere notion of running into Debra every day was excruciating. Luckily, Debra didn't seem to notice Eileen's wide eyes before she turned her attention to Chris. She pointed out her concern that Chris' newborn baby had a broad nose and drooped lips that resembled those of his pastor at The Newberry Tabernacle and she was "only looking out for Chris' interest" as she put it. The look on Chris' face was enough to make Eileen change the conversation to the prices of rice and corned beef, subjects which Debra weighed in on with great gusto until Chris reached his destination. A few moments later, Eileen breathed a sigh of relief when she deposited Debra just up the road from the funeral home. Holden had taken the short walk from his house and was waiting for her in front of Davis and Sons by the time she arrived.

Holden got into the car, his omnipresent ledgers and diary in tow. He gave directions before becoming engrossed in a tangle of figures, tallying and reworking numbers as the wind whipped the pages of his books.

Wicklow Gardens was a tidy row of houses on a narrow lane in a rural community. The James family lived at the end of the cul-de-sac in a small white bungalow next to a patch of grass where black belly sheep grazed for hours before walking two abreast back to their pen. Holden walked across flagstones to the verandah and rapped on the wooden louvres. Lydia's mother came outside, clad in a pink housecoat that hung forlornly on her reduced frame. In a matter of weeks, she'd become an economical version of her former self, as though picked apart and reassembled using the least amount of material possible. Eileen's heart sank when she saw what grief had done to Ernesta James. She waved at her through the window and asked how she was doing.

"Holding on," Mrs James said with a slight lift of a bony shoulder as she held out a tattered envelope to Holden. Her fingers lingered on the edges of the package before she bit her bottom lip and looked away.

"Thank you very much, Mrs James. It's unfortunate that we met under these circumstances, but I wish you and your family all the best." Holden handed her the receipt for her final payment. "I hope that we offered you some comfort during this difficult time."

Mrs James shook her head in disbelief as she stared at the envelope. "I was saving that for Lydia to go overseas and study to be a chef."

A tear slipped down Eileen's face. She saw Holden look at it as though unsure what to do with it now that he knew the funds symbolized her child's hopes and dreams. "I'll bet she was quite the cook," was all he could say.

"Yes… she was talented with food. Last thing she did was get a little part-time job to pay for her plane fare."

Holden bowed his head. "They say that only the good die young. In this particular instance, it's painfully true."

That was too much for her mother; Ernesta excused herself and went back into the house. Holden took his time coming back down the path to get into the car.

"Lydia was my age," Eileen said slowly as a muffled wail came from inside the house. "When I took this job, I only thought about old and sick people; not healthy young women with so much potential."

Holden looked at her, his eyes speculative, and rested his hands on his knees. "This isn't easy, and neither is it what you'd imagine it to be. The hard part about these situations is that those who remain are left to puzzle over what they could have done."

Eileen exhaled, sorry gripping her heart as she asked, "Don't these things haunt you?"

"It's not the dead who haunt you; it's the living with their tears and worries and problems. You'd be surprised what people confess when their minds are heavy with grief. I'm both a mortician and a counsellor. Someone who relieves their pain, but also easily aggravates it. It's a difficult thing to straddle this line between the living and the dead."

"How do you do it?"

His smile was benign, his eyes patient. "By listening, but not absorbing. Sympathizing, but not empathizing. There's a lot of freedom in this job if you let it be so."

She eyed him warily. He snickered at the look on her face.

"Yes: freedom. Death is the point at which the living reconcile everything. It's the finale; no longer is hindsight 20/20 because there are no other options to exhaust. So..." he clasped his hands. "...instead of focusing on how sad a family is, I learn from them. What did the deceased do right in life? What financial mistakes did they make that I can avoid? Are marriages of convenience worth it? Did particular circumstances cost them their life?"

Eileen bit her lip and considered his words. She couldn't deny the wisdom behind it. She had assumed he would revel in the macabre given his line of work, but Holden's optimistic outlook surprised her.

"Yes, I see what you mean," she conceded. "But how do you get past the emotion to arrive at the lessons?"

"This business makes me boil everything down to one question: who and what would I need to sustain myself if I were stranded on a desert island? When I think of it like that, life isn't so hard anymore."

* * *

THAT NIGHT, Eileen gazed out the window at the bushy pasture next to her apartment. Sandflies buzzed against the dusty mosquito screen, fluttering in the light winds that blew in from the northeast. Downstairs, the baby awakened his mother at 1 a.m. to feed and the bus driver who lived next door entered his house with a weary yawn an hour later. A police car took its time traversing the potholes on the bumpy road, one of the nightly patrols that had started since the police force had realized a serial killer was at large. Eileen had grown accustomed to this new monotony of the night, a dark reality that she resented having to embrace. She had poured a glass of brown rum as she watched the news, a recent addition to her nightly routine. Each night she grew more jittery about turning on the TV. The headlines could go either way: another woman could have been found, or the killer might have been apprehended. Tonight, neither option materialized. The only assurance that the commissioner offered to the public was that the police force had stepped up neighbourhood patrols and they were was still investigating the serial murders.

After she had turned off the TV, her nerves were still on edge as she thought about her day. Many parts of it stood out, but more than anything else, her mind replayed Holden's words: "Who and what would I need?" It was a statement so childishly parabolic, that at first, Eileen didn't think much of it. But as the day went on, the universe conspired to illustrate his point.

Earlier that evening, as Eileen walked out of the funeral parlour, a little girl toddled away from her mother and stepped into the path of an oncoming bus. The wheels turned, the gears shifted, and the bus picked up speed as that little person kept moving further into the driver's blind spot while she blew spit bubbles with her mouth. Inertia gripped Eileen. Her chest grew tight and her stomach flipped. And then everything happened in slow motion. The mother flung her handbag and a crate of eggs on the sidewalk and scooped up the child, instincts kicking in long before the tears did. The woman's emotions came out as a scolding garble of words and tears that competed with the startled child's red-faced sobbing.

The mother retrieved her handbag and went on her way, the broken eggs abandoned and laid waste on the sidewalk. Still in shock, Eileen watched the eggs go from floating balls of sunshine to a muddled mess that mixed with two fat wads of pink chewing gum before they slid down the rain gutter.

How many times did people say they'd grab a treasured photo or memento if the house was burning? When forced to pare down our possessions, how many things does one have to leave behind for the good of a healthy future?

Her past felt like that crate of eggs. Theoretically healthy, but Eileen didn't even like eggs, nor was she proud of the choices she had made if it came down to it.

She looked around the apartment and cringed at the state of her existence. She saw it in the pile of unread books, the unhung art on the floor, the junky closet with the previous tenant's belongings. Her thoughts drifted to Holden. As much as she poked fun at him, she found him to be fascinating. Eileen was impressed by his wisdom, and his diplomacy was enviable: he didn't sugar-coat things and his habit of weighing his words was one that Eileen wanted desperately to learn from. If only she'd exercised that caution with her words, her life might have been very different today.

Making extra money and getting her life in order had to become a priority. She got up and dug around in her bag, extracting a cloth and a length of wire that she pulled taut. Now was the time to surround herself with the things that she wanted her life to manifest.

Chapter 7
Mouth Open, Story Jump Out

In the six weeks that Eileen had been at the funeral home, Holden noticed that she sat outside on the picnic bench with Clifford every Friday evening to drink beer. More than once Holden had stayed behind to peer at them through the bathroom window, feeling like a churlish schoolboy whenever he did. He'd considered wandering outside to join them more than once, but he worried that Clifford would find his actions odd and say something. Finally, on the sixth Friday, fortune smiled on him when at four o'clock, a call came for a collection at the geriatric hospital. He waited until Clifford had driven off the lot and into the evening traffic before he picked up two beers and pushed open the back door. Eileen sat atop the table with her feet resting on the bench and eating biscuits out of a plastic bag when he joined her.

"Want a beer?"

She raised an eyebrow. "One: I'm off the clock and therefore within my rights to cuss, so don't be alarmed if anything slips. Two: I didn't know you drank beer."

Holden had a penchant for fine champagne, well-aged cognacs and even the occasional Irish whiskey if he was feeling particularly rambunctious, but it wasn't for Eileen to know that. "Whatever gave you that notion?"

She smirked. "Let's just say that if I was a betting woman, I doubt I'd lose my shirt on that particular wager."

"Why is that?"

Eileen bit the inside of her lip, but her eyes were alight with mischief, reminiscent of the twinkle in her eyes on the night he'd hired her. "You forgot the opener."

Holden looked down at the beers and realized with dismay that they were indeed covered with bottle caps.

"You don't know how to open them without an opener, do you?" She reached over and took the two bottles, flicking the caps against each other so quickly that Holden had no idea that she'd opened one of them until he heard a metallic ping when the cap landed next to him. She took the other beer and a soft carbonated hiss sounded when she prised off the cap with her back teeth before she handed it to him.

"Now you know *two* ways to open beer bottles."

Holden grunted. "Not really; still not sure what you did with the first one."

Eileen broke into a fit of giggles. "I like that you're honest."

Holden sipped the beer and smacked his mouth as though he'd swallowed a mouthful of grey mopping water. "A well-aged cognac, this is not."

Eileen grinned. "Biscuit?"

Hoping that the sweet flavour would help to untie the knots in his tastebuds, Holden reached inside the bag and said in surprise, "But they're broken."

"I know. That's what makes them taste so good." She looked at him quizzically for a moment before she said, "You've never had broken biscuits from the biscuit factory? It's practically a right of passage for every Bajan."

Holden studied the biscuit in his palm with the imprint of a tiny chattel house etched in its golden surface. He enjoyed sweet biscuits but usually, when they looked like this, he'd already taken a bite.

"I can't say I have." He nibbled the biscuit and his eyebrows shot up. "You're right… but *why* does it taste better?"

Eileen smiled. "I have no idea, but why fight it?"

He grinned and sipped his beer again.

She chewed and tilted her head back to catch the last rays of dying sunlight. “I’m kinda glad you came outside today. I saw you watching us from the bathroom and I figured it’s gotta be kinda lonely — not to mention, smelly — in there.”

He averted his eyes. *How the hell had she seen him?*

“I didn’t say that to embarrass you or anything.”

“And yet, you’ve done just that.”

“Sorry,” she said, sincerity etched on her face. “I’ve realized recently that I’d do well to take a leaf out of your book and think before I speak, but I admit that it’s a work in progress.”

“I don’t think there’s anything wrong with how you express yourself; rough honesty is better than a gentle lie. But I’m glad you feel inspired.”

“Yeah… I’m learning a lot from you and Clifford.”

Holden’s face soured. He shook his beer gently and said, “I take it that Clifford’s company is scintillating enough that you spend your evenings here instead of with your…loved ones.”

Eileen shrugged. “I’ve only been here a few weeks and I’ve got some bills to catch up on; I can’t exactly be blowing my money on wild hobbies.”

Holden had to hand it to Eileen; she had responded, but she didn’t answer.

“So do you have any hobbies…maybe some that you like to do with…others?”

“I go to the library on Saturdays and I spend Sundays reading and cleaning.” She looked across the car park toward Buckworth Street. The after-work rush had subsided and now only a handful of vehicles went up and down the road. Eileen dusted her hands on her skirt and handed Holden the biscuits before she descended from her perch on the table. “I’m going to skedaddle now that traffic has eased up.” She smiled as she reached for his empty beer bottle. “I’ll take that. And…it was nice talking to you. I had fun.”

She took both bottles with her to the car, started it and drove off, honking the horn twice as she careened down the road. Eileen had grown more and more perplexing as the days went on. Her afro was as big as her attitude and Holden had never been exposed to antics as quirky as hers. He'd hoped to learn more about her but all he'd been able to gather was that she was thrifty; she'd probably taken the empty bottles to claim the deposits at the bottle depot. But he had to admit that he'd never imagined that he could have so much fun drinking beer and eating broken biscuits.

* * *

THE NEXT DAY was quiet. Clifford and Holden were at a funeral and Eileen was left to lock up since they wouldn't return until after closing. It was the first time Eileen had experienced such quietude at work. With no incoming calls or filing to do, the solitude soon turned to boredom and Eileen spent the bulk of the afternoon spinning in her chair and staring at the ceiling.

Later in life, Eileen would question if fate intervened when she accidentally spun too quickly, sending her chair crashing into Holden's desk and knocking over his treasured obituary book with a heavy thud. Yellowing scraps of news-sheet checkered the book's white pages like a deathly chessboard as it fell open on the floor. Lydia James' face smiled back at her, a pretty pawn in a madman's game. Eileen bit her lip as she picked it up. She'd never looked at it before; she found the idea of keeping pictures of dead people to be creepy and she was never entirely sure why Holden relished the notion. Eileen flipped through the book until she found the

Slasher's victims, each of them barely separated by a few pages. She shuddered. With no way to predict who else might attract the killer's attention, who knew how many more young women would soon fill the book's pages? The thought sent a chill down her spine.

The only connection between the victims was that they were young and came from humble neighbourhoods. Using that profile, half the island was at risk, including herself. Eileen massaged her forehead and glanced at the time. Mercifully, the clock on the wall told her it was time to lock up and go home.

Traffic was intense: buses, trucks and cars were at a standstill on the busy road. Only a snow-cone vendor was able to wend his way through the tangle of vehicles, his even pace propelling his bicycle and its large ice-box mounted on the front. Down the road, a man was loading animal feed onto a donkey cart as the supermarket manager pulled the sliding doors together and secured them with a padlock and a heavy chain.

Eileen tossed her bag into the car and slid behind the wheel. As she was about to pull onto Buckworth Street, a hand snaked through the open passenger window, flipped the lock and yanked open the door. Eyes wide, Eileen was about to slam her foot on the gas when in tumbled her nosy neighbour, Debra.

Chest heaving and arms sweating, Debra flopped down on the seat with two large grocery bags.

"Oh…g-good evening," stammered Eileen.

"Good thing I see you before you pulled off," Debra wheezed as she settled into the seat. She glanced at the sign on the building behind them and her eyes lit up. "Wait...one of your family dead? What you doing at the funeral home?"

"Oh, well, I..." Eileen hesitated, wondering if to risk karma's wrath in case the universe punished her for lying. "...I was just turning around in the car park."

"Oh... alright," Debra pouted as though juicy gossip was more important than if Eileen's family was alive and well. "Thanks for offering to drop me home," Debra said as she shoved her handbags onto the backseat.

Offering? Eileen raised an eyebrow. Debra would only worsen her headache. Eileen had to find a way to get her out. "But I'm not going home yet. I've got a stop to make and I don't want to keep you."

Debra's eyes lit up. "That's perfect. I was wondering why you does leave home at all hours of the day and night." She beamed at Eileen. "You could explain as you drive."

Eileen rolled her eyes as she eased her rumbling car slowly into the traffic. "If you don't mind, I've got a headache and don't really feel like talking."

Debra nodded knowingly. "Probably from trying to figure out what happened to Anna, the girl who lived in your apartment before. But, don't worry; I'm gonna tell you now."

"Uh-huh," said Eileen. Her temples started to pound.

"She is one of them girls that get kill by the Cane Slasher."

Eileen's ears perked up. "The serial killer murdered someone who lived in my apartment?"

"Yes, girl," Debra effused with the air of someone with a captive audience. She smacked her lips and leaned in as she stage-whispered, "The day she went missing, I see a man lurking in a car by the apartment. A tall, slim fellow. He waited outside for over an hour."

"Did you tell the police?"

Debra snorted. "Them ain't ask me nothing, so how I going to tell them?"

Eileen made a mental note to mention this detail to Holden so he could pass it on to Derricks. It might just be the clue the police needed to make the country safe again.

"Had you seen him before?"

"No, that's why I noticed him. This fellow looked real twitchy like he didn't up to no good. He had on a brown uniform, kinda like what the road works men does wear. Name tag say he name J. Walker."

"How did you see his name tag?" Eileen was flabbergasted by the depth of Debra's details.

"How you think I know he was waiting for Anna? My mother always used to say if you want to know, you would ask. So I went and ask him what he was doing there."

"What kind of car was it?"

Debra pursed her lips, glanced at Eileen's cracked dashboard and said, "It was old and rusty like this, except it was brown."

Eileen ignored her and asked, "Anything else you remember?"

"Yeah, he hair coulda use a good combing." Debra gave Eileen a knowing look. "A man who looks that rusty is capable of anything."

Chapter 8
A strange request

"I didn't realize so many people died until I took this job," Eileen mused the following Friday as they drove north on the island's tiny west coast highway. The sunset's golden light filled the car and occasionally, just over the top of a galvanized paling, glimpses of the Caribbean sea came into view, the gilded surface shimmering under the lowering sun.

Holden smiled. "Life is a cycle. But, maybe it just *seems* like a lot because we handle government collections. Oddly enough, before we did it, Happy Home had the contract." He puckered his mouth. "Our families used to get along very well before, sharing resources and materials until we outbid them for the government tender. That's one of the reasons Lloyd doesn't like our family very much anymore. Dorothy, on the other hand, realizes it's just business and never took it personally."

Eileen glanced at Holden. "Yikes. I used to think morticians were just as dull as librarians except they actually got to see naked people, instead of just reading about them."

He chuckled. "Death is a whole industry which means it comes with its fair share of backstabbing and high-jinks. There are stores for it, schools for it... I went to university in Britain for four years to become a mortician. You have seen for yourself how much more there is to it than just embalming bodies."

Eileen nodded as she turned off the highway and onto a narrow road. He was right about that. In just over two months,

Eileen had instituted cost and time-saving measures and made suggestions to increase business. Holden had been impressed with her business savvy, declaring her a valuable asset to Davis and Sons. Clifford agreed to an extent, jokingly saying that her 'hot-coal typing' was the only thing keeping her humble. The three of them had morphed into a well-oiled machine, functioning so seamlessly that Holden no longer went into fits of melancholy when the bills arrived.

"So why do you go to almost all of the pick-ups if Clifford is already going?"

"It's an old practice called touting — basically face-to-face advertising. Some mortuaries post touters outside the hospital's A&E to solicit the relatives of new decedents. They do their best to outbid each other and can be a rather unruly bunch."

Eileen cringed. "That's heartless."

Holden agreed. "Which is why I do it myself and offer a more sympathetic ear. But touting is good business. If I'm there to listen and offer advice to the bereaved, I'm more likely to get the job."

"Ah…" Eileen smiled. "…so that's why you needed an assistant with a car?"

"Yes. It's bad form for Clifford to be dawdling with a corpse while I try to drum up business. A family may wonder what sort of indifferent brutes we are."

Eileen laughed.

"By my father's logic, a family may open the yellow pages and pick whomever they see first. Due to the disadvantages of alphabetization, 'Davis' isn't the first name on the list."

Not for the first time, Eileen realized how much she regretted not having met Holden Senior. “Your father was a regular renaissance man, wasn’t he?”

"That he was. This is the turn we're looking for."

They were driving through an overgrown area that was so unkempt that the grass formed a bushy blanket over the sidewalks. Holden pointed to a narrow gap ahead of them. “Slow down by the lime grove opposite the cane field and you’ll see an old mill as soon as we turn in.”

Eileen manoeuvred the car onto a rocky lane. Above the treetops, the funnelled tip of a mill wall loomed like a dark shadow in the waning light. Plumes of white dust coated the car as the tyres bobbled down the gritty track. On both sides of the lane, tall trees grew wide branches that melded overhead to form a bright yellow arch that extended the entire length of the driveway. Warm sunlight illuminated the bright yellow blossoms, making them glow like tiny comets as they fluttered down into flowery drifts on either side of the path.

The leafy tunnel opened up to a wide courtyard, complete with a rustic villa that looked as though it had been freshly plucked from a natty little vineyard in the French countryside. Clifford and his son were closing the back door of the boxy white van at the foot of the flared staircase. Next to the circular fountain, two police officers spoke to a harried-looking middle-aged woman and Dr Thorpe, the Crown's pathologist. Even without him turning around, Eileen recognized Derricks from his broad-shouldered build. She was surprised to see the commissioner at a collection for a man who died of a stroke. But then again, this was no routine collection.

Holden said, "Eileen, I'm sure you remember Commissioner Derricks from the office and Dorothy Greaves of Happy Home Funeral Parlour."

"I'm very sorry for your loss, Ms Greaves," Eileen said as she reached out to clasp Dorothy's hand, but the woman merely nodded and clutched a lacy handkerchief to her nose as she wrapped her other arm around her midsection. Dorothy's stocky frame was clad in a pale pink dress with far too many frills, her grey wig trembling as she shuddered. Eileen stepped back awkwardly. Dorothy had been warm and friendly the first time they'd met, but her brother's death had made her cold and distant.

"I can't believe it," said Dorothy, her deep voice a sad murmur. "I thought Lloyd had overslept. But when I shook him this afternoon I realized how cold he was."

"Yes, yes… rigour had already set in by the time I arrived," offered Dr Thorpe as he adjusted his glasses on his nose. "Truth be told, it's not unusual for someone with Lloyd's history to have a stroke."

Dorothy sniffed. "High blood pressure runs in our family."

Holden's face was pained as he looked at the older woman. "Dorothy, if you need anything at all, you call us. We'll handle Lloyd free of charge."

Dorothy squeezed the handkerchief in her fist and shook her head. "No need. He wanted to be cremated."

Dr Thorpe fished a slip of paper out of the top pocket of his shirt jac and scribbled a note. "Very good. I'll write up the certificate tonight so you can organize the paperwork and ship him to Trinidad."

Derricks tapped Holden on the arm. "Davis, now that you're here, there's something I've been meaning to discuss with you." He tilted his head toward the covered verandah and tipped his hat to the rest of the group. "If you'll excuse us." He strode away and Holden followed in his wake.

"Love, I real sorry 'bout this," Clifford said soberly as he wrapped an arm around her shoulders. "Don't think twice to call if you want to talk or need any help."

Eileen wasn't sure if her eyes deceived her, but Dorothy seemed to recoil slightly before she smiled feebly at Clifford. It just went to show that even people in the business of death weren't immune to grief.

* * *

HOLDEN AND THE COMMISSIONER stepped carefully around the multitude of plants Dorothy kept in the verandah, hoping that he wouldn't be there too long. He never liked the tense energy Derricks gave off, and it was especially profound in the gathering darkness beneath the flickering overhead bulb.

"What's going on?"

"This is a delicate matter. I don't want to be difficult, especially since the man is ready for retirement…" started Derricks. He glanced across as Dr Thorpe drove his pristine Mercedes Benz slowly out of the courtyard. "I'm not trying to make him lose his pension, but I'm finding inconsistencies in Thorpe's reports."

"Oh?" Holden twisted his mouth in confusion, unsure as to why Derricks was telling him this. "Just let Lynch verify them."

"Dr Lynch is on holiday and won't be back until Thorpe retires in two weeks so I'm stuck with the old man until then." Derricks scrubbed his beard. "The thing is that I normally wouldn't be so uptight about it, but there are certain things — little things — that he didn't list in the report for the girl we found in the factory."

"Like?"

"Well, I saw some yellow dust on the side of her face. There are photos of it and everything, but Thorpe didn't mention it in the report so I have no idea if it's chalk or paint flecks."

"It was pollen. My assistant saw some of it in the victim's ears and washed it out. Along with some mud that was under her fingernails."

"Hmm… pollen," mused Derricks. "Do you know what kind?"

"No…and to be honest, we had to do more washing than we usually would when Lynch sends a decedent." Holden raised an eyebrow. "Don't forget that we work under the assumption that the pathologist has already done his job by the time we get involved."

Derricks heaved a deep breath. "Look, I normally wouldn't ask, but would you be willing to submit reports for the crown's cases? Just for two weeks so I can create some redundancies." His face was serious, his voice earnest as he leaned in. "Thorpe is a good man, you know. It's just old age and the drinks. Plus, he's been a little off since his wife left him. So just help him out a bit."

"Well…I…" Holden wasn't sure it was a good idea. A lot could happen in two weeks. "By the way, that tip my assistant had shared about the man in the brown car... did that yield anything?"

Derricks flicked his eyes toward the courtyard where Clifford and his son had left Eileen alone with Dorothy. They stood six feet apart, Eileen swatting sandflies and Dorothy looking as though she wished the sandflies would eat her alive. "Do you know how many budget cuts I had to manage when I took this post? I don't have the manpower or money to track down every hare-brained tip. I suspect that her and the nosy neighbour just like blabbing for the sake of it. Try and keep this thing with Thorpe quiet for now. Your assistant is clearly a talker."

Holden frowned at Derricks. If anything, Eileen was more clandestine than Holden was, which was unusual in and of itself. Derricks clapped him on the shoulder and said, "Thanks, young Davis."

The commissioner jogged down the stairs, calling to the station sergeant who had driven him to the scene. Dorothy also got in her car and in a few seconds, both engines roared to life and the headlights cut a wide swath across the courtyard before they both drove away.

Fruit bats screeched overhead in the ring of trees around the courtyard, camouflaging the crunch of Holden's footsteps on the gravel as he walked toward Eileen. She had been watching the cars leave and she startled when he touched her shoulder; he dropped his hand, wondering if he had been out of line for touching her. As much as he wanted to tell her about what Derricks had asked him to do, he felt now wasn't the time.

"Let's go. I'm sure you don't want your chariot covered in bat guano," Holden gestured toward the bats overhead. "Plus, it's going to rain." Eileen glanced at the grey clouds that gathered and nodded.

The engine wheezed the way it always did whenever Eileen turned the key.

Except this time, it didn't start.

Chapter 9
Between a Rock and a Dark Place

The Baygon tin tucked behind her seat was empty. Holden had given her a small raise the previous week, but it was nowhere near enough to buy a new starting motor. Eileen was grateful, but between rent, petrol and utilities, her desires often eclipsed her assets. There were many other things she would have loved to upgrade, like the threadbare bedsheet at the window that kept the sun from roasting her to a crisp every morning. She sighed.

"There's a phone booth at the gas station on the main road. I'll go and leave a message at Thorpe's office. He can tell Clifford to come back for us," Holden said as he reached for the door handle.

"Oh, geez." Eileen leaned onto the steering wheel and looked around. Her eyes caught the lurking shadows in the broad verandah and her ears heard the branches that creaked and twisted in the whistling wind. Fear curled in her belly, resolute and indifferent to her pride. Being with a man as tall and strapping as Holden should have made her brave, but her fear of the Slasher was too strong. Yes, they needed to leave, but she wouldn't feel safe walking between two cane fields on that lonely road. Nor would she ask Holden to go alone because that meant staying in the car by herself. She imagined him returning to find her gone, leaving only a trail of bloodstains that disappeared among the drifts of yellow blossoms until she turned up a week later.

"Can't we just…" her shoulders sagged; she felt like a child scared by the Heart Man. "…stay here?"

"Here? All night?" Holden was confused. "Why ever would we do that?"

Eileen stared at him like he'd asked for directions to Mars. "There's a serial killer on the loose. I don't want to wander in the dark."

He rubbed his face and said, "I'm like a bull in a verbal china shop. I mean well, but my words are clumsy. It's one of the reasons I don't talk much; I save time by not having to explain what I meant to say ten minutes after I said it."

Eileen sighed. It wasn't his fault that he wasn't taught to be fearful the way she had been. She wondered what it was like to be a man, given respect and privilege just for the sake of it. Still, she couldn't discount that being a beneficiary of a system didn't make Holden a victim, even if it made him unknowingly complicit.

"It's stressful always looking over your shoulder when you've done nothing wrong," Eileen said, shaking her head at the injustice of it.

"You're not wrong, but I didn't think you'd be okay with being in the dark all night. I assumed going for help was the wisest thing to do."

She felt guilty for jumping to conclusions. "It's not that dark." Eileen motioned to the flickering light in the verandah.

He cocked an eyebrow at her. "I guess. But if you change your mind, it's not a long walk. We just have to hope that it doesn't rain too much since this area is prone to flooding."

No sooner than he said the words, it started to pour. Eileen sighed. She was caught in the no-man's-land of bad decisions where no matter what you did there was a downside.

He shook his head in disbelief. "As much as it pains me to quote Clifford, a few years ago he mentioned that scientists created a phone you can use anywhere. 'Practically fit in yuh pocket, boss' he'd said. One of those would be perfect now," Holden said, raising his voice above the din of the rain that pounded the car's roof and rattled the windows.

Eileen imagined stuffing a rotary phone in her purse and knocking on doors to ask strangers to use their wall sockets.

"How would they even work?"

"Radio frequencies. That's what makes them completely portable. Clifford predicts that in thirty years, everyone will have one."

"I can't picture my bag ringing when I'm in town." She frowned. "And who on earth needs to use a phone all day?"

Holden wrinkled his eyebrows. "For Clifford to call and ask for orange money all the time? I could do without one."

Lighting forked and split the sky with thin silvery cracks of electricity overhead and gave Eileen second thoughts about waiting out the storm. She peered through the heavy rain at the house's covered verandah and wondered if they shouldn't wait it out there.

"You're a man of science. Should we be inside a tin can when there's lightning?"

"We're fine as long as we don't touch metal." His eyes lingered on the door's hanging rods and the exposed ceiling where the roof-liner used to be. "So make yourself small."

Eileen giggled.

A hint of a smile played on Holden's face. "The last time I was caught in a storm like this, Paul and I got our asses cut for tracking mud inside the house."

In her mind, she wanted to smile and nod, but her mouth had different plans. "Then why do you hate him so much?"

"I don't hate Paul. Well…maybe it seems like I do," he said resignedly. "I hate how easy he's had it. He went to a better mortuary school and stayed there twice as long because he didn't focus on his studies. If that were me, my father would have shouted at me to get back to Barbados however I could, because he wouldn't encourage slacking off with his money. Then Paul got the new funeral home in the will." He bit his lip so viciously Eileen thought he would draw blood. "*That* was the one that hurt."

She thought about what he said. "It does sound like you got the dirty end of the family stick. But 'the Lord don't put more on a man than he could bear', as the old people always say."

"Yeah, maybe."

She smiled. "One lesson I've learned from working with you is that every emotion has its uses. Sometimes, bitterness can help drive us forward because we become so determined to have the last laugh. You never know; what you're supposed to have in this life might be even greater."

He grunted the way one does when words have too much wisdom to deny, but sting too deeply to easily accept. "These things take some getting used to. I've often considered just splitting the two businesses, letting him keep his building and I keep mine instead of having him leech off of me. But... I guess maybe I find comfort in feeling like I'm looking after him."

Eileen took a deep breath. "All we can hope is that these things are worth it in the end."

Holden searched her eyes with his. His voice was low as he said, "It's hard asking for what you want in this life while feeling you have no right to it."

Her heart skipped a beat and she regretted the infinitesimal moment when her lips parted and she held her breath. Was she reading too much into what he said? Or was there truly more to it?

"What is it that you want?" Her nerves got the better of her and she hastily added, "From your brother, that is."

He tore his eyes away and looked down at his hands. "You've seen the bills; you know by now that I'm paying for Paul's fancy facility." Resentment tainted his voice as he said, "I co-signed the loan while Paul was studying overseas. I didn't *imagine* my father could die if that makes any sense. Putting people in the ground every day can make you detach yourself from the fact it will happen to you."

Eileen was hesitant to ask, but the solution seemed so simple that she had no choice but to make it tangible, to give it wings so it could float into the air and alight in Holden's ears. "Can't Paul help to pay the loan?"

He snorted. "My father made me promise to look after Paul." He chuckled dryly as he mimicked a deep voice. "'Son, I named you after me because you're the next best thing. Don't forget it.'"

Despite the misery with which he said it, she laughed and observed, "Your father was very wise."

Holden looked at her again. In the glistening moonlight, his eyes glowed back at her, focused and unrelenting. "He's a brilliant man. Was." He shook his head self-consciously, his eyes drifting to the tangle of tree branches that shivered overhead in the deluge. "I'll be honest; he wouldn't have wanted me to hire you. He would've said you'd be too much of a distraction."

Eileen stared at him, her brow furrowing. "Am I?

"Yes," he said, softly. "One I needed."

Eileen looked down, her cheeks aflame.

"Eileen?"

"Yes?"

"The rain stopped."

* * *

SO IT HAD.

Holden checked the time. Two glowing hands spread wide across the watch face in the dark and his eyes flew open. "It's almost ten," he said.

"Do you think it's too late to walk to the phone booth on the main road?"

Holden was surprised, but not because of the late hour. As Eileen had rightly pointed out, he was a man — that kind of fear wasn't ingrained in him. What unsettled him was that they had spent three hours talking in a dark car. Three hours with no food, wine, or other amusements and yet he felt sated and free. The desert island he had waxed so philosophically about had materialized and he was on it with Eileen. He glanced at her, thoughts foaming in his head like bubbles, each one fraught with peril if he were to let them escape.

In some ways, Eileen was a complete mystery to him. Her cadences were artificially hardened, like those of a catholic school girl who had ended up on the wrong side of the tracks one day after school and never went back. She was insightful and sharp but gritty around the edges. She was well-read, having an absurd amount of pop culture knowledge coupled with historical and social theories. He'd heard her cuss more than once and seen her drinking beer with Clifford. All of it only served to make her more intriguing.

She turned to him, eyes questioning because he hadn't responded. He opened his mouth, ready to say the words on his mind when headlights beamed through the windshield, dousing them in sharp light. In unison, they raised their hands to shield their eyes. The oncoming vehicle rocked closer and closer on the dark road, splashing through puddles on the uneven gravel driveway and, for a brief moment, Holden felt Eileen's hand clasp his. "Oh, my — is that Clifford?"

The van jerked to a stop and a loping figure emerged, sauntering in front of first one headlight and then the other as he traipsed around to the passenger side of the car. "Boss," he nodded. "Eileen," he grinned. "Y'all ready to go home?"

"Clifford, how'd you know we were still here?"

"I ain't see y'all come back. I had a mind that Ol' Faithful wasn't so faithful," he chuckled and tapped the rusty car door. "That Baygon ain't save you tonight, girl. Let we go home."

Eileen grinned and got her bag from the back seat. "Good thing he's so nosy, isn't it?"

Holden was silent as he got out of the car and walked across the wet gravel driveway. He didn't think Clifford's nosiness was a good thing at all.

* * *

LATER THAT NIGHT, his mind troubled, Holden lay naked on his bed at the Davis family home. It was a sprawling great house, painted in warm brick red and bordered by a ten-foot wall. He felt like an old man whenever he reflected how he came to live there alone. First, his mother had died. Then Paul moved out to marry a socialite who came from plantation money. A few years passed before his father also died. Now only Holden remained. Since then, he'd toyed with the idea of renting the great house and moving into the living quarters above the funeral home. The savings would be immense, but Holden suspected that memories of residing above the business were more alluring than rental income.

Like most traditional merchant buildings in Barbados, the parlour's second floor was outfitted as living quarters. His memories of living in a happy home were strongest there. He remembered his mother lighting the kerosene lamp at night and if it were warm, she'd pad silently across the wooden floor to throw open the jalousie doors to cool the house. Holden would trail her in his little pyjamas and beg for permission to sleep on the verandah like a big boy. She'd make up a cot for him, telling him to be careful even though she never went too far. His mother would spread a blanket across a chair by the door and watch as he stretched his little hand through the wooden rails to count the stars until he fell asleep. He would dream that he was high above the world, carefree and happy as he played in the sky. But what he looked forward to most were the mornings.

Before sunrise, he would wake up early to watch as the dray carts came down from the country laden with fruits, the donkeys' hooves clopping in a rhythmic beat on the road. They'd be joined by vendors who pushed boxed carts full of vegetables to the outdoor markets. Merchants would open their louvred double doors for business, one after the other, like a row of dominoes, tipped over by an unseen hand. Large trucks with barrels of rum would pass on their way to the careenage to be shipped overseas. The barrels were stacked so high that Holden tried to reach them as they passed by. Holden had loved living on a such a lively street.

He was seven and Paul was five when his mother pressed his father to buy a family home. For years she complained that the living shouldn't sleep under the same roof as the dead. In the end, his father was persuaded. He often said his wife poured so many libations to keep the spirits at bay that the living room smelled like a vat of overproof rum. So, to keep the peace, his father purchased the great house and converted the second story home into storage space.

For a few months, Holden had faced the very real possibility that if business didn't improve that he'd have no choice but to climb the dusty stairs and clean out the cobwebs on the second floor. But then Eileen arrived and things picked up considerably. Eileen was organized and full of great ideas. He made many more grief visits and the bills were paid on time. Her make-up skills were exceptional and soon, word spread that if you wanted your relatives to look good in the hereafter that Davis and Sons was the place to go. She had recently suggested that with her artistic talents and the unused refrigeration space, she could easily start creating wreaths for retail, a venture which she forecast could bring in hundreds every month. She was also shrewd enough to suggest that she be paid a handsome commission for each piece, an observation which Holden didn't argue with. Truth be told, it gave him a slight thrill when she was so assertive with him; at times he found himself being difficult on purpose just so she'd square him up.

Work had become an effortless hobby. Eileen was smart, funny and so energetic that she made him yearn to spend his days in the warmth of her smile. At first, it was unthinkable that he would find her sassy antics endearing. Now, he felt he couldn't live without them.

He had avoided broaching the line between passion and professionalism with her before, but earlier that night, he had felt himself heading perilously toward the void. Maybe it was the intimacy of the dark or their close confinement inside the car, but either way, he didn't like it. His stomach churned when he thought about men with an endless stream of secretaries that they took for mistresses. It was contemptible when men tampered with their businesses and jeopardized their marriages. His father had been a captain of commerce above all else and never approved of such base behaviour.

"Six children in four houses, a wife and two outside women that can't stand him," Holden Senior had said to his boys at one shipping merchant's funeral. "His daughters won't trust men and his sons won't respect women. What a lovely legacy he's left." Holden Senior shook his head in disgust before escorting the coffin down the church aisle. As the casket went by, Holden remembered the outside women looking daggers at each other from opposite pews at the back.

Holden never wanted that kind of life for himself. He sighed as he stepped into the shower. He pressed his hands against the wall and leaned forward, letting the warm water flow through his hair and down his muscled back. Eileen drove him crazy in more ways than one. Sometimes he worried that the allure of an illicit desire might be to blame for his attraction to her. He truly hoped it was. Because the alternative — that he might have deeper feelings for her — was terrifying.

Chapter 10
Two of a Kind

It was too late on a Saturday night for the phone to ring. And yet, at 9 p.m. it jangled in the darkness, rattling a loose linoleum tile on the apartment floor. Eileen rubbed her eyes, her mind caught between sleep and wake. It was Holden calling to say that another body had been found in a cane ground. "Do you need me to pick you up?" she asked as she swung her feet over the edge of the bed and fumbled for her clothes in the dark.

"No. Clifford and his son left already." The line went quiet, with only the gentle ticking of Eileen's alarm clock counting the seconds that passed.

"Hello?" she said, after a moment.

"I'm still here," he replied.

On the surface, his response seemed ordinary, but the heaviness in his voice told her it wasn't.

"Holden?" she said. His name sounded strange coming out of her mouth, the first time she had ever uttered it. She had never liked the idea of calling someone her "boss"; it didn't seem like a smart thing for a woman to imply to a man that he owned her. But the flip side of that was not calling him anything at all. Holden had become known as "he" when she mentioned him to Clifford or "excuse me" when she spoke to him directly.

He exhaled as though releasing a breath he'd held for hours instead of seconds. "It's just...," he faltered and tried again. "…sometimes descriptions and situations can make you presume the worst."

Eileen was baffled for a moment before recognition flooded her consciousness. She squeezed her eyes shut as the image of a moonlit cane field took shape in her mind. The bent body of a woman with light brown skin and a shock of thick curly hair lay among a patch of young green plants. Glassy eyes identical to her own stared back at her.

She blinked.

The scene vanished and the bedroom floor and wardrobe slid back into place, her nightgown clinging to her body and the cold telephone receiver gripped in her hand.

"You thought it was me."

"Yes."

A chill crept through her body and with a start, she realized she'd been holding her breath as she waited for his answer.

"I'm fine," was all she could finally whisper. It was a trite thing to say at that moment, the bed still warm enough to remind her that her life and all of its inherent potential were safe. The fragility of her existence exposed itself, laying bare the entitled ease with which she assumed she could do things in that flimsy theoretical place called tomorrow. For the young woman who resembled her, tomorrow, with its procrastinated promises and deferred dreams would never come.

"I wanted to know you were okay." He sighed, the noise coming through the receiver like a sad gust of air. "Goodnight, Eileen."

There was a clatter and the line went dead. Eileen hung up too. Being presumed dead was stressful. Suddenly, every unfulfilled task was thrown into sharp relief, impatient to be fulfilled. Every noise outside the house was magnified and menacing as time ticked by. Eileen spent every minute of it wondering when and why it became acceptable for women to live in a world where they were forced to worry about their safety. Finally, Eileen dozed off again.

A deep slumber begrudgingly agreed to gather her in its warm embrace, but the universe mutinied. Flashes of a doppelgänger, bloated and crawling with maggots that worked their way through her flesh and flies that laid eggs in her ears haunted her as she slept.

As the sun crept higher in the sky, the morning heat baked itself into the wall next to her bed and warmed the room, drawing sweat and leaving a damp outline of her body pressed into the sheets. Hot and restless, she woke up and wandered into the bathroom. She splashed cold water on her face and stared into the mirror, searching her eyes to reassure herself that her nightmares were unfounded.

The serial murders were perplexing on their own, but the fact that this woman looked like her piqued Eileen's curiosity even more. Eileen was an orphan after all. What if the latest victim was a relative? A sister or a cousin perhaps? What if she could find out more about her mother and her real family? The possibility was too great to pass up. Eileen downed a cup of scalding hot tea and pushed her feet into red rubber slippers before she headed out the door.

Just a few houses down the narrow lane was a clapboard chattel structure with flaking brown paint that housed a shop at the front and a residence at the back. The shop's bifold wooden door was topped by a faded sign declaring it to be the property of Mr C.J. Briggs, licensed seller of liquor. Despite the unassuming facade, the business was the village's hub, a place where residents could get gum, gossip and rum just a stone's throw away from home. Inside the packed shop, women bought pork chops, chicken backs and rice by the pound, ingredients that would find their way to modest kitchens to be heavily seasoned, stewed and baked. One woman with a skirt pulled over her breasts gossiped with a lady decked out in neatly pressed church clothes. Two men were huddled in a dark corner, the window above them closed tight so the sunlight wouldn't sting their rummy eyes. The large glass case on the counter was devoid of the usual ham cutters and cheese cutters. They wouldn't sell on the Lord's day when pots bubbled merrily on every stove with Sunday food. Next to the glass case, two stacks of newspapers were weighted down with chunks of wood that had been rubbed smooth after being handled by Briggs and his father for almost sixty years.

The headlines screamed '4TH WOMAN FOUND DEAD' and 'CANE SLASHER STRIKES AGAIN'. Eileen greeted everyone, picked up a newspaper and pushed a worn red one dollar note across the counter. Briggs nodded, pocketed the bill and puffed on his cigarette all without interrupting his argument about the pitfalls of the West Indies cricket team.

Eileen read as she walked. Last night's victim had been discovered. The details were almost identical to the previous victims: her body was dumped in the cane field after being murdered elsewhere. A couple was out for a late-night dalliance when they found her body and reported it to the police. The article continued on page four, but even on that page, there wasn't a picture of the victim. A brisk wind blew, fluttering the pages of the newspaper and snapping Eileen back to reality. She glanced around, her nerves on edge, but saw nothing except the houses on her left and the field on her right. The canes across the road were young, but the bright green leaves rustled irritably in the wind like footsteps on dry grass. She tucked the paper under her arm and hurried home.

* * *

THE NEXT MORNING, Eileen got to work extra early and waited in the car park for the others to arrive. In the time that went by, she read the rest of a book, painted her nails and considered getting a jheri-curl. The afro she saw in her car's cracked wing mirror was an unruly tangle of pencil-sized curls that spread out around her face like a fuzzy halo. She twirled a lock of hair around her finger and pulled it taut until it touched the tip of her nose. Instead of staying in the middle of her forehead the way Michael Jackson's did, the hair sprang back up and lost itself in the tawny pile on her head.

"Girl, that hair just as disruptive as you. Try and stop forcing it to be something it ain't," came Clifford's taunt as he swung onto the lot and parked neatly next to her. Eileen scowled but didn't retort as she gathered her things from the back seat and headed into the building.

"You very early," Clifford observed as he unlocked the back door. His voice betrayed nothing, but suspicion lingered in his eyes.

"I've got a lot of filing to do."

When Clifford walked past her desk to unlock the door and windows at the front of the building, Eileen saw him raise an eyebrow at her neat desk.

"You mussy think I is Queen Isabella," he mumbled.

"Pardon?"

"Columbus convinced a rich woman to finance a trip to a place he wasn't sure existed to bring back things he didn't know were there. That was genius. This…" He gestured to her paper-free desk, "…is just sad."

Eileen's face reddened. Clifford whistled as he picked up his yard broom on his way through the front door, pausing briefly to greet Holden who had just arrived. Holden didn't make eye contact as he said good morning, choosing instead to sit at his desk and make himself busy doing nothing. Eileen wondered if he felt uncomfortable after their late-night conversation. His discomfort only served to increase hers and for four hours, both of them tried to pretend the other wasn't there. Their interactions took on the stilted, overly polite rhythms of two strangers on a bus who wouldn't verbalize which one of them wanted the last seat.

At lunchtime, the radio news came on. Both Eileen and Holden listened with rapt attention as the police commissioner asked the public to remain calm and cooperate with officials as they investigated the murder of Michelle Jones who had been found over the weekend. Of course, mass panic and speculation ensued. The public's anger was palpable on the call-in programme that aired immediately after the news. Callers blasted the police and politicians, the former for doing too little and the latter for doing too much.

"Somebody high-up killing these girls! That is why dem ain't catch them yet."

"All of this foolishness about amnesty! The government put way the hangman last year and since then this place gone to the dogs."

"I got two young daughters and dem can't even go outside. That murderer want lashing with the cat-o-nine."

Holden's mouth stayed in a firm line the entire time. At one point he glanced at Eileen the way a hummingbird hovers above a flower - quickly and timidly - before tapping the desk and saying, "I talked to Derricks yesterday morning. He told me he's never seen anything like this. The only thing that lets them know it's the same person is the cut on the girls' necks."

Eileen thought back to the neatly stitched gash on Lydia's neck that she had covered with make-up and a high-collared shirt. It had felt like a masquerade the way they had trotted her out so dewy fresh in a crisp black suit that still had the tags when her wailing mother handed it to Eileen.

Eileen remembered that day vividly. She had gone into the cold room and pulled back the white sheet before picking through the make-up, mixing powders and tints until she had created the perfect shade for Lydia's pretty dark skin. Eileen had purposely avoided the puckered skin under the stitches until the rest of Lydia was brushed and blushed to perfection. She hadn't wanted to touch it, that narrow egress through which the young woman's life had drained and left her an empty shell. In the end, Eileen gritted her teeth and painstakingly covered the thick black thread, building and blending the make-up until it looked like no more than an old scar.

Holden had been impressed and asked if she'd be willing to do all of the make-up since she did a better job than Clifford. "He's hit or miss. Sometimes they're okay but, other times they look like they're wearing Kabuki masks."

Eileen had tried hard to forget Lydia's gash but now her throat grew dry as she asked, "L-shaped cuts?"

"Yes. Derricks is working under the theory that the killer may have a disability like a missing thumb or something, which may stop him from holding the weapon properly."

She shuddered. "What about the brown car I mentioned outside Anna's apartment?" *My apartment*, she thought anxiously. "Did that help?"

Holden bit his lip and tapped a pen on his desk before he leaned forward and cleared his throat, "It seems that lead wasn't as concrete as he would have liked. But on the plus side, the toxicology report came back for the last victim and it's clean."

"What's a toxicology report exactly?"

"The coroner takes blood, skin, hair samples, etcetera and tests them. They checked her for things like drugs or alcohol, but they didn't find any in her system."

"Oh," comprehension dawned on Eileen's face. "I had wondered why there was a bald patch at the back of her head. I didn't realize the coroner shaved it."

Holden stared at her. "Bald patch? Thorpe only plucks a few hairs so you'd never even notice."

"But I saw one at the back of Lydia's head when I washed her hair."

"Hmmm," Holden mused as he stirred his tea. "Might be a bad haircut." He shrugged.

Eileen raised an eyebrow. She doubted any teenage girl would submit to a haircut that left a shiny patch of scalp staring back at the world.

"I finished a book on serial killers this morning. Many of them take souvenirs from their victims. Do you think that's why Lydia's hair was shaved?"

Holden considered it. "I wouldn't doubt that. Any person that does these things repeatedly must have deep-rooted compulsions."

"So after all of this time, they still don't have any other clues?"

He shook his head slowly. "I know if they have anything to go on other than the similarity of the wounds. Plus, I doubt Derricks would tell me everything. It is a police investigation after all. I'm sure he's withholding some information."

Eileen didn't like the sound of that at all.

Traffic sounds, a tinkling bell and a gust of air signalled that Clifford was back. He closed the door behind him and side-stepped the grey partition to enter the open-plan office.

"I forgot to ask: how did it go over the weekend, Clifford?" Holden asked.

"It rained so hard I thought the mud would keep my shoes. Thorpe said if the family sends her this way that she should be ready before the end of the week."

The preceding forty-eight hours played itself over in Eileen's head. A dead woman who might be related to her. The police butting their heads against dead ends. The two facts boiled together and bubbled over and the urge to learn more about Michelle Jones gripped Eileen.

"Speaking of the young lady… we've got a busy day ahead, so I'm ready when you are."

Holden's lips pursed in the middle of blowing his tea and he squinted at her. "Really? I don't recall any appointments."

"The victim from over the weekend, remember?"

"I was thinking to just give them a call. There's an art to touting. Showing up at the crime scene — that's official. Knocking on their door two days later — that's creepy."

Eileen gazed into the distance and sighed. "I just thought that since you quoted your father so often that you'd want to carry on his legacy. I guess you *do* wait for opportunity to knock on your door." She shrugged and turned back to the typewriter, poising her fingers over the keys even though she knew full well she had nothing to type on the blank sheet of paper.

Out of the corner of her eye, she saw his jaw go slack and his hunched shoulders straighten. He gulped his tea in one swallow and fastened the buttons on his jacket. "Let's go."

Chapter 11
Suspicion

They made their way to a modest cookie-cutter housing development on the west coast. Dubbed "the Venezuelan houses" by locals, each was indistinguishable except for the forgotten toys or overturned tricycles left to rust on patches.

Michelle Jones' house was painted an ugly green. Its mossy steps and unkept garden seemed ready to take over the property at any moment, and very much resembled a lost cottage waiting for the inevitable despair that would settle over it some day.

Holden rapped on the door. A few seconds later, a tall dark-skinned lady with uncombed hair and a tear-stained face opened the door. "Good morning, are you Lena Jones? I'm Holden Davis of Davis and Sons' Funeral Home. Let me say how sorry I am for your loss. I know how difficult these situations can be and, as I was in the area, I decided to pay a visit to see if you need assistance with Michelle's arrangements."

Lena heaved a weary breath and turned away as though she was too tired to respond. She flopped down on the brown sofa, blinked her puffy eyes and stared at Holden and Eileen before she started crying.

Holden and Eileen glanced at each other as they stood rooted to their spots just inside the door. Lena's head lolled back and then fell forward, as though the weight of the tears off-balanced her. She then leaned over with vicious momentum to gather a handful of photos that had been splayed out on the coffee table and clutched them to her chest before her weight sank into the cushions once again. Eileen took a covert glimpse at the ones that remained. Yellow with age, they all showed the same light-skinned girl at different stages of life. In one fuzzy photo, she flashed a gap-toothed grin with her lucky dip prize at a school fair. In another, she showed off an unbroken row of white teeth as she clutched a graduation scroll. Based on Holden's description, Eileen understood why he had assumed it might have been her instead of Michelle Jones in that field. But this girl had a heart-shaped face, thin lips and a rounded nose; Eileen's skin tone was lighter and her oval face featured wide brown eyes and full lips. The only thing they had in common was their thick afros. Eileen's heart sank. She didn't think she was any relation to this girl. She glanced at the mother then, hoping to see something telling her they were kin, but given Lena's dark skin and sharp features, it was clear that Michelle took after her father. All that was left were memories cast in ink on photo paper that Lena held in her damp hands. Eileen felt sick: Lena's sobs were loud and her grief was fresh, her body not yet digested by fatigue and anguish like Ernesta's body was. But Eileen knew it was only a matter of time.

Holden took a deep breath. "Ma'am, is there anything we can do? Maybe get you some water?"

"She's good," answered a gruff voice from behind a beaded curtain. A dark hand pushed aside the beads and a stocky man stepped into the light of the living room. "I'm Errol, Michelle's stepfather. Lena ain't taking this too good. Let we go outside and talk," he said leading the way out the front door.

"Sir, we're very sorry…"

Errol shooed away Holden's apology as though it were a swarm of flies. "First things first: another fellow from Davis already talked to us yesterday. What sort of jack-leg place are you running that wunna don't talk to each other?"

Holden shot an annoyed glance at Eileen. "Well...we're very thorough, you see. How are you holding up?"

Michelle's stepfather shook his head. "It ain't easy. Michelle split her time between here and her boyfriend's house. She left a week ago to go there." He shook his head bitterly. "We thought she was fine. Not once did that ignorant fool call to say she was missing."

Errol's eyes grew steely. "If you ask me, I think he killed her. I told her not to get mixed up with fellows like that. Only when the police called did we find out that she was missing for days."

Eileen was taken aback by Errol's candour but had to admit that he had a point. Over his shoulder, movement caught her eye. Lena was standing behind the white lace curtain that slowly swayed to and fro at the front door. She looked like a ghost with her dead eyes and blank face as she watched them. A breath hitched in Eileen's chest.

Errol leaned in and said in a low voice, "I wouldn't doubt that the boyfriend killed the other girls too. People like him are funny."

"Would you say Michelle was afraid of him?" asked Eileen.

The man glared at her. "You's the police? I thought wunna was from the funeral home."

"We are," Eileen said quickly. "But what you tell us can help to eliminate certain bits of evidence we may come across."

Holden's eyebrow was raised and his jaw was tight. Normally the scope of their conversations wasn't so intrusive. Eileen could only hope that Errol didn't know enough to know that funeral homes weren't supposed to be actively involved in forensic investigations.

Clearly, he didn't.

Errol shrugged. "Not really… he just doesn't fit in, if you get what I mean." He gave Eileen a meaningful look.

"Hmm…where does he live?" asked Eileen.

"Does a funeral home normally need to know that?"

Holden's gaze was impassive, but Eileen knew he wouldn't let this go once they got back to the car. "Nah. But I started talking to a new chossel and I want to make sure it isn't him." She smiled sweetly at Errol and winked. "A pretty girl like me can't be too careful."

"Oh, geez," Holden muttered. Errol didn't seem to hear though. He looked Eileen up and down and — concluding that she was indeed a pretty girl — answered with a lusty smirk, "Ronald O'Riley. He lives on Sea Breeze Hill."

"I knew you'd look out for me," Eileen said with a sly grin. She thanked him and sashayed back to the car.

Holden stormed along in her wake. "Listen to me," he fumed as he got in and slammed the passenger door. "We're not Cagney and Lacy. I don't know what you're up to, but solving crimes isn't my job. I bury dead people!"

Eileen started the car. "Then tell me who *should* solve these crimes. Because this is the fourth victim they've found and I have a feeling that if you and I work together that we'd find the killer."

"Why? What on earth would possess you to get tangled up in police business?"

She narrowed her eyes at him. "I'm a woman and I'm tired of trying to pack eight hours of sleep into my lunch hour every day since I'm too afraid to close my eyes at night. Because I could tell from the way you answered earlier that Derricks thought I was just a busybody and didn't take my tip about the man in the brown car seriously. The way I see it is that if we gathered some more evidence and gave it to Derricks they'd be able to find the killer faster. That's why."

Holden drummed his fingers irritably against the sharp crease in his pants. Finally, with a disgruntled shake of his head, he said, "Fine. Solving this would give a lot of people some peace of mind."

Eileen put the car in gear. "Excellent."

"We're going to Sea Breeze Hill, aren't we?"

"Yup."

* * *

THE PINNACLE OF SEA BREEZE HILL was a rocky little mound on the island's east coast that cast long afternoon shadows on a quaint chattel village. On one side of the road was a gully where green monkeys ran rampant during the day. On the other side, patches of cassava, sweet potatoes and cane were interspersed with candy-coloured chattel houses. A query at the variety shop led them down a dusty lane to a ramshackle dwelling with a backyard enclosed by a rusty paling.

They knocked on the wooden windows until a young man opened the door. His skin was deeply tanned, a stark contrast to the sad green eyes that peered at them beneath a tangle of sandy hair. Lanky and long-limbed, he looked more like a tourist marooned on a surfing vacation than a murderer.

"Ronald?" asked Holden.

"Yeah. Who are you?"

"We have some questions about Michelle's death."

His jaw hardened. "Her stepfather sent you too?"

"Well…he gave us directions, but…"

"Listen… Errol has problems with me, not with how I treated her," the young man fumed as he made to close the door.

"We're here to help," Holden said gently as he looked the young man in the eye. "I don't believe you had anything to do with her murder."

Holden could sense the young man's reluctance as Ronald's eyes flicked between the two of them. Finally, Ronald ran his hand through his tangled curls and sank onto the moss-covered chunk of coral that served as the front step.

Holden knew he still had to tread carefully, even if Ronald did seem compliant. "What did you mean by Errol having problems with you and not how you treated Michelle?"

Ronald stared up at him with disgust. "If I was a rich white boy with family money I bet Errol wouldn't have a problem." He gestured to his dilapidated home and the weeds that surrounded it. "I loved Michelle and thankfully she could see past this." His grin was sardonic, his eyes angry as he said, "Hmph…my mother always said that the more things change, the more they remain the same."

"Is that your car?" Eileen asked. She pointed to a brown hatchback partially covered by a bank of river tamarind trees further along the grassy lane.

Ronald met her eyes and said, "Miss, I can't even afford Rediffusion. Where would I get money to put gas in that or any other car for that matter?" He stupsed. "Besides, that old thing ain't moved from there in years."

Ronald had a point. Holden knew Eileen was taken aback by a white Bajan living in a place that looked like this. Many of the local whites had deep roots in plantation ownership or mercantile endeavours. Generational wealth allowed them to own huge swathes of land, myriad businesses and an incredible amount of political clout that ordinary people didn't have. Ronald's home, with its missing window panes and the mixed breed pot-starver who peered through the rusty paling, probably wasn't what she expected.

"Do you think that's the only reason Errol said we should talk to you?" asked Eileen.

Ronald's mouth folded into a tight line. "Tell me what other reason it could be. He sent police here at two o'clock yesterday morning to bang on my door like I'm a criminal. They dragged me to the station and questioned me for six hours without food or water. I told them Michelle was here for a few nights, but she left for a job interview that morning. I don't have a phone so I thought she went home when she didn't come back."

"Did anyone have problems with her?" asked Eileen.

"No. She was quiet, hard-working, liked to read," said Ronald as his eyes grew damp. "Michelle wasn't riff-raff."

It was too much for Ronald. He broke down sobbing. Holden patted him on the shoulder and told him they were sorry for intruding before helping him back inside the house.

Once they returned to the car, Holden exhaled. "I have a good feeling that he's not the driver of the car that was outside your apartment. I'll make some calls and see if I can find out which companies have brown uniforms for their male staff. The good thing about a small island is that it's not hard to pinpoint these things."

"I wonder if the guy with the car is what these girls all have in common," Eileen mused. "Lydia and Michelle seem like model citizens."

He nodded thoughtfully. "Which might explain why Errol didn't care for Michelle's relationship with Ronald."

She shrugged. "He has that beach-bum-surfer aura to him, but I suspect he's alright otherwise."

Holden shook his head. "That's not what I meant. Ronald is what Bajans call an ecky-becky."

"What's that?"

"Imprisoned Irish slaves who worked on the plantations."

"I thought only Africans were slaves here."

"Actually, the Irish were enslaved before blacks were. Oliver Cromwell was behind most of it, shipping the Irish here by the thousands to work the plantations until Africans replaced them."

Holden rolled down the window to let in the fresh breeze as they drove along the narrow country thoroughfare. He gestured to both sides of the road where red poll cattle grazed behind rail fences. "After the Irish were freed, some became farmers and that type of thing, but others formed insular little communities like the one Ronald lives in. The problem is that many rich whites look down on them and some blacks do too."

"But why?" she asked.

He scratched his chin. "I'm no anthropologist, but maybe it's because they don't fit within society's construct. They have skin that should allow for privilege, but not the money. It's a difficult space to occupy."

She was bewildered. "If they're so insular, how did he end up dating Michelle?"

"Times are changing. Young people are intermingling more. It's not just about race or class. Plus, he said they were in love." Holden smiled ruefully at Eileen. "'Every piece of cloth in town got an owner' as the old people say."

"I don't know if I believe that," Eileen said. "Michelle seems so serious and he looks so easy going. How could two people who are so different be in love with each other?"

Holden was silent for a moment as though contemplating how best to answer her question. Finally, he stared out the window and sighed, "It's one of life's most vexing mysteries."

Chapter 12
The Genesis of the Truth

On Tuesday morning, dressed for work with her thermos in hand, Eileen knocked on her neighbour's door.

"Shh!" said the woman as she stepped outside. Eileen had only met the young woman named Ingrid once before when she had first moved in, but their paths hadn't crossed since. She looked Eileen up and down, touching her matted hair and brushing her hand self-consciously over the wet yellow stain that glistened on her T-shirt. "What's the matter?"

"Morning, Ingrid. I'm not sure if you remember me. I'm Eileen from upstairs."

The woman stared back at her with eyes that had known no peace since giving birth. "The baby's asleep now. Sorry if he woke you," Ingrid said as she turned to go inside the house.

"That's not why I'm here," said Eileen. "I wanted to ask about the tenant who used to live upstairs before, Anna."

Ingrid scratched her head. "What about her?"

"Did you see her the day she disappeared?"

"Why?" Ingrid asked, eyeing Eileen suspiciously.

"It's important. I think I found something that may help the police figure out who killed her."

Ingrid's eyebrows shot up as she stepped back. "I ain't talking. I've got my son to raise and I'm minding my — let go of my door!"

Eileen took a deep breath and slowly lowered her hand from the knob.. "I promise that I won't tell anyone that you said anything, but I need to know if you saw Anna that day."

Ingrid glanced around and lowered her head before saying, "I went into labour the day Anna disappeared and spent six days in the hospital. I didn't find out she was gone until the police came here asking questions."

"Did you know much about her personal life?"

Ingrid shrugged. "Not really. Mostly she talked about her family from up north and money being tight. I helped out at first, but after I got pregnant, I didn't have the energy anymore."

"Helped with what?"

"Smocking. Anna's fingers got sore from doing it at the garment factory all day. What made it worse was that she had so much work, she had to bring it home sometimes and sew until midnight." Ingrid shook her head in disgust. "Anna hated it. The irony is that the last time I saw Anna alive, she said she had good news to share when she got back. Next time I saw her was at her funeral." Ingrid quirked an eyebrow at the irony.

"Did she hint at what the news could be?"

"I don't know. She was rushing to catch a bus, so we didn't have the chance to talk," Ingrid said. She glanced pointedly at her watch.

"Someone told me a man waited hours for Anna that day," said Eileen, hurriedly. "Did you see anything?"

In the other room, the phone rang and woke the baby.

Ingrid squinted at Eileen and her voice was tight as she said, "I was rolled up in bed with labour pains. When they put me in the ambulance on a gurney, I wasn't studying my surroundings." The baby's wails crescendoed and Ingrid rolled her eyes in frustration. "Look, unless you're going to nurse him, I have to go," she said irritably. With that, she slammed the door.

Eileen frowned as she walked across the gravel lot and got in her vehicle. She might have to give Ingrid a bit of time before she darkened her doorstep again.

Holden was waiting in the car park behind the funeral home when she arrived, eager to leave for a grief visit in the country. Ten minutes later they were following Clifford in the white van to collect an old lady who had keeled over in the middle of choir rehearsal. Sadly, the woman's nephew was also a mortician. He sneered at Holden before explaining in no uncertain terms that he would be handling his aunt's arrangements, thank you very much. Eileen snickered at the nephew's tone and to her surprise, Holden grinned back at her as they made their way out of the church. It was a stark contrast to the other times they had missed out on business.

They drove on winding roads bordered by big banana patches and across small concrete bridges that overlooked lush gullies, the wind whipping through the windows with such force that Eileen thought she'd misheard him when he asked out of the blue, "Are you hungry?"

"To hear Clifford tell it, I'm always hungry."

"I thought a luncheon would help us to get better acquainted, since you're still new to the business."

"Oh really?" she asked. "A lot of business owners aren't so nice."

Holden cleared his throat. “Well… yes, I try.” He gestured to a weathered stone sign ahead engraved with the words ‘Highland Club, 5 KM ahead’.

“Have you ever been?”

“No.”

“Well…if you have time we can have that luncheon now so I could properly welcome you to Davis and Sons.”

She turned to look at him. “Oh… I thought everyone attended.”

“I would have invited Clifford, but he’s headed to the morgue and today is his day for polishing the walls, so it will be just us.”

Eileen laughed. “I really like him, you know.”

“Yes, Clifford’s free-wheeling nature tends to have that effect on the ladies,” Holden said wryly as she swung the car onto the narrow road.

It was the kind of day that photographers rushed out to capture for the postcards that filled souvenir shops at the airport. The sky was a storybook blue that stretched as far as the eye could see. Coconut trees stretched high above fields where yellow butterflies flitted from flower to flower. Eileen savoured the country air; it was much lighter and sweeter than the bus fumes that crept under the door at the funeral home.

Her deep breaths didn’t escape Holden’s notice. “You like the country?”

“I was raised in Ten Men’s so maybe I gravitate to something different just to be contrary,” she said with a cheeky smile.

Surprise registered on his face. "The fishing village up north? I wouldn't figure you for a girl who grew up smelling melts all day."

Laughter erupted from Eileen's throat. "Well, I did and I loved it. Every evening after school, I used to run across the road to play on the beach. Vendors like Miss Fray and Miss Lucy would make sure I didn't go into the sea and drown."

"I've always been envious of people whose upbringings were full of fun and frolic," Holden sighed. "I spent my childhood handing tissues to widows and holding condolence books."

In spite of herself, Eileen couldn't shake the image of a tightly wound boy dressed in a tiny suit as a wizened old woman cried on his shoulder. She folded her lips to hold in a smile.

"When I was young, children used to play in Southbury Cemetery after school. One evening, some boys were upping a kite just outside the chapel door. My father had left me to mind the coffin of an old man, telling me to stand between it and the church door and above all, *don't move*." He shook his head in amusement. "I don't need to tell you that a little boy would rather fly a kite than babysit a coffin."

"My father turned away, so I figured I'd just nip out to get a little fly off the kite." A smile played on Holden's lips. "There I was, jacket off, running with the kite when I heard shouting and noticed something moving along next to me. I figured the kite's owner had changed his mind and didn't want me to fly it anymore so I ran faster. The thing picks up pace and passes me before I realized it was the coffin speeding down the incline with my father running behind it. It turns out that the wheel-lock on the coffin trolley was slack."

Eileen's chest heaved and tears streamed down her face. Holden joined in and both of them were rolling with laughter when they pulled up to the Highland Club.

The modest country road had opened up and split in two, curving to meet under the high porté cochère of a wide coral stone building. Two stewards in black coat-tails appeared from behind round columns as soon as the car screeched to a noisy halt under the covered arch. Eileen liked them immediately; neither batted an eyelid at her car even when she showed them how to jiggle the gear stick to put it in park.

A few minutes later, she and Holden were seated on the oceanfront terrace at a table laid with polished silver that glinted in the afternoon sunlight. The view was breathtaking, and it was instantly clear to Eileen why the club was one of the most exclusive spots on the island. A sandy knoll beyond the low balcony was covered with tangled green vines struggling under the weight of ripe fat pork. Sea breeze whistled through the vines that thinned out as they crept closer to the sand only to be replaced with stubborn tufts of salt-bleached grass and small crab holes. Rough waves raked foamy fingers across the white sand beach, dragging seashells and pebbles back into the Atlantic.

"Is this the kind of scenery you're more accustomed to in Ten Men's?" Holden asked, jutting his chin at the view.

"Well," Eileen said as she draped her napkin over her lap, "it's missing an old woman who shouts at strangers while she plays with stray cats, but I guess it will do."

She'd had no idea he could smile so broadly; for the first time, she realized he had a dimple in his left cheek. That tiny detail added a boyish charm to his handsome face. His black jacket was tossed over the back of the chair with his tie neatly folded inside the pocket. He had unfastened the top two buttons of his white shirt and folded back the sleeves. Eileen fidgeted in her chair. How could the absence of a tie and jacket make her feel like she was on a date instead of a business lunch? She hid behind the menu to conceal the blush that crept up her face. Since the stormy night when her car had broken down, she'd replayed their conversation in her mind, wondering if Holden could possibly have any interest in her. It wasn't lost on her that she happily rushed out of the house whenever he called her to go on grief visits or that she enjoyed embalming bodies with him in the intimacy of the chilly prep room. She wondered if he'd noticed her furtive glimpses or realized that her fingers lingered when she handed him pens and syringes.

"How do you like the job so far?" he asked.

"I feel bad for saying this, but it's fun," she said, wrinkling her forehead in bemusement.

"Why is that bad?" Holden replied, his eyes worried.

Eileen quirked an eyebrow. "It's a funeral home, not a circus. It isn't the kind of place people hang out when they're looking for a good time."

He chuckled. "You're not wrong. For me, it's all I've ever known so I don't associate it with any particular feeling. But I understand why people see it as a place of despair."

Holden sipped his champagne and pursed his lips, pleased with how the tiny bubbles tickled his palate. "As a boy,

I wondered if that's why other children avoided me. They acted like I'd eat their organs at lunchtime."

"That doesn't sound nice."

"When Paul started school I realized it had nothing to do with my father being an undertaker. Paul had friends by the bushel. I know now that being so tall and not skylarking at break-time was the reason." He tilted his head to one side as though amused by his own revelation. "What was life like growing up in a fishing village?"

"Fishy."

Holden cocked his head to the side as a smile tugged at his lips, as though he would have been disappointed if she had answered any other way. "And?"

"It was nice but I didn't have many friends." She bit into her rosemary bread and chewed. "I'm a barrel baby, so you know how the rumour mill goes crazy when that kind of thing happens."

"Barrel baby?" His face betrayed confusion. "What do you mean?"

"I wasn't born in a barrel if that's what you're thinking. At least I don't think I was," she said, pondering her words for a second. "I was raised with things that came out of a barrel from overseas. Those big cardboard-looking containers that Bajans in the States send back with rice, games, flour, school shoes and anything else they can squeeze into them."

"Oh, I get you now. So your grandmother raised you?"

Eileen pursed her lips. "I don't know my mother or grandmother. All I know is the lady who raised me and her cousin."

"Don't you have any relatives?"

Eileen tapped the butter knife against the table and avoided his eyes. “Yes… but we never met. I spoke to them on the phone once. That conversation didn't go very well...so I haven't heard them since."

"May I ask why?"

Her eyes met his. "They lied to me. But...a part of me regrets how I acted. I’d still like to get to know them."

"I can understand that."

"When you called the other night..." She hesitated and rubbed her thumbnail against her lip. "I thought that if the victim looked like me that maybe she was a relative."

Recognition lit his eyes. “That’s why you’ve been trying to find out who killed the girls. Because you thought Michelle might be related?”

“It started that way, I guess,” she relented. “But there are other reasons. Speaking of the victims, did you hear from your contact about the twitchy guy in the brown uniform?”

“No. But if you want to change the subject, you could say that directly.”

Eileen sighed. *Darned Holden and his sharp insight*. “I didn’t grow up rough, despite what you might think. I went to private school, did art and ballet on weekends. The lady who raised me was one of the sweetest people you’d ever meet, but it’s not the same as having a mother, is it?”

Eileen saw the way Holden’s face changed. She hated having to sing for her supper. She made a mental note not to go to any more of these office luncheons.

She raised an eyebrow at him. “The truth doesn’t need pity.”

Straightening his cutlery, Holden thought for a moment before he said, "You're very unusual in some ways. There's no pretence about you. It's refreshing."

She smiled. "Thank you."

Their meal arrived, and for a few minutes, there was only the roar of the ocean and the tinkle of cutlery to fill the silence. Eileen looked out to the water while Holden chewed, his expression thoughtful before he said, "Your life seems very interesting despite what you say. You're smart and you've had a solid upbringing. So the bigger question is..." he looked her in the eye. "What's keeping you at the funeral home?"

"The economy for one reason."

"I see." He sipped his champagne and when she didn't add anything else, he picked up his fork and went back to eating his fish. "Very well."

She didn't know if he'd resigned himself to minding his business or decided she was no longer worth the trouble. Either way, the outcome was the same. She wasn't sure if she liked that very much.

* * *

WHEN THEY RETURNED TO THE OFFICE, the phone rang non-stop. Four funeral requests came in, and Eileen became engrossed in her work. She feared she would have to work late, but Holden picked up the slack and helped her complete her tasks well before closing time. She breathed a sigh of relief when she finally leaned back in her chair. "Thanks. I know you're paying me to get all of this done, and I appreciate that you took the time to help."

Holden averted his eyes. "It's nothing, but I admit that I had an ulterior motive for wanting you to finish early. Do you have plans this evening?"

Eileen's heart skipped a beat. Holden's face was eager, his tone earnest when he spoke. Would he ask her out for dinner? The luncheon had been a professional one, but there would be no mistaking his intentions if he asked her out for dinner. The thought made her cheeks warm.

She shook her head. Her mind whirled over the possibilities of how the night would end. She imagined telling her grandchildren about this day, clutching his wrinkled hand in hers as they reminisced about the spark that ignited their love.

He tapped his desk in triumph. "Excellent! I found the guy in the brown uniform. My contact said he'll be at a rum shop in Lord Town now."

Eileen's face fell. She turned away so Holden wouldn't see how red her cheeks were. She was the one who had dragged him into tracking down the Slasher so why was she disappointed that he had come up with a new lead? As Eileen gathered her belongings she wondered what on earth had compelled her to jump to the conclusion that her boss was asking her out on a date.

Chapter 13
Lord Town

Lord Town was the epicentre of every immoral behaviour known to man. It was a seedy enclave surrounded by a bus station, bank and outdoor produce market that thrummed with illicit activity all year round. Drugs, prostitution, drinking and gambling were always in heavy rotation, making it so that a man could easily hop from vice to vice without ever having to pick a struggle. The area's ability to thrive among reputable businesses might cause a cynic to question if such disparate lifestyles could only cohabitate because one supported the other.

Eileen never had a reason to frequent Lord Town before, and her first impression was that it smelled of baby powder, fried chicken and gutter water. It was more of a small district than a town, split into four quadrants by two narrow roads. Most of the structures were so tightly packed that you could spit through your window and be certain it would land in the neighbour's bathroom sink. Shops were constructed in the traditional merchant style: tall and narrow with wide verandahs propped up by long wooden braces, while residences were modest chattel houses topped with gable rooves.

Holden and Eileen walked past a general store, a basket maker, and a flock of yard fowls that pecked around in a small front yard as a woman with a bag balanced on her head talked to the heavyset woman who leaned through her window.

Holden and Eileen soon found the place they were looking for: a large beige building emblazoned with logos for beers and rum at the end of a urine-soaked alley. Its front doors were barred shut, but Holden noticed a man coming out of a side entrance and pointed it out to Eileen.

The smell of baby powder was even stronger in the dimly lit space and Eileen could see why. Women sat on men's laps and cackled on cue at everything they said. At the end of the bar, one woman, her chest doused with a heavy coat of talcum, sat between two men who ogled her full breasts as they shared a bottle of white rum. A burly man with a shiny bald head who looked as though he'd been squeezed into his polo shirt was washing glasses behind the bar. He eyed Holden and Eileen with suspicion, perhaps unaccustomed to seeing a man bring along a woman to an establishment such as this.

"What can I do for you?" he asked.

"I'm looking for a fellow who comes in sometimes. He drives an old brown Cortina and wears a brown uniform."

"You mussy mean Jerry," said the proprietor as he wiped droplets off the polished bar top. "He's upstairs with Mary," he grinned. "He don't take too long though, so just give him a few minutes."

Just then, heavy footfall clattered down the stairs as a man's tan boots came into view. Right down to his unkempt hair and dirty fingernails, he matched Debra's description to a tee. Jerry's eyes landed on Eileen, and a sly smirk crossed his face as he looked her up and down. Holden stepped in front of her and asked, "You're Jerry?"

The man straightened his shoulders and said, "Yeah… and you?"

"We want to know why you were outside Anna Brown's apartment the day she went missing."

Jerry bristled and his jaw clenched. "Two of you don't look like police."

"We're not," Eileen said. "But you either tell us what you know or we'll send them to find out."

"Hmph." Jerry pointed to the door and led them outside to a corner of the alley. It was littered with empty beer cases and a pile of flattened boxes.

"Look…I work in government so I don't want no trouble," he started in a low voice. "Yeah… I went to pick up Anna, but I didn't do anything to her."

"So why are people describing you as 'twitchy'?" asked Eileen.

He bristled. "Twitchy? I work in government's maintenance department, and I go to different buildings to fix things. I drive my own car so I can nip out and do a little taxi work in between. Only problem is that I'm not supposed to be doing another job on the government's time and I ain't got no hackney license."

Holden frowned. "So that's why you didn't come forward?"

Jerry nodded. "I can't explain what I was doing there unless I admit that I'm breaking the law." He shrugged. "Things hard and I got bills to pay."

Eileen raised an eyebrow. "Mary's bills or yours?"

Jerry's lips peeled back over his teeth. "Bills is bills, darling."

"But why did Anna call you in the first place? Where were you taking her?" Eileen wondered aloud.

Jerry rubbed the back of his neck. "She got my number from another girl that I take around sometimes. Anna had an appointment on the west coast. She would gotta catch three buses to get there and she didn't want to be late. I waited for a while, but she didn't show up."

"Why not?"

Jerry cast his eyes downward. "Well…truth is that I was here with Mary longer than I planned so I got to Anna's apartment late. I knocked and then waited in the car for a while. When Anna didn't come outside, I told myself that she caught the bus instead."

Eileen caught Holden's eye. Jerry sounded genuine. To Eileen's mind, his biggest problem seemed to be his addiction to Mary. Which meant they were back to the drawing board. They thanked Jerry and left.

"This is another dead end," groused Holden as they retraced their steps through Lord Town. "But my father always used to say that 'the more you look, the less you see'." Holden said. "When we least expect it, something will shine a light on this mystery."

Eileen chewed on her nails, a habit she had developed when she realized that she slept in the same bed as one of the Cane Slasher's victims. She was feeling similarly defeated, but she was desperate to find the killer before he found her.

* * *

HAVING DEPOSITED HOLDEN AT HIS HOUSE, Eileen drove home. She parked the car and craned her neck, squinting at the shadows by the stairs before she ran across the gravel patch and up to her first-floor apartment. She slammed the door behind her and pressed her hand to her thudding heart.

She'd never liked the dark, a slight phobia that had started during her childhood, but as she had grown, her distrust had morphed into a mild inconvenience. In the past few months, her fears had resurfaced. She felt her lungs expand with the stale air trapped inside her apartment and fell sideways into the chair next to the door. That nightly dash was mentally and physically exhausting.

When Eileen fell asleep, she dreamed. At first, the vision was relaxing: the room was cool, the way it always is after heavy rains wash away the heat of the day and gentle breezes caress your skin like freshly washed fingertips. A faceless man, tall and broad with muscled forearms grabbed her by the neck, dragged her out of bed and threw her over his shoulder. His clothes smelled of soil and grass, and were slick with the blood of women he had killed. She felt it seeping through her nightgown and onto her skin, leaving bloody streaks on her chest and legs. He carried her across the road into the cane field, his heavy boots thudding an ominous rhythm as he walked. He tossed her on the ground and raised a knife high above his head, his features obscured by the moon behind him. Eileen saw the curve of the new moon in the night sky. She felt the rush of wind as the knife came down. She heard herself scream as her eyes flew open and she sat bolt upright in bed.

She clutched her chest and looked down. In the light that filtered through the thin bedsheet at the window, her nightgown clung to her flesh, but it was soaked with sweat and not someone else's blood. Her heart beat so fast that it hurt to breathe and a shuddering sob escaped her throat as she put her head between her knees.

Adrenaline filled her veins like drugs, leaving her too wired to go back to sleep. She glanced around the apartment, searching for a distraction to soothe her anxiety. She had no new books. The lone TV station had finished the night's broadcast. Rainbow-coloured bars stretched across the screen to accompany a tonal pitch that droned through the TV speaker.

Eileen's eyes landed on the darkest corner of her room and she decided that moment was as good as any to face at least one of her fears. She picked up the bottle next to her bed, downed a mouthful of brown rum and flicked the light switch.

When Eileen had first viewed the apartment, that gloomy little alcove set into the wall had reminded her of the cupboard under the stairs in her childhood home. It was used as a larder and lined with shelves where Christmas black cake mix, biscuits and canned goods were stored, but there were also times when she heard grunts and deep groans coming from behind the closed doors. Those noises had terrified her, forcing her to return to bed and wet herself more times than she cared to remember. It was only after Eileen reached adulthood that she theorized that those sounds were more sexual than sinister. The lady who raised her had a teenaged niece who sometimes came to babysit Eileen. When the lady worked late shifts at the hospital, the girl would promptly put Eileen to bed. Early one morning, Eileen saw a young man clambering through the window and realized what was afoot. But that didn't change Eileen's dislike of dark cupboards. It was why her room looked like a thrift shop with a bed in it since she kept her clothes on wall hooks.

The cupboard's hinges creaked and the door traced a wide arc along the worn linoleum tiles as a musty scent wafted out when she pulled it open. She blinked quickly, willing her eyes to adjust to the dim light in the shallow space. She had tucked the previous tenant's belongings into the cobwebbed corner. Now a thin layer of dust covered two tattered pairs of slippers and a cardboard box filled with odds and ends that the landlord said the family would return for but they never did. It felt intrusive going through the dead woman's possessions, but Eileen hoped a clue to her disappearance and death would emerge. There was a nearly full tube of S-curl, two cassette tapes, plastic bangles and neon eye shadow. She pulled out a pet rock, bottle caps for a competition and the classified section of an old newspaper. Eileen sighed. She had hoped for extensive diaries, bloody fingerprints or some other smoking gun that would point her to Anna's killer. It was no wonder that the young woman's family hadn't returned for these items. They were easy to forget.

Eileen dragged out the boxes, piled the shoes on top and then swept, mopped and dusted the closet until it was free of spiders and smelled faintly of lavender disinfectant. She gathered everything in her arms and took them to the grey dustbin in her verandah. No sooner than she'd opened the door, a brisk wind whipped the sepia-toned sheet of newspaper out of the box and slapped it into her face.

"Pfft!" Eileen pulled it off her forehead and was about to throw it back into the box when she noticed a circled want ad. Ringed with red ink was a small classified listing with thick-set black type seeking a seamstress. Along the newspaper's deckled edge was a scribbled note: "Thursday 2 p.m."

Her breath hitched in her chest as she checked the date. The tiny month and day in the top right corner matched the time Anna had gone missing. Eileen bit her lip as her mind whirred. An alarm bell in her head went off, and her stomach flipped as she considered the grungy classifieds in her hands. She tipped the rest of the items into the bin, rolled up the paper and took it back inside.

* * *

EILEEN WAS LATE FOR WORK the next morning. By the time she flew through the door, her cheeks flushed as she lugged her heavy handbag, the echo of the tenth gong from parliament's clock hung in the air. Holden raised an eyebrow at her. "Thought you weren't coming in, boss."

"Yeah, I almost didn't," she replied absently as she rummaged through her bag.

Holden stared at her as though she had gone mad. "Eileen, I'm a tolerant man, but you're playing fast and loose with my easy-going nature."

Eileen regarded him for a moment as though wondering if it was worth it to retort. She clearly decided against it, as she stepped over to his desk and pressed a worn newssheet onto the wooden surface. She pointed to the circled ad. "The girl we picked up two days ago — Michelle — didn't her boyfriend say that she went to a job interview?"

Holden put down his teacup and peered at the crinkled page. "Yes," he replied slowly. His eyes flicked toward the date in the corner. "But this paper is from months ago so this can't be the ad she responded to. What's this about?"

"I found this paper while packing away Anna's things that were left in my apartment. When did she go missing?"

Holden wrinkled his forehead. "I can't remember. Why are you asking me all of this?"

"Wasn't it six months ago?"

Holden grew more flustered by the second. "I don't know. Eileen, what are you going on about?"

Eileen grabbed Holden's obituary book. His brows arched when she licked her fingers and thumbed through his precious book until she found Anna's extract. She spun the book around so Holden could see the dates. He looked at both clippings: the obituary and the ad. The date of her death was one week after the ad's publication. "If she went to the meeting on Thursday, that would have been a week before she was found."

Out of her handbag, Eileen pulled a stack of bright white sheets of photocopy paper. The grainy black and white facsimiles were a jumble of front page articles and want ads for carpenters, fortune-telling and common entrance lessons. On each sheet, there were fat blue circles and names scribbled in Eileen's handwriting: Anna, Lydia, Nora, Michelle.

"I went to the newspaper archive office and cross-checked the dates the girls went missing with the dates these ads appeared. The phone number on Anna's ad also matches ads that were published a few days before Lydia and Nora went missing. I checked the archives up to a week before Michelle disappeared but I still can't find an ad with that number that she may have answered."

Holden's eyes grew wide as he calculated the probability of Eileen's evidence. It made sense. Derricks had said the girls had never crossed paths otherwise. It was a cunning trick — with the economy the way it was, the promise of a paying job would lure many women.

"And look at this." She opened a colourful tourist map on top of the photocopied ads. It crackled beneath her palms as she smoothed it out, her hands running over pictures of snorkelling dives and mini moke rentals. She had highlighted four spots in red marker, creating a trail of scarlet dots on the west coast of the island. Between each point was a thin stroke that joined them together. Holden's eyes flew open. Eileen's finger traced the wiggly outline. "It's a circle," she said, pointing to the dots. "Which means that he's purposely dumping them around a place he's familiar with."

Holden's bottom lip disappeared as he bit down on it, his eyes flicking between the ads and the blood-red dots on the map. "Derricks said there was no real evidence to link them other than the marks on their neck and the fact that the killer dumped them in cane fields." His eyes met Eileen's. "I could be wrong, I think you've cracked the case."

Chapter 14
The Paper Trail

"I feel like I'm in a horror movie," Eileen said as the car bumped its way down the dark cart road that night.

"That's expected if you come to a lonely cane field in the middle of the night," Holden said with a slight grin on his face. "How do you expect to be Nancy Drew with an Afro if you're so afraid?"

Eileen cast him a withering look. Her fear was palpable, even though it had been her idea. She wasn't sure when Holden had gotten hold of a funny bone, but his teasing wasn't welcome in this particular instance. After showing him the map and classified ads, she suggested they visit the crime scene to see if they came across any other clues which the police may have overlooked. "I know it was three days ago, but Clifford said it was wet; there's a good chance that there may be tyre tracks or something got stuck in the mud." To her relief and surprise, Holden had agreed.

She shook her head. "You know we couldn't come when the sun was out. One: the police were still here going over the scene. Two: we don't want them to know what we know until I'm sure."

A thick plume of smoke rose from the sugar factory's chimney in the distance, filling the air with the sweet scent of crushed cane. The crescent moon hung overhead, covering the field of gangly plants in soft white light. Eileen knew they were carrying out reconnaissance for wholly different reasons: she was there because she could have easily suffered the same fate if she had answered one of those ads. Holden, on the other hand, may have been there because a part of him relished the idea of risky behaviour that was so foreign to him. Growing up in a good neighbourhood, going to good schools and having a business to inherit probably meant that the idea of going against the grain thrilled him. Eileen glanced at him. Holden bopped his head in time to the radio, something she had never seen him do before. She seldom saw him outside of his tailored black suits and tightly knotted ties. Tonight he was especially striking, dressed in a soft navy polo shirt and neat slacks that hugged his body. She shook her head ruefully. Imagine that he waited until he hit thirty to start rebelling.

Even in the dark, it was easy to find the spot they were looking for. The rain had softened the packed earth and made it easy to follow the tyre tracks. Police vehicles and the funeral home's body van had crisscrossed the area with muddy chevron lines that encircled a stone well in the middle of the field. The car's headlights illuminated a large square of yellow crime scene tape that fluttered with the same rhythm as the cane arrows. They alighted from the car, leaving the engine idling in case they had to make a quick getaway. Eileen pulled a flashlight out of her bag and with a soft click it came on, breaking the darkness and lighting the way across the crackly cane trash toward the well. Large round wells with metal grates were a common feature in many cane grounds to alleviate flooding. Eileen had recently become very wary of them when she realized that the folk song 'Millie Gone to Brazil' was an ode to a missing woman who was thrown into a well. Eileen remembered swishing her skirt and dancing from side to side with her friends in the schoolyard as they sang:

Millie gone to Brazil,
Oh lawse, poor Millie,
With a wire wrap round she waist,
And a razor cut up she face.

It wasn't until she listened to a call-in programme that Eileen had properly considered the lyrics. A local historian had phoned to bemoan the few times that the island's peaceful existence had been shattered by violent acts and mentioned Millie's murder in the 1920s. Millie's husband had killed her, dropped her in a well and told everyone she went to Brazil to account for her whereabouts. Her husband had assumed he would get away with it because so many other Barbadians had left to find work in South America and were never heard from again. Eileen had shuddered at the thought and told herself she would never again sing folk songs with such great abandon.

Her heart pounded as she aimed the light inside the circular stone structure, but thankfully, she saw nothing in its depths. She knelt close to the base of the well and circled it, moving the flashlight up and down the wall as she went. She found nothing. Holden kicked a pile of cane trash around, shifting it with the tip of his shoe when he suddenly said, "Look here."

He kneeled and fished a sodden scrap of newspaper from the pile with a broken twig. It was the size of a saucer and had been crudely torn off a larger sheet. Eileen took it off the stick.

Holden shook his head at her. "You should be wearing gloves, you know. We learned at mortician school that gloves have been standard crime scene issue since Emily Kaye was murdered in Britain in 1924."

Eileen raised her eyebrows at him. "We didn't come here to picnic; why didn't you bring some?"

Holden shrugged, a sheepish look on his face. "I didn't think we'd find anything."

She shook off the excess flecks of mud and leaves before she held up the paper and spotted the flashlight on it. In the upper right corner was an ad almost identical to the one she had found with Anna's belongings except this one was seeking a receptionist. It listed a different telephone number and the date on the newspaper was almost two weeks earlier. Holden stood behind her and read over her shoulder. He exhaled loudly and said, "This is odd; the number is different and so is the job description." To further complicate matters, the number's prefix indicated that it was in an entirely different part of the island to the original phone number. Her blood ran cold as she looked at him. Was it possible that more than one killer was on the loose?

They got back in the car and sat in silence, both of them wearing worried expressions on their faces. Holden's mouth was pressed in a grim line. Eileen stared through the windshield, considering how easily she may have come into contact with a murderer during her first week on the job.

"I could have been one of these girls," she said softly.

Holden turned to her, his face questioning.

Her chin trembled as she said, "I saw an ad the day after you made me dig the grave." Tears welled up in her eyes and spilt over her lashes and down her cheeks. "I was going to call."

Holden clenched his jaw in anger. "What if something had happened to you?"

The tears came faster ."But I didn't realize a murderer was running ads."

Holden was flabbergasted. "I thought you liked being at the funeral home."

"Being there?" Eileen was flustered. "It's not a hobby, it's minimum wage work. It's fine for now...but I don't want to work there forever."

He went quiet then, his face pained as though she had hit him.

She wasn't sure why but the look on his face only made Eileen cry more.

* * *

HOLDEN BARELY SLEPT THAT NIGHT. After Eileen had dropped him off, he flipped through magazines, wandered the corridors and eventually ended up in bed watching shadows move across the ceiling. He didn't care for the uneasiness that coursed through him whenever Eileen was around, the subtle anxiety that ground away at his nerves as he wondered if she knew how he felt about her. It was times like these when he missed his father most. Holden had done his best with the business, avoiding foreclosure despite Paul's fiscal ineptitude, but he was out of his depth in figuring out how to manage his affection for an employee.

Holden thought back to the night he met Eileen, remembering her cheeky responses for everything he said. He sighed, finally admitting to himself that from the time he laid eyes on her, he knew he was attracted to her. If he could turn back time, he would have told her that the post had been filled, but perhaps they could go out for a nice meal instead. It would have been far less gut-wrenching than seeing her almost every day and missing her every night.

Holden had hoped she would find the job too macabre, too daunting and eventually resign. In his dreams, he imagined Eileen winking at him before suggesting that he take her out for dinner. Then, their romance would begin. He imagined her teasing him about it in later years, chuckling with mild deference as Eileen served tea on the great house's wide verandah.

He cursed under his breath. Instead of fulfilling his fantasy of spending his life with Eileen, his antics had nearly driven her straight to the edge of a mad man's knife. All because he didn't want Clifford to believe Eileen was getting special treatment. He hadn't planned to make Eileen dig the graves, but Clifford had shown up with the shovels that night and Holden was too embarrassed to admit that he didn't want to make her do it.

It had irked him to make her undertake such laborious work, but he sometimes felt like Clifford was watching him in his father's stead. Many times, that feeling of perpetual supervision caused him to overcompensate, overriding knee-jerk reactions in favour of sound business principles. Mostly, it augured well. But not with Eileen.

Holden regarded Clifford as an uncle and he felt a distinct shame at the thought of the older man realizing that he was attracted to Eileen. Holden sighed and rubbed his eyes, telling himself that daylight would bring the answers he so desperately needed.

* * *

HOLDEN WALKED TO THE PARLOUR early the next morning, intent on putting his restless mind to good use instead of roaming the halls of the great house like a forlorn ghost. It was just after seven when he let himself into the building which meant he'd have a whole hour to do the book-keeping before everyone arrived. He pulled out his ledgers and balanced the columns, writing neatly on the lined pages. He always found book-keeping to be calming and stable; there was no grey area; things were either an expense or income. Less than an hour later, he heard the key turning in the lock.

"Morning, boss. Why you're in so early?" Clifford asked as he traipsed into the kitchen to start the kettle.

"Morning. I'm catching up on some book-keeping," replied Holden distractedly as he transcribed figures from a stack of bills into the ledger.

Clifford came out of the kitchen and sat on the edge of Holden's desk. "Ain't see you come in this early since business was slow."

Holden stopped short and looked up at Clifford. "Meaning?"

"That I know you since you were a little sprat. You work late when you got things to do; you come in early when something's bothering you."

Holden turned back to his ledgers and pinched the bridge of his nose. "Nothing is bothering me."

Clifford rubbed his chin. "That probably means it's about Eileen."

Holden's head snapped up with such force that Clifford broke out laughing.

"I got two eyes, young Davis. I can see that you got aspirations on her."

The younger man dropped his head in his hands and rubbed his eyes with the heels of his palms. "I've really stepped in it this time, Clifford. I can't express my feelings for her without seeming like a letch."

"Yeah...you was better off hiring them cranky old women with the bunions." Clifford shrugged. "Except for the fact that they used to turn off customers with them nasty attitudes and couldn't do the work, them was alright."

Holden glared at him. He wasn't in the mood for sarcasm. "No need to rub it in." He looked at Clifford, his eyes pleading. "Should I tell Eileen how I feel?"

Clifford stood up and clapped Holden on the shoulder. "Life is short. As your father used to say: a moment of discomfort or a lifetime of discontent."

In spite of himself, a weak smile crept across Holden's face. His father truly did have a saying for everything.

The phone rang and Holden let out a breath before he answered. It was Dr Thorpe calling them to collect a decedent whose autopsy was finished. The pathologist's office was only five minutes away so by the time Clifford returned with the old lady's remains, Eileen was walking through the front door and greeting them in her usual cheery tone. Holden knew it wouldn't do to profess his feelings for Eileen over a corpse. He would talk to her later. For now, he'd keep it casual.

* * *

"I BET YOU WERE A PREFECT at school, weren't you?"

They were attired in their usual white frocks in the chilly prep room, deftly handing each other tools and liquids without prompting as they worked. It had taken a few weeks, but they had developed a seamless preparation routine since the day Eileen had almost brought up her lunch on the spotless floor tiles. Now, instead of enquiries about embalming and requests to hand him a syringe, their conversations had become more casual.

She grinned. "Of course I wasn't. I'm too short and I always look like I'm up to no good. They only give badges to the tall, serious-looking children — like you. I imagine that's the same reason the police force has a height requirement; it's society's way of saying that height means authority."

Holden considered her theory as he pushed cotton inside Mrs Holmes' mouth. "So they didn't make me a prefect because of my roguish good looks?"

She laughed. "Probably not."

He tutted and sighed as though deeply affronted by this new knowledge. "My father's donation to the library fund probably helped to shore up my appointment as well, didn't it?"

Eileen smiled benignly and raised a shoulder. They both knew it did.

"You know..." Holden said as he massaged Mrs Holmes' face to set her features. "... back then, I really did believe that I was rewarded for following the rules." He frowned. "Which makes no sense because Paul was head-boy."

She giggled and asked, "Was he brighter than you?"

Holden scoffed. "Brighter? Paul barely flickers." He shook his head in amusement as Eileen broke down laughing. They were polar opposites in that way. Holden's humour simmered below the surface while Eileen's bubbled over.

She wiped tears from her eyes and said, "But if we're being honest, life isn't set up to be fair."

He took a small sponge from her and replied, "You're right. My father used to say, 'Son, rule lovers get a pat on the head. Rule breakers get a pat on the back.'"

Eileen broke into another fit of laughter. It was hilarious the way Holden would drop the timbre of his already deep voice to mimic his father.

"What does that even mean?" she asked through giggly hiccups.

Holden's gloved hands moved deftly, almost robotically as he worked on Mrs Holmes. He didn't answer until he had finished the internal embalming. He never spoke while doing that part. When Eileen had first started working there, she thought he was ignoring her, but she soon realized that he always picked up their conversation as soon as he closed the veins. "Look at history: average citizens go to their graves as 'nice people'. It's the renegades and pioneers whose memories live forever."

That was the thing Eileen liked best about Holden. The most gruesome day spent filling people's veins with chemicals could turn into hours that were wiled away in laughter and wisdom. But she quickly sobered when his statement about average citizens triggered a thought she had the night before.

"About what I said last night…" she bit her lip. "It's not that I don't *like* working here. I appreciate having a stable job and I like learning from you and Clifford. But what you said just now about average people…it pretty much sums up how I feel about where my life is right now."

"Meaning?"

"It's my dream to do something creative, something that will transcend my lifetime and exist forever. Something that I'll be known for." Eileen opened her hands apologetically as she gestured at the equipment in the sterile room. "I can't do that here."

"You are quite good with the make-up and the floral arrangements." He looked up at Eileen and said, "But far be it from me to stop you from your heart's desires. You're ambitious, even a daft person can see that."

She reached for the stainless steel tray next to him. "Thank you," she said as she started sterilizing the tools. "I'm glad you're not offended."

"No…why would I be? I don't imagine that everyone desires to spend their lives surrounded by the dead."

His face was a mixture of sadness and acceptance as he shrugged. "I understand."

Eileen had grown accustomed to working with Holden. But she'd started to put her plan into motion, to work toward her life she wanted for herself. Her hours at the funeral home were too erratic to allow her another job, so she'd found a way she could make more money by creating floral arrangements. Thankfully, Holden had sanctioned it without hesitation. Despite the fact that the post of parlour assistant wasn't her dream job, her stomach sank at the idea of never seeing him again.

Chapter 15
Dead Ends

Eileen's life was in limbo. It had been three days since their trip to the cane ground and two days since Holden had handed over the evidence they had gathered to Derricks. She had some measure of comfort in knowing she had done a good deed. But under that, clawing at the surface, were doubt and impatience.

To pass the time, Eileen tried calling both phone numbers from the ads, but eventually she gave up on the newer of the two when no-one answered after many calls. That was the problem with something as light as a piece of newspaper at an old crime scene. It could just blow into the middle of a place and be irrelevant. But she felt similarly frustrated with the older number; whether she called early or late in the day, no one answered. Eileen concluded that it couldn't possibly belong to a business, forcing her to question her theory. Every day she checked the classifieds looking for similar ads. She even went back to the newspaper office and extended her archive search from seven to ten days before the other victims had disappeared. Her efforts were in vain.

She tried the phone company to no avail. The operator told her they could find the number attached to a name, but not a name attached to a number. By the end of the week, Eileen was at her wit's end. There was one other lead they hadn't fully fleshed out and despite Holden's assertions that the killer might find out that she was asking questions, Eileen wanted to continue looking.

The Friday after their visit to Lord Town, Holden and Eileen stood in front of the Mutual Building, waiting for the Hampstead Village bus to arrive. The buses were quaint little things with bright colours and rustic appeal. Commuters sat on long benches enclosed by wooden rails, putting Eileen in mind of circus attractions behind stout parallel bars whenever she saw them. Buses were in high demand since so much of the populace didn't have cars which meant that seats were always at a premium. Two schoolboys ran past her to grab the rails on the bus so they could squeeze between the bars and cobble a seat before the bus got to the depot. A policeman chased them with truncheons, landing stout whacks that left bright whales on their brown legs and arms, but both Eileen and the police knew that efforts to discourage dangerous onboarding would be forgotten by the next day. Many of the boys did so in imitation of the conductors who were adept at navigating the slippery sideboards and fenders on the outskirts of the bus without ever once stepping inside the speeding omnibuses to collect fares. Neatly dressed in khaki uniforms, they hung off the sides, their sharp eyes seeing every passenger who hopped on. Shortly after, they'd shuffle along the sideboard with a leather pouch slung around their shoulder that jingled merrily with its cache of coins.

Soon, the Hampstead Village bus rounded the corner, trundling up the street until it pulled to a stop in front of the Mutual Building. As people disembarked, the conductor hopped off the wheel flares and tipped his hat to them. He eyed Holden's three-piece suit and asked, "Wunna is the inspectors?"

Holden shook his head. “No. We came to ask you about Anna Brown. I’m Holden and this is Eileen. What’s your name?”

“Raymond.” The conductor nodded grimly. “I remember Anna. Nice girl who always looked sweet in her clothes.”

“Did she catch your bus the day she disappeared?” asked Eileen.

“Yeah, it’s the only bus on that route.” He looked her in the eye. “But you should know that…it ain’t you that move into Anna’s old apartment?”

Eileen was surprised. “Well…yes. But I never met you.”

The conductor’s face coloured. “I like red women so I would always notice you. I’ve seen you in the neighbourhood.”

Holden cleared his throat. “So did Anna get off here that day?”

“Nah,” said Raymond. “She got off by the post office and told me she had to catch another bus for a meeting on the west coast, so she had to hustle.”

“Who was she meeting?”

Raymond shook his head. “She never said. When she was found, I talked to the guys on the west coast route and asked if they had seen her. Don said she caught his bus and got off by the secondary school. When he didn’t see her again, he figured she came back to town on another bus.”

Holden raised an eyebrow. “So what happened to her after that?”

Raymond shrugged and said, “If I knew, I would tell you, but right now the bus is full so I gotta go.”

Raymond jumped onto the sideboard and tipped his hat to them again before the bus disappeared around the corner.

"So she did make it to town that day," Eileen said, her mouth twisted with worry.

"Yes," said Holden. "So she was abducted either before or after her interview."

Eileen nodded. "The question is…who took her?"

* * *

EILEEN SPENT THE AFTERNOON making wreaths while Holden balanced the books. It was their second week dipping their toe into the floral arrangement business offering wreaths and bouquets for all occasions. Business had been robust and Holden smiled broadly when he saw the numbers. They'd done wreaths every day since they started, not to mention bouquets for guilty husbands who forgot birthdays and anniversaries and were their most frequent customers so far. As Eileen had predicted, their central location was a huge boon, a great place to get a last-minute token of affection. It wasn't lost on Holden that sometimes orders were upsized because of the pretty lady who prepared the bouquets. He wasn't discounting her artful persuasion, but men were men, and they constantly tried to impress her by doubling their orders. He didn't care for the extra attention they showered on Eileen, but she put her foot down after one man reduced his order to a single red rose when Holden tried to intervene. "Stop helping! I'm working on commission and you don't have boobs".

He wasn't pleased with how she got results, but never before had an assistant put so much care into him or his business. It was so unfamiliar and profound that it filled him with a joy that felt like it was pried from deep within his shoes. She said she didn't want to work there much longer, but maybe Eileen would be willing to stay with him. Provided he could get his head out of his ass and finally tell her how he felt.

"I think this is my best work yet," she effused as she floated into the office with two massive pink wreaths. The scent of lilies and roses wafted around her as she laid them on his desk.

Holden was impressed. "They're stunning."

"Why thank you. Oh, the postman came?"

"Yeah, he left the letters on your desk. I know you have your system so I didn't touch them."

"Aww. I'm not that uptight, but thank you," she said, patting his hand warmly.

Her smile almost made him melt. He'd come to realize that pleasing her had become his favourite hobby. He tucked his head and looked at his ledger, trying to hide the look on his face.

As she sorted the letters, he noticed a square white one in her hands addressed to H. Davis Jr.

"Just throw that in the garbage," Holden said when he saw Eileen looking at it.

She frowned and glanced at it before extending it to him. "It doesn't seem like a chain letter."

"It's an invitation. I never go so just throw it away."

"Oh…okay," she said. She was about to toss it in the trash when she noticed the return address. "But…it's from Paul."

Holden stopped writing for a moment and looked up at Eileen. The two wreaths on his desk lent a hazy, dreamlike glow to the office, making Eileen look like she were abed on a pink cloud. Would going to the party really be so bad? Perhaps it would be the excuse he needed to get her in a more casual environment and tell her what was on his mind.

He cleared his throat. "Well, it's Paul's birthday party, but he treats it like an annual ball. Clifford loves that kind of thing. Would you like to come too?" As much as it pained him to invite Clifford, he knew it was necessary to keep the optics above board. Plus, Clifford never turned down a chance for free food and booze.

Eileen grinned and bounced on her heels. "Yup. It's tomorrow, but that's okay. I've already got a pink dress that would be perfect."

* * *

EILEEN COULDN'T SLEEP THAT NIGHT. She drank water, ate a slice of sweet bread and still couldn't calm her mind. She'd had that dream again, the one where she was dragged out of bed.

Eileen wanted to feel better, to feel less alone and afraid. There was only one person she could think of at that moment, one person who could lighten her mood and make her laugh. She leaned over the edge and felt around for the phone. Never before had the urge to hear Holden's deep voice been so strong. She began dialling his number and then caught herself. It was almost midnight and she didn't even have a plausible excuse for calling him so late. Plus, she didn't know how — or with whom — he spent his nights. She slammed the phone back on its cradle, frustrated by the idea of him being with someone else. In an instant, her irritation turned to rage.

Her brain ticked and before she knew what she was doing she pulled out the slip of paper she kept folded in the side pocket of her handbag, even though she had called the Cane Slasher's number so often that she knew it by heart.

Bitterness coursed through her. She hoped the phone woke everyone in his household. If she was right, and the number was residential, a wife or elderly grandmother wouldn't want that annoying trill in their ears. She held her breath, praying that the odds were in her favour.

The phone rang eight times before someone answered. But instead of a woman's sleepy mumble, a man's drunken voice asked, "Is this Jesus?" Wind blew into the receiver, muffling his response as whistling frogs and crickets chirped so loudly that Eileen thought they were right inside the telephone.

"Uh no…" Eileen was caught off guard but she quickly said, "I have an urgent person-to-person call from someone important. What's your name, sir?"

The man wept and said, "Um is an angel. The Lord sent you. This is a sign. I gonna stop drinking right now." Glass smashed on the ground and echoed through the line as the man slurred, "See?"

Eileen wrinkled her brow. If he was drunk, there was a good chance that he'd rat himself out. Her heart beat faster. Catching the serial killer might be so much easier than she thought.

"Yes…that's very good. But what's your name?"

"Them does call me Skunk," he rasped with a drunken giggle.

How clever, Eileen rolled her eyes. She didn't doubt that his nickname alluded to him always being drunk like a skunk. "Where are you, Skunk? I can come and get you."

"But you know where I is," came the petulant reply. "You is an angel."

"Yes, but I want you to tell me so I can make sure you get help." In the background, a clock chimed loudly and her heart beat so fast that she feared she would faint.

Skunk stupsed. "You ain't no angel. All you do is frig me up and make me throw 'way my rum for nothing." And with that, he slammed the receiver down and ended the call.

Despite not getting an answer, Eileen had heard enough to know that not only was Skunk not the killer, but he was at a payphone near the parliament building.

Chapter 16
Family Feud

Paul's home was an uptight Victorian affair that looked like a replica of Angela Channing's house from Falcon Crest. It was set on a sprawling hilltop with an unencumbered view that spawned miles of shoreline on the west coast. The home was ablaze with lights and loud music poured through the windows as clusters of people in long black gowns and tuxedoes entered the mahogany double doors. Even from her vantage point in the cobbled stone courtyard, Eileen could see the huge jewels that sparkled on the necks of the female guests. She looked down at her knee-length sheath with its sweetheart neckline. She sighed; this was the only nice dress she had. She stepped back, intent on turning around and going home, but bumped into something big and solid. Two hands held her arms and a voice said, "Careful, Eileen."

She twisted around and her words caught in her throat. Holden was handsomely decked out in an immaculate black suit that fit his body not unlike how a mango's skin conforms to its shape.

"You look…good," she stammered.

He chuckled and tugged on the lapels. "I'm out sharp tonight, aren't I? He gestured to her figure-hugging dress, his eyes glittering as he took in her outfit. "You look beautiful." She blushed and he struggled to take his eyes off her before he cleared his throat and held out his arm. "We can't party out here so let's head inside."

Her face flushed. She shook her head and muttered, "I'm not properly dressed. I don't want to embarrass myself."

"Codswallop! These stuffy bats have old money, but no style. Besides," he said grimly, "Clifford is parking the van. No-one will question your ensemble when they see his."

Arm in arm, they joined the steady stream of people on the pathway that led to the foyer, Eileen tugging her hem as they walked. Soon they reached the mahogany doors where Paul was patting men's shoulders and kissing women's cheeks with unstoppered zeal.

Backlit by the sparkling crystal chandelier, the difference between the brothers was more pronounced, perhaps because they were dressed in almost identical outfits. While Holden was broad-shouldered and warm, Paul was a curtailed version, lean and angular, his pinched features giving him an air of haughty austerity.

He shook Holden's hand enthusiastically and slapped him on the back. "Brother! I wondered when you'd come to see The Manor. I'll give you the grand tour as soon as I finish greeting my guests." His eyes flicked over Eileen's curvy figure and her dress before he smiled and said, "Aha, is this the lady to whom we owe the pleasure of your company?" He hugged Eileen, then stepped back and pressed his forefinger against his lips. "I must admit...something about you seems familiar, but I can't put my finger on it."

"Jesus, Paul, you met her at Earl's house."

Paul's eyes scanned Eileen's shapely figure greedily and he said, "No...I don't think that's it."

"Well, I'm sure you'll work it out soon enough," Holden snapped. "We'll be moving along now."

Paul's smile faltered for a second before he plastered it back onto his face and patted Holden's shoulder a bit too heavily. "Ever the diplomat, my brother." Something in the distance caught Paul's attention and his grin widened. "Ah. Here's Clifford, colourful as usual."

Of all the outfits Eileen had ever seen on Clifford, this one was the most spectacular. A broad-rimmed tie-dyed hat, a lime green suit jacket, woolly leg warmers and a worn pair of jeans were paired with a beaded peace sign that bounced against Clifford's bare chest as he ambled up the pathway.

"Oye, this is a real shindig," Clifford said as he sidled up behind them, hitching his pants higher on his slim waist. Paul beamed. Holden rolled his eyes. Eileen smirked.

Clifford cracked his knuckles and surveyed the scene. Inside the foyer, waiters wafted through the crowd with canapé-laden silver trays high above their heads and a pianist played music in the corner of the massive room. "I shall be wining and dining 'til the cock crow." He caught Holden's stern face and added, "Or 'til you ready to leave, of course."

The three of them made their way through the crowd as the sounds of clinking glasses and clattering cutlery filled the air. Clifford waylaid a passing waiter, retrieving six fishcakes in the process. He popped one in his mouth before pressing two fishcakes into Holden's hand. "Try these, boss, you gonna like them."

"If you say so, these things must burn like Hades' ass."

"Nah, them taste good." Clifford threw another in his mouth, chewed twice and swallowed.

Holden raised an eyebrow. "I'll take my chances with the crudités." Clifford shrugged and ate another fishcake and handed the rest to Eileen. Holden plucked two tiny vegetable stacks from another waiter's tray and tasted them, commenting that they were very flavourful. Clifford raised an eyebrow but said nothing as his eyes assessed the females at the party like a hungry man at a buffet. A full-figured woman with hair like Whitney Houston's waved at Clifford from the other end of the terrace, beckoning him to come over. She was dripping in jewels and attitude, but her face glowed like a teenage girl's when she saw him wink back at her.

"Excusez moi, s'il vous plait, I'm being summoned." He sauntered off like a cowboy into the sunset to join her, throwing a wink over his shoulder at Eileen. She laughed, wondering what these hoity-toity women could ever have in common with Clifford.

Piano music floated through the doors from the large hall beyond the french doors that led outside to the terrace. The black and white marble floor glinted under the soft yellow light from the brass sconces that lined the terrace's exterior walls.

Eileen took in the decor, the beautiful tropical gardens, the bright moon. Eventually, his crudités eaten, Holden leaned over and asked, "Having a good time?"

"I am."

"Good. Good." He cleared his throat and asked, "Something to drink?"

"A 7-Up, please."

Holden nodded and disappeared through the crowd. He returned shortly, bringing along a stocky gentleman that he introduced as John Wilson, a bank manager. Soon a handful of others, including Dorothy Greaves, the owner of Happy Home, joined as well. Dorothy looked even more pitiful than she had the last time Eileen had seen her, dressed in a shapeless black dress and orthopaedic shoes. The older woman's manicure was atrocious and her wig was in desperate need of a good washing. Eileen's heart went out to the grieving woman.

"My dear, I'm sorry I was so cold the last time we met. It was a very trying day." Dorothy smiled and pulled Eileen into a hug.

Eileen patted her back. "You don't have to apologize. I know it can't be easy."

"Yes…yes…" Dorothy's eyes skimmed the crowd. "Is… Clifford here?"

Eileen wrinkled her nose as she looked about for Clifford. "I last saw him just off the terrace. I can go and get him if you'd like."

"Oh no," Dorothy grabbed Eileen's wrist and then fixed a tight smile on her face. She flexed her rose-coloured nails and said apologetically, "I just asked." Eileen heard what Dorothy said but her grip had been too insistent for her query to be casual. Whether Dorothy liked it or not, Eileen would mention it to Clifford.

The rest of the group was chattering away about all manner of things: investments, politics, history and art, traipsing seamlessly from one topic to the next. Eileen sucked it all in, glad that she had stayed.

She glanced at Holden covertly as the night went on. His flushed cheeks, ready smile and hearty laugh looked strange on him, like a new outfit, but they suited him marvellously. She blushed and looked away when their eyes met. Out on the gazebo, Clifford was holding court, a flock of chattering middle-aged women surrounding him and laughing out loud at everything he said. His gaudy outfit and outrageous antics were like catnip to those high society women in their baubles and silk gowns. One of them stroked his arm lightly, sipping champagne as she looked at him with star-crossed eyes. Eileen laughed and waved at him. He waved back and motioned to her that he was coming over in a minute. In her periphery, she noticed Dorothy Greaves watching Clifford, her eyes inscrutable as she followed his every movement. Eileen looked away, deciding to finally try the fishcake that Clifford had given her earlier.

"Oh my…" Eileen sputtered as she inspected the pillowy insides of her fishcake. Flecks of bright red scotch bonnet pepper stared back at her. Her eyes watered, and the burning sensation at the back of her throat made her cough. How on earth could Clifford enjoy anything so spicy?

Holden looked at her in concern, a wordless question clear in his raised eyebrows.

"Need water," she mouthed to him as she stepped away.

The bar was on the far end of the terrace. *Probably so the rich people won't have to mingle with the help*, thought Eileen wryly. Mouth still smarting, she retreated to a dimly lit section of the terrace, sipping the water and dabbing the tears that formed in her eyes. "These fishcakes really are as hot as Hades' ass," she gasped.

A long silhouette stretched across the black and white tiles and Eileen looked up to see Paul come through the french doors. For months that moment would replay itself in Eileen's mind; the bass-like tremor of his shoes crossing the floor, the yellow light from the sconces casting half of him in shadow as he came toward her.

Paul's approach was viper-like; Eileen could tell that he had sought her out, waiting until she had slipped away to follow her.

He stood at arm's length, his face vaguely pensive as he tapped his fingers against his lips and said slowly, "You know, Charlene… I just remembered how I know you."

The look on his face made Eileen's heart skitter to a stop. He smiled too sweetly and blinked too slowly, awaiting a reaction he was sure would come.

She laughed giddily. "It's Eileen. And I have one of those faces. We never met before."

Paul's lips smiled, but his eyes hardened. He rested his hand on the wall, leaned in closer, his back hunched like a predator about to pounce as he put his mouth in line with her ear. His cologne and the brandy on his breath intermingled, nauseating her. Her face paled as he whispered, "You're funny, even with your clothes on."

She felt a shift then, the way every hair on her body rose like quills on a porcupine. She remembered his lips on her neck and breasts as he pressed into her over and over again. Her hand fluttered up and covered her cleavage that had suddenly grown cold in the evening air. Breathing became painful, unfamiliar. "Mr Davis, I always have my clothes on." She stepped back and brushed against the brick wall behind her.

"The last time I picked you up from Buckworth Street, you didn't." She stared back at him, her eyes glassy with wet rage as he went on, "My brother and I don't usually have the same taste. He's such a fucking bore with his morals and all of that shit." He looked her up and down with a poisonous smile. "But, I guess the apple never falls far from the pussy tree."

Eileen didn't mean to cry, but she couldn't help it. Tears ran down her flushed face until they dripped onto her hand that was still pressed against her chest. "Leave me alone."

"Oh… you want me to pay you," Paul said as he fished around in his pocket. In a flash, he pulled out two twenties and fanned them in her face. Eileen squeezed her eyes closed. It wasn't what Paul said that upset her. She'd started the night feeling insecure about her dress. She'd progressed to enjoying sophisticated conversation with cultured people. Now he'd found a way to cheapen her and drag her back to the lowest night of her life.

In the blink of an eye, spittle flew from Paul's mouth as a fist crashed into his jaw and a sickening crunch like a thunder clap echoed across the terrace. Paul fell to the ground as Holden stood over him. Both brothers were breathing heavily, their eyes riveted on each other as anger crackled between them. Paul touched his face, shifting his lower jaw from left to right trying to determine if it was broken. Holden's hands were clenched and he bit into his lip, trying to quell the rage that moved through his body like a low frequency vibration. Eileen had experienced Holden's crankiness, frustration and restlessness before. But she'd never known his anger, never witnessed the all-consuming furore that turned him into a broad-shouldered beast.

The money slipped from Paul's fingers; a stiff breeze caught the bills and blew them across the lawn where they landed in a bougainvillaea bush. Paul got unsteadily to his feet and stepped away from Eileen, his spidery bearing harmless once more. He stuck his hands in his pockets and gave his brother a wide berth before he sauntered through the french doors whistling the Bonanza theme song. Holden said nothing as Paul went inside. He gazed at Eileen, a mixture of anger and disgust on his face.

She licked her lips. How much had he heard? Did he believe what Paul had said? Holden stepped slowly toward her and said, "I suggest we talk privately for a moment."

She nodded numbly and hooked her arm in his. He didn't retrace their steps through the large living room and the foyer where the pianist played a lilting ballad. Instead, Holden guided her to the garden, leading the way down a mossy path through the lush grounds and out to a small utility gate. Eileen's lip trembled and her face burned with embarrassment as she imagined what Holden would say. *He'll fire me*, she thought miserably. Her eyes started to leak tears again. It was a childish thought, but all she could think was that it wasn't fair.

At the end of the path, he released her arm and pressed his back against the rough bark of a tamarind tree. It was hard to read the look on his face as he folded his arms across his chest. For a while, he stared down at his feet as though willing them to speak for him. She'd seen him do it before, weigh his words so they properly conveyed what he wanted to say. Eileen's anger bubbled as she watched him. *Why drag this out?* she wondered as her impatience grew. His fingers traced a line around his mouth and she was just about to tell him what he could do with his job when he held up a hand and said, "I'm sorry about Paul. He was an ass and I'll deal with him tomorrow." He exhaled and looked at her. "But what I want to know is why you didn't tell me."

The rage inside her deflated like a balloon and turned to exasperation. She threw up her hands and asked, "Tell you what? If I was packing shelves at the supermarket, would you have wanted to know that too?"

He shrugged. "Yes."

Hands on her hips, she glared at him. "No, you wouldn't. I don't have time for all of this long talk. You're gonna fire me, but you know what? I don't even care."

She could barely see him in the darkness, hidden as he was by the tree's shadow, but his deep voice was even and patient. "When did I say that?"

Eileen squinted at him in the dim moonlight trying to read the expression on his face. His question caught her off guard. Was he playing the diplomat and trying to make her quit?

"Eileen, I'm not a man of many words. I have my quirks. But that doesn't mean that I consider you less of a person because of what you did before."

"That's what you say now. But in the end, you'll always judge me." Tears stung her eyes, but she refused to cry again as she paced next to a rose bush.

"Eileen..." Holden stepped out of the shadows with his hands pushed deep into his pockets. "...have you ever considered that I always knew?"

Eileen spun around to face him. He couldn't be serious. But in the soft moonlight, Holden's face betrayed no laughter or mirth, just hopeful sincerity. It was one thing to be accepted; it was another to not have to *seek* acceptance. Eileen bit down, squeezing words between her teeth like an angry hiss. "You're a liar."

He blinked, looked down at his feet and then at hers. "It's your shoes. I heard you pacing the corner that night. Same rhythm, same clicking heels. I had my suspicions, but the first morning you came to work and I heard you walking across the floor, I knew. You saw the sign I had stapled to the wall outside the building, didn't you?"

Her lip trembled, but she nodded.

"I didn't want to hire you at first — not because of what you did — but because you took my breath away when we first met. I didn't want —" Holden threw up his hands and pressed his knuckles against his forehead. "The point is that I don't care what you did before."

Eileen started to cry. "But everybody else will know."

Holden waved his hand dismissively at Paul's house. "Ignore them. They'll stew in their bitter juices until I or some other undertaker collects them."

He held out his hands to her. Reluctantly, she rested her hands in his, savouring the warmth of his large hands clasping hers. "The long and short of it is that I don't want you to leave. You do a really good job. Plus, you actually brighten up that gloomy funeral parlour. Clifford is entertaining in his own annoying way, but you're different."

Eileen's heart fluttered in a way it never had.

"Will you stay with me?" he asked, stepping so close that there was not even a hair's breadth between them.

Eileen felt faint. She had imagined this moment. Dreamed of being this close to him. She felt his breath on her lips, surrendered to the desire inside her that had yearned for him for weeks. His arms wrapped around her waist and their lips touched. Every nerve in her body tingled as his tongue slipped into her mouth. Eileen had never felt that much heat or intensity from a kiss before, never known the unadulterated pleasure that came from a tongue caressing her own. She pressed her hands against his chest, felt the muscles tense as he sighed with lust. Even his moan was delicious, an ardent plea to deepen the sensations to which they freely surrendered.

The heat between them built and their desires grew feverish as they explored each other's body. Holden pressed Eileen against the tree, his hands roaming over her waist and hips as the tree bark pressed into her back. She wanted him. All of him, right there in that moonlit garden while the party was in full swing less than a hundred yards away.

But, as though he read her mind, Holden pulled away and said breathlessly, "This isn't right. We can't do this here." He glanced toward the house, light blazing from the windows and piano music drifting into the garden. "Not that I don't want to…I sense that memories of this moment would delight me in my old age."

Eileen bit back a smile.

"I want to date you properly first." Holden touched her cheek as he looked into her eyes. "If, of course, that's what you want too."

If her heart could have burst, it would have. Hot sex in the garden would have been amazing, but she couldn't deny that a storybook romance had its own appeal. "Yes." Eileen blushed. "I'd love that."

A cloud shifted overhead, unveiling the moon and washing the garden in silvery light. "How about we leave this place? Maybe get some fried fish from Astor's Road?" He grinned. "Our first date."

Eileen smiled and nodded. "Yeah. I'd like that."

Chapter 17
Something is fishy

They got two juicy steaks of fish fried to perfection over a wood fire from a sidewalk vendor whose coal pot was still aflame at that late hour. It was a typical Friday night on Astor's Road. Similar to Buckworth Street, the road was heavily traversed with buses and cars, but instead of accountants and pharmacies, it had more than its fair share of rum shops and shoe repair businesses. At night, the street transformed into a drive-through food court with vendors setting up brightly painted trays and coal pots to ply their trade. The fish vendor they visited occupied a small soot-stained corner, her bright yellow stall a stark contrast to the corona of dark, smoky residue that framed her location.

She heaved her generous figure off the flaking yellow bench, taking bits of shiny paint for a ride on her ample backside when she got up to prepare their food. Two fat steaks of dolphin were stuffed with a heavenly homemade herb seasoning, then doused in flour and dropped into a pan of oil that bubbled merrily on the fire. The aroma of frying fish was enough to make Eileen dizzy with hunger.

"My child father make this coal pot, you know," she said as though Holden and Eileen had asked. "Yes, he gimme some pretty red-skinned daughters. Got good hair and thing," she added as she checked the fish.

Holden winked at Eileen and whispered, "This is why I like vendors; they're so amusing that it's like free dinner theatre."

The woman returned to the bench and sat on the opposite end so gently that Eileen wondered if her robust frame was a suit, so graceful were her movements.

"Yeah, that is an old gearbox housing that my child father rigged up to cook the fish. But it is my seasoning that does make it taste good. Best fish in Barbados," she bragged. Her grin was cocky as she rubbed her hands and turned the damp flour into moist balls that clung to her fingers like tiny white barnacles. She shook her hands, releasing the flour balls and giving them a new home on Holden's crisp black suit. The vendor didn't notice though; she was too busy looking at the frying pan. "Ah, it ready."

She returned a moment later with two steaming strips of foil and plastic forks. The fish tasted as good as it smelled. Eileen couldn't imagine a better first date with Holden: delicious fish in the cool night air with the stars overhead and a chatty vendor who skipped nimbly from one subject to another while they ate. There wasn't much the vendor missed from her busy street corner. She knew which paros had gone to university and fallen prey to drugs, which politicians drove by on Friday nights with their outside women. She even knew where Holden could get stolen picnic hams in time for Christmas. The vendor shrugged like it was a given that anyone in their right mind wanted picnic hams at half price. No? Well, that was Holden's business because she certainly wanted a stolen picnic ham. It was for the children, of course. The daughters with the good hair, she reminded them as she dusted more flour onto Holden's pants. To Eileen's mind, she could have eaten that fish and laughed at the vendor's quirky monologue every night and never gotten bored.

They wiped their mouths and Holden handed the lady a hundred dollar note. She dug into her apron pockets, but he held up his hand. "No change needed. Get the ham for your girls." The woman's face lit up as she looked at the hundred dollar bill. Holden reached out to shake her hand. "And you're right; it is the best fish in Barbados."

"You's a good man." She grinned and then caught sight of the flour crumbs that coated the left leg of Holden's pants. "Don't mind that flour. It sends my children to school, so it is a blessing." Eyes wide, she cocked her head to the left, her sharp ears attuned to a sound that Holden and Eileen didn't catch until a few moments later. "Wait… you hear that?"

It was a siren, growing louder and louder as a police car sped by. Two more cars soon followed, all of them heading west. Eileen's eyes met Holden's. There was a very good chance that their date had come to an end. They thanked the vendor and left.

Stomachs full, they wondered aloud what had happened as they drove the five minutes to Holden's house. Just as Eileen pulled the car to a stop, they heard the phone ringing inside his house, breaking the quiet of the night air. He looked at her briefly. She nodded and cut the engine as he rushed inside to answer.

A few minutes later, he walked back down the stairs, loosening his bowtie before he leaned through the car window and said, "The Slasher struck again in St. James. Derricks said that they found something at the scene that they need to investigate further so we can't go there just yet." He stuffed his hands in his pockets and rocked on his heels. "Seems we have some time to kill," he said.

Eileen sighed. Holden didn't fool her with his attempt at striking a casual tone. Her fantasy of turning their night into something special was dashed. Not to mention the fact that it would be her first Cane Field murder scene. "We do," she said with a glum expression.

Holden raised an eyebrow and said, "I haven't sat in the garden for a long time. How about we do that?"

Eileen followed him down the walkway and through a trellis covered with bright yellow allamanda vines that glowed neon in the moonlight. Beyond the trellis, soft lights flickered inside coral-stone lanterns that trailed the length of the winding flagstone path. At the end of the path was a gazebo surrounded by ferns, red ginger lilies and hundreds of fireflies.

Holden gestured to the bench before sitting on the structure's wooden floor. Eileen took a deep breath and sat down.

"So…how is your night going?"

Eileen grinned. "It had some fits and starts, but it's gotten better." She winced and said, "Oh... I forgot to tell Clifford that Dorothy was looking for him."

"Was she now?" Holden asked with a sly grin.

"What's so funny?" His smile was contagious and she couldn't help the giggle that bubbled up as she awaited his response.

"Clifford and Dorothy have a…chequered history."

"Meaning?"

"They're casual lovers. Whenever they're bored or attend the same party, they end up in bed."

"Dorothy and Clifford? Nah…I don't believe it. Plus, she's kinda…"

“She’s not conventionally beautiful,” admitted Holden. “She’s got that squarish build and a deep voice, but Clifford has always preferred a more robust lady.”

He wasn’t wrong about that; Eileen had seen the way those other women glommed on to Clifford. But when Eileen tried to imagine tall, slim Clifford in the throes of passion with sturdy Dorothy, she just couldn’t.

Holden laughed. “Stop wrinkling your face like that. ’Every piece of cloth in town got its owner’ as the old people would say. They’ve been knocking around together since they were teenagers and I don't think anyone ever understood their attraction." Holden chuckled. "Do you know how her brother Lloyd found out? One time, he stood on a chair to spy on them through those cross-ventilation squares close to the ceiling. The chair broke and Lloyd fell on a kerosene lamp. He got a cut on his arm and minor burns.”

Eileen grimaced. “That sounds painful. But why didn’t it work out if they were fooling around for so long?”

Holden plucked a piece of spindly grass that waved in the light breeze and spun it between his thumb and forefinger. “Clifford said he loved Dorothy and wanted to marry her. But he had some…difficulties overseas and Dorothy’s father forbade her to marry him.”

“Sounds like one of those old-fashioned novels. That probably explains why she kept watching him all night.”

“It’s true. Unrequited love is one of those stories that you read about and hope never happens to you.”

Eileen’s heart skipped a beat. She searched her mind for a new topic to discuss, desperate to shift the conversation's course. The last thing she wanted to focus on was heartbreak.

"I love them, you know," she said pointing to the flecks of light that floated around the ferns just out of her arm's reach.

"Fireflies?"

"Yes. When I was a little girl, I used to catch them in jars and keep them next to my bed. I'd put tiny flowers at the bottom of the jar and pretend the fireflies were fairies in a magic forest. I liked watching them in their little see-through world."

Holden twirled his blade of grass again. "They're amazing insects," he admitted. He caught Eileen's eye and said, "Not many creatures can make their own light and shine it on the world. You can't blame someone for falling in love under those circumstances."

His voice was low, earnest — the way a man speaks when his words are the only channel his soul can find.

Holden wasn't like other men who told their imagined war stories so often that you wondered what the truth looked like in its embryonic stage. He was smart, thoughtful, kind, ambitious and probably deserved better than a smart-mouthed wild child like Eileen. Now that Eileen's ardour had cooled, she realized that this wasn't a passing fancy for her. She hoped the same was true of him.

Inside the house, the phone rang again. Holden's frown soured his face. He sighed. "I guess it's time to go."

Chapter 18
Revelations

Anna Brown's dump site had been Holden's first exposure to the Cane Slasher's machinations. At the time, Holden assumed it was a lover's quarrel gone wrong and believed the crime would be solved quickly. Now, a deathly sense of dejá vù overtook him as he watched an almost identical scene unfold in front of him. The police tape, the camera flashes, the young woman's contorted body among a pile of cane trash and withered blossoms were all the same. The only difference was the victim, Donna Green. Bile rose in Holden's throat.

He was a voyeur to this spate of killings, an outsider with a front seat to the carnage wrought by a deeply disturbed person. A few feet away, the young woman's family held hands as the girl's mother quivered in agony at the centre of the group. Next to them, Dr Thorpe was packing away his bag after administering a sedative to the mother.

"How could a man wake up every day with so much anger in his heart that this is normal to him?" Holden mused.

Eileen shook her head distractedly, her eyes glued to the family. She leaned close to Holden and whispered, "Did you notice the young guy with them?"

"What about him?"

"Is he wearing pyjamas?"

"It's hard to tell since it's so dark, but they look like hospital scrubs to me."

"Didn't you say that you thought the killer had medical expertise because he kept hitting the jugular all the time?"

Covertly, Holden raised his eyes to look at the young man again. He was close to the family yet distinctly apart from them. Instead of commiserating with relatives, his gaze was focused on the scene, watching with interest as investigators took photos and wrapped the young woman's body for transportation.

"Are you sure he's with them?" Holden's question was tinged with doubt.

"Yes. When we first got here, I saw the girl's mother talking to him."

"I guess we'll find out soon enough what's going on. Look."

The commissioner had ducked under the yellow tape, his face grim as he braced himself to offer the police force's sympathies and update the family, before beckoning to Holden and Eileen.

"This is Holden Davis, owner of the funeral home that will safely transport your loved one to the coroner," Derricks said with practised fluidity. Knowing Derricks as he did, Holden suspected that he had crafted and memorized a multitude of mini speeches which he could rattle off to journalists and grieving families at will. Derricks was nothing if not practical.

Holden reached forward and shook the matriarch's hand. He ignored the wetness of the damp handkerchief clutched in her palm.

"He said you do funerals too. We ain't got much, but how much is it gonna cost for you to — to..."

The end of the sentence dangled in the air. It always did. No parent wanted to say “bury my child”.

The tears were still streaming down her face, but her eyes looked glassy and numb. The sedatives had begun to kick in. Holden knew she needed to rest. He patted her shoulder and said, “I can visit you tomorrow to show you some options." Donna's mother simply stared at him until one of the relatives — a sister perhaps, based on their resemblance — guided her to a small hatchback to rest and compose herself.

Just then, the hum of a heavy engine and two square beams of light broke through the night as Paul’s Camaro travelled toward them slowly across the rutted earth. Out of the corner of his eye, Holden noticed Eileen’s mouth tighten. They had only left the party three hours earlier; her disgust for his brother was still fresh.

Paul was dressed as though on his way to an eighteenth-century cotillion, clad in a top hat and coattails that fluttered behind him as he walked. He tipped his hat to the policemen and said, “Good evening, folks. To the bereaved, I’m very sorry for your loss.” He cast a dark look at his brother and added, “I’m the co-owner of Davis and *Sons*.” Holden didn’t miss the emphasis Paul placed on the last word, but he also knew that he didn't have the patience or time for a public argument. Holden excused them and steered Paul back to his car.

“What are you doing here?” Holden asked through gritted teeth.

“You know full well I’m supposed to get half of the bodies. But you and your little floozy have been swooping in and taking almost all for the past few months,” Paul fumed as he shook Holden’s hands off his shoulders.

"Half of the *government* collections — which I might add, you don't even want in the first place since you always tell them to call me. It's up to you to organize your own funerals."

"Since when do you dictate what my half of the business gets to do? From now on I want my share of the collections or I'm calling my lawyer."

Holden cocked a haughty eyebrow. "You're only hot and sweaty about these collections because the hospital served you a cease-and-desist," Holden said, his voice carrying a dangerously cool undertone.

Paul bristled. Holden had struck a nerve. For years Paul had paid touters to stand outside the A&E to solicit funerals, a practice which Holden was firmly against. One touter had followed the mother of a recently drowned child to her car and offered to go home with her, saying grief was nothing a little sex couldn't cure.

The hospital board was livid and the woman's husband, a big-shot lawyer, claimed severe emotional distress and sued. Not only was Paul's most lucrative income generator gone, but he also had a looming lawsuit that could wipe him out. Much to Holden's dismay, Davis and Sons had been listed as the plaintiff.

Jaw clenched, Paul's words came out as mere whispers between his teeth. "I own fifty per cent."

"Then do fifty per cent of the *bloody* work," retorted Holden. "Start by paying the massive loan for the fancy building you occupy or cutting back on the huge staff you have. Maybe pull your balls out of your back pocket and do an embalming or two. Then you could do something other than dressing like a ringmaster to drive a carriage."

If Paul's skin were any lighter, Holden would have seen the blood drain from his face. But knowing his brother as he did, Holden also knew that Paul would rather pursue an irrational argument than listen to reason.

Paul was enraged. "You know…at some point, that stick up your ass is going to rupture your spleen. But long before then, I'll have made you pay for this."

He stalked to his car and revved the engine. The wheels spun and a shower of muddy splatters rained on Holden's pants as Paul shifted the gears and sped off.

"That was unnecessary," came Eileen's voice from behind Holden. She pulled a cleaning cloth from her handbag and set about wiping the stains.

Holden bit his tongue. Paul wasn't the most reliable when it came to time or ethics, but his spite had a way of being consistently punctual. Holden could handle anything his brother dished out, but his real fear was that Paul would harm Eileen. For decades, he had struggled to get along with Paul, brushing everything aside for the greater good. But Paul would cross the line if he harmed Eileen. Holden would see to it.

He took the cloth from her and wiped his shoes before he straightened to his full height and looked at her. Holden knew with certainty that his feelings for her had overtaken him. Not in a gentle way like the caress of a soft wave over your toes at the beach, but gradually, forcefully like thick vines that snake their way over a forgotten cottage, covering every window and door until the cottage became no more than a large trellis, a mere microcosm of the forest that engulfed it.

Chapter 19
Eye Witness

A train of puffy clouds swept across the sky, moving in time with the jacket Holden had draped over Eileen's shoulders as it flapped noisily in the breeze. The echoing wind magnified the clicks of the photographer's camera, the rustle of the cane arrows and the chirps of the whistling frogs, transforming the night's sounds into an ominous rhythm. Eileen shivered as she surveyed the scene. A man in a plastic coat was hunched over, partially hidden by swaying cane stalks as his gloved hands panned the area with a magnifying glass. The wind shifted, allowing Eileen to catch snatches of the investigator's conversation with the photographer.

"Can you get a picture of this?" he asked, pointing at the section of the cane trash where the victim had been found. He grunted as he stood up and massaged the small of his back.

Eileen screwed up her eyes to see what he was referring to, but she was too far away. "What am I taking pictures of?" queried the photographer.

"This little pink thing right here. Looks like a fingernail to me, one of those fake ones women wear when they go out."

The photographer shrugged. "Ain't ever seen one before, but it might be." He adjusted the camera's aperture, leaned in and clicked the shutter twice before he adjusted the settings again and snapped a few more shots.

"How soon can I get back those photos?"

"A few days. I've got urgent ones to push through first."

"Fine," grumbled the investigator. He gingerly picked up the shiny pink thing and dropped it inside a bag, sealed it and put it in his case, a pensive look on his face. "That girl had fake nails?"

"Dunno," said the photographer as he swapped out the used film for a new roll. The investigator squinted at him like he wanted to gouge his eyes out with the tweezers in his hand. Eileen shook her head in amusement. Even she could see that the photographer was there to do his job; no more, but preferably less if he could get away with it.

Holden came up behind her. He had spent the better part of twenty minutes chatting with Clifford and Derricks before Clifford had left to go to the morgue. "We've both had a long night and there's nothing more we can do here. Let's go home."

The cane field was part of a large plantation, crisscrossed with sunken cart roads made by fat tractor wheels. The easiest thing to do was to head south, going deeper into the cane ground until they came out to a small village on the other side. Once in the car, Eileen turned the steering wheel and drove down the narrow lane flanked by tall stalks of cane. The humps in the middle of the track were covered with thick patches of grass that flicked the metal underbody so it sounded like thousands of tiny pings echoing throughout the car's interior. "I could never understand why tractors compact the earth to the point where the grass in the middle is like a long island," Eileen grumbled as she drove.

"They fill the tyres with water," responded Holden.

"Really?"

"Yes. Water acts as a ballast which the tractors need for stability."

"Hmm." Eileen considered what he said and then asked, "How do you know so much?"

Holden smiled. "I read. You read a lot too, but mostly those classic novels where the people never even heard of electricity so you wouldn't know about tractor tyres."

Eileen laughed and wiped the windshield with the sleeve of her shirt, trying to erase a smudge that blocked her view. It barely helped the visibility. "Geez, it's dark," she mumbled. Ahead of them, the headlight's beams illuminated the cart road but left the fields on either side doused in heavy darkness. The thickness of the night pressed against the car doors, threatening to swallow them whole.

A chill went down her spine as she gripped the steering wheel tighter.

Holden's voice was gentle as he asked, "Afraid of the dark?"

She smiled ruefully. "A little bit. The night always felt like a time that wasn't entirely safe."

"I see," was all he said.

"I know it may seem odd to you given the circumstances, but I was always afraid of the night because of strange sounds. And now, with everything going on…" her voice trailed off.

"I can understand that." He cleared his throat. "What led you to your previous line of work if you don't mind me asking?"

She sucked in her bottom lip and blew a breath through her nose. "I found out that the lady who raised me was keeping a secret from me and we had a big falling out. A few months later, she moved to America and I had no way to reach her to ask for help."

Holden frowned. "Sounds like a bad secret indeed."

Eileen's mouth soured. "If lying to someone for their whole life constitutes a bad secret, then it's abhorrent."

Holden raised an eyebrow, his expression grave as he contemplated her words.

Eileen sighed. "I told myself that it wouldn't be that bad. I regret doing it now." She bit her lip and shook her head. "There aren't a whole lot of choices for females out there. Which is kind of obvious given that these women were killed because they were desperate for jobs," she added soberly. "By comparison, being afraid of the dark is something I can get over."

Holden thought quietly for a moment before nodding his head. "Start with the little fears and the big fears fall in line. Even people like my father had their share of doubts about their ability. He once confessed that he almost didn't start the business."

Eileen tried to remember a time when the peach building hadn't served as a landmark. She couldn't imagine a world without Davis and Sons.

"What did he do?"

"He said that he learned the hard way that fear wasn't his friend. He said you've gotta kick it in the nuts and chase it away."

The man's wisdom was on point as usual. "What's your fear?" Eileen asked.

"I can't think of any." Holden shrugged.

The car jerked to a stop as Eileen pressed the brakes in the middle of the field.

"Want to drive?"

Holden looked at her and then the steering wheel as though trying to connect the dots. "But I haven't driven in a long time."

"Because?"

He was about to respond when he stopped himself and looked at her. The moon had come up, full and round in the sky, and dusted everything in sight with pale light.

His laugh was sardonic as he muttered, "'Son, everything you've ever wanted is on the other side of fear'."

To Eileen's surprise, he got out, walked around the car and waited until she climbed over the handbrake before sliding behind the wheel and shifting the car into drive. Hesitation and doubt evaporated and Holden looked like a brand new man behind the wheel, one prepossessed of himself and his capabilities. At the end of the cane field, he turned the car onto the road, his capable hands manoeuvering the car through the village and toward the highway. They drove past shops, small chattel houses and men playing road tennis under a streetlight.

"Do you want me to take you home?" Holden asked.

Eileen bit her lip, her mind warring with itself as she considered the implications. Did he want to spend the night at her house? She pursed her lips and said slowly, "I'm not sure what you mean."

"It's late; you shouldn't go home alone given the current climate. I can drive you there and come back in the morning to take you to work."

"Oh...yes...that would be very nice."

Damned him for being such a gentleman, she silently fumed as he followed her directions.

"I'm sorry about Paul," said Holden as the wind whipped through the windows. "He was a full ass tonight."

Eileen's cheeks coloured; she had pretended not to hear his floozy comment, but her ruse hadn't fooled Holden.

"Don't worry about it."

"I have to worry about it. Paul has been getting away with murder for years and it's got to stop. Everything with him is pure luck. Do you know that he signed up for the Vietnam war and they called it off before he even got a uniform?"

"That *is* lucky," Eileen agreed as she turned his words over in her mind.

"You're telling me."

"Now that you've mentioned your brother…" Eileen cleared her throat, trying to frame her words carefully. "…I had the chance to talk to the young man in the scrubs. He's Grenadian and he's studying at the medical school here."

Holden raised an eyebrow. "So what's his relationship to them ?"

"He's the victim's cousin and he said something interesting when we were chatting."

"Oh." Holden's interest piqued.

"He said she was heading to a job interview."

Holden smacked the steering wheel. "We're definitely on the right path."

"As a matter of speaking," she said slowly before she cleared her throat. "He went to a study group in the north, and when she got off the bus, a black car was waiting for her. He couldn't see the driver, but he said the car was fancy."

"What did he mean by 'fancy'?"

Eileen looked Holden in the eye. "He pointed to Paul's car."

Chapter 20
The Reckoning

Maybe telling him wasn't the best idea, Eileen reflected the next day. She should have known that Holden wouldn't race to the nearest police station and have his brother clapped in irons. But on the other hand, his brooding anger didn't seem like a natural progression either.

He'd left the car at her house and taken a taxi home, choosing to wait outside in the verandah as he stewed silently in the humid night air. By the time Eileen got to work the next morning, Holden had been there long enough to drink two entire pots of Earl Grey, evidenced by the mound of used tea bags in the bin. His tone was clipped as he dictated two letters and he left work long before lunchtime. She bit her lip. In the months she'd been there, Holden had seldom left on time, far less early.

She'd always heard that blood was thicker than water but she was an orphan; she had never been forced to test the theory. Almost every story Holden told involved Paul flouting rules with impunity. Holden had said it himself: his brother was accustomed to getting away with murder. What if it was literal this time?

Her feelings for Holden warred with her disgust for Paul and it left her stomach in knots. If she could gather enough evidence to implicate Paul she would ensure that he faced the consequences of his actions, because there was a good chance that he was the culprit. Not only did Paul have medical expertise, but an eye witness had connected Paul's car to his cousin's disappearance. She rifled through the telephone directory after Holden left, but neither of the listings for Paul's home or funeral parlour matched the other numbers on the photocopied classifieds she kept in her handbag. Despite that small snag, she knew that it had to be him.

Eileen was still pondering the situation an hour later at the picnic table under the tree when Clifford sat across from her. Unlike Eileen, Clifford ate outside every day, claiming that Barbadian weather was perfect whether it rained or not. But that afternoon was particularly nice: a light blue sky and fluffy clouds perfect for outdoor lounging.

He straddled the wooden planks with surprising grace, and popped the lid off his homemade pudding and souse. Eileen stared at the little hairs on the flap of the pig's ears and the mound of brown pudding swimming in pickled cucumber juice. She could never stomach that particular Saturday tradition and it showed on her face.

Clifford laughed as he plucked an ear out of the bowl and chewed it. "You don't like souse, little starling?"

"Not really," she said disdainfully as she put away her half-eaten lunch and picked back up her book.

Clifford chuckled and peeked at the cover. "'Little Women'? First time you reading that?"

"No, but sometimes I check it out from the library and re-read it."

Clifford nodded and pulled out a pig foot. "You ever read 1984 by George Orwell?"

Eileen shook her head.

"Well, you're only a year late so you could still read it," he said, winking at her.

She giggled. "What's it about?"

"Dystopian novel 'bout a world under too much government control. Good book."

Eileen nodded, not sure if she should ask what 'dystopian' meant. Clifford side-eyed her, his eyes dancing as he said, "'Dystopian just means gloomy fiction. That's all, little starling."

Eileen smiled. "Are you saying starling or darling?"

"Starling. It's a bird."

"Oh…is that a good thing?"

"Them real smart. Could talk better than parrots, even. Pretty feathers too. I had one."

"Really? I'd like to see them. Do they live in the gullies?"

"Them ain't from 'bout here; you find them in Europe, Asia... those kinds of places."

"How did you get one?"

"Used to live in Europe. You think I was always uncultured swine like this pig?" he asked, flapping a half-eaten pig ear at her. He laughed at the look on her face.

She had to admit that Clifford's laid back style and attitude weren't the only clues that founded her assumptions. He spoke roughly and his lunches usually looked like the dregs of something a cat coughed up.

"Sorry," she said sheepishly. "Did you like it there?"

"In a way. Didn't get to see much of anything 'cause I was always working or studying. I was almost a doctor, just didn't do the last exam."

This time the look of shock on Eileen's face was much harder to hide. She peered at him, searching for the distinguished features that people usually associate with doctors. Instead, she saw the weathered face of a man who wouldn't ask much of life if it didn't ask much of him. The questions piled up inside her head, questions that Clifford knew she would ask.

He nodded, his face smug. "Probably wondering what I'm doing here, helping young Davis dress up duppies and sweeping the yard, nuh?"

"W-well… it's honest work."

"You full of shite, Eileen. Just talk straight." His eyes were serious for a moment before he pressed the cover back on his container and stared at it for a moment before he spoke. "Life in those places as a doctor wasn't for me. I tried too hard to fit in and the drugs didn't help. Lucky for me, I came back home and hit rock bottom. I say lucky because it had to happen so I'd clean myself up and realize I only want to be myself at the end of the day."

Eileen bit her lip. It took real courage to strip oneself down like that. It made her admire Clifford even more.

"This is a step down from doctoring for some, but I still get to deal with anatomy - that's a fancy word for bodies in case you didn't know." He grinned at her. "Holden Senior hired me and I've been here ever since. I get the weekends to deal with my little farm and I like it here with young Davis."

"So you've known the family for a long time," Eileen said carefully.

"Well… as long as anybody could." Clifford watched Eileen with interest. "Why do you ask?"

"The brothers are just so different, you know?" She shrugged, not entirely sure how to explain what she wanted to say. “But I guess even though they don't get along that they still love each other.”

“Ah.” He stared back at her with knowing eyes. “Sometimes love is more about duty than affection. Even though young Davis resents his brother, that doesn’t mean he won’t do the right thing. No matter what the right thing might be.”

Eileen scratched her head. She could only hope Clifford was right.

Chapter 21
Complications

Holden looked up at the building and flexed his fingers against the chill of the night air. The taxi had left him in the gravel courtyard that surrounded Eileen's apartment building and now Holden stared at it with his heart in his throat. Five minutes had passed since he'd arrived, and he'd considered leaving more than once. He had seen how headstrong Eileen had become about finding the Cane Slasher. In others, her focus would be considered obsessive; in Eileen, it was just one example of how determined she was about everything she did. But her theory about Paul had forced Holden into an untenable position. He knew that this might be his only chance to fix things before Eileen went off on a tangent and did something that couldn't be undone.

Holden took his time going up the stairs, his mind whirling as he walked to the threshold. He rapped on the door twice. Shuffling footsteps approached before he saw her eyes glare at him from between two wooden louvres.

"Good evening," she said. The chill in her voice stabbed at the pit of his stomach like an icepick. In the space of twenty-four hours, he had gone from feeling the warmth of her body against his to being greeted like an encyclopedia salesman with bad breath.

"I tried calling, but you didn't answer the phone. I hoped I could come inside and talk for a minute."

Eileen raised an eyebrow as she sighed and unlocked the door before stepping back and gesturing him into the apartment. That was when he first noticed the marks on her hands.

From afar, they looked like bruises on her caramel skin, extending from her right wrist almost up to her elbow. But when Holden stepped into the apartment's light, he realized they were paint blotches; a mixture of blues, purples, greens and blacks that had coalesced to form angry blemishes on her hands and forearms. He was about to ask what they were when he caught sight of the living room.

"I didn't know you were such a good painter," he said in surprise.

But in the back of his mind, the cogs turned and he realized it was the only thing that made sense. The hand-painted sign to advertise the floral arrangements. The cleaning cloths. The tiny brush she carried around to dust things.

Her paintings leaned against the walls, like foot soldiers guarding the throne room of a beloved queen. Every canvas was complex and layered, wrought out of something so deep that Holden wasn't sure where the art ended and Eileen began.

The portraits featured some of the island's iconic settings like Broad Street and the Garrison, but it was the people that stood out. There were solitary young women on lonely beaches or in open fields. One square canvas focused on the rear view of a woman walking naked down a busy city street. No one stared at her, and she seemed oblivious to everyone else as she walked blithely out of a luxury store, her arms weighed down with shopping bags. Despite not seeing her face, there was a lightness in the woman's step, as though being happy with herself was the only thing in the world that mattered.

Yet, the one that captivated Holden was the scene at the Garrison Savannah that hung above the chair, the only decoration on the otherwise bare walls. In the background, the colours of the centuries-old military post and its race track were more subdued than in real life, the hues muted and demure. A woman walked on the race track's loose golden sand carrying something swaddled in bright blue and yellow folds. He pointed at the painting. "This one is stunning."

Eileen stepped in front of it so that her head and shoulders covered part of the canvas and said, “Yeah…I paint sometimes.” She put her hands on her hips and met his eyes. “But that’s not why you came here.”

“Err…yes.” Holden rubbed his hand across his forehead, suddenly remembering why he had dared to enter the lion’s den. “I’m not going to lie. I was caught off guard by what the Grenadian student said. As much as Paul and I don’t get along, it’s another thing to believe that he's a serial killer.”

She stared at him blankly, her eyes clearly telling him that she was so far unimpressed with his speech.

“You think I want to cover up for Paul, but that’s not the case." Holden squeezed the nape of his neck and started to pace. "Look, you have to understand…I’m in a ticklish position and I got angry because I felt like this was just another bunch of crap Paul created that I have to clean up.”

“Meaning what? That you want me to keep my mouth shut?”

“No. When I left today, I went to talk to Paul.”

“You did what?” Eileen’s mouth hung open and her hands balled into fists at her sides as she glared at him.

Holden folded his arms across his chest and looked her in the eye. As angry as she was, he also knew that he had done the right thing. "Just wait a minute. I didn't tell him what you said. I asked him some questions, and I truly believe that Paul has nothing to do with these killings."

"Oh, so I'm supposed to believe that? Should I just keep locking my door and hope that the Slasher picks another young woman to kill instead of me? That's how you want me to protect myself?"

"Please lower your voice." Holden let out a breath. "I know Paul didn't do it because he suffers from haemophobia. He gets sick or faints whenever he sees blood. Why do you think Clifford and I always say something is a 'bloody' shame when we talk about Paul? It's because we're making fun of the fact that Paul hired a mortician. That's why Paul only drives the hearse and that stupid carriage." Holden pressed his lips together. "It's also why my father put so much pressure on me to look after everything after he died."

Eileen squinted at Holden, her comprehension at odds with disbelief. "Is that why Paul was at mortician school for so long?"

"Yes…at first my father thought Paul was just playing the fool. But when Paul kept failing and getting sick, my father finally gave up and told him to come back home." Holden rubbed his head with both hands. "All of those girls were cut; if they had died in another way, then I'd be more inclined to consider Paul as a suspect."

"So why did you question Paul if you didn't believe it was him?"

“I wanted to know if he was loaning his car to anyone. He said he hadn’t. Not even his wife drives it.”

Eileen shifted from one foot to the other. “As much as I want to 'drop a dime on someone' as they say on TV, I guess we’ll have to keep looking.”

Holden was relieved that Eileen didn’t think he was trying to cover up for his brother. For too long, he had paid for Paul. He didn’t want to spend the rest of his life regretting that doing so had caused him to lose her.

“Is there anything else?” Eileen’s raised eyebrows were clear in their meaning: she’d listened, but she wouldn’t simply swallow his explanation. Holden stood there for a moment, suddenly aware that as much as he wanted to stay, he couldn't do so without a plausible excuse. He couldn't blame Eileen for wanting to mull over what he had said; he would have to give her time. “Well…the taxi left. Do you mind if I use your phone to call another?”

While he waited for his transportation to arrive, Eileen offered him a glass of juice. And as he sipped, Holden looked at the paintings. His eyes hopped from one to the other, unable to choose a favourite. Finally, he asked the obvious question, even though he knew he would kick himself if it sparked action on her part.

“Why aren’t you a full-time artist? Your work is very good.”

“I don’t think so,” she replied as she glanced critically at the canvas closest to her. “This one needs something…a detail that would make it sparkle.”

“I’m not very artsy,” he admitted. “But they make me feel something deep in here,” he said, touching his chest.

She blushed.

“I’m not against nudity. It’s uh…very pleasing,” Holden gestured vaguely at the painting of the woman on Broad Street. "But why are so many of the women naked?”

Eileen smiled and cocked her head to the side as she studied her art. “I think they’re me. Or at least the me I want to be.”

Holden averted his eyes. It wouldn’t do to stare at a painting depicting a nude employee, even if they had shared a kiss. He wondered if it would be any less immoral to buy a painting and keep it at home. Surely no one could judge him then.

“What do you mean?”

“She’s herself…not a slave to fashion or society’s expectations. Who knows? Maybe I'm so idealistic that I have to paint a world that gives me the freedom this one won't."

Holden grinned at her cocky retort. An idealist forced to live without perfection was a difficult space to occupy without some sort of release. “It certainly explains how you’ve managed to carve out job satisfaction at a funeral home.”

She threw back her head and laughed.

“It’s true. The makeup, the flowers…you’ve certainly got an eye for these things.”

“Why, thank you.” Her smile was enough to warm his heart.

“So why didn’t you ever tell me that you painted?”

She lifted a shoulder half-heartedly. “I don’t know. I wasn’t sure if they were good. Plus, I never planned for the world to see them.”

“Why not?”

She sighed. "Some people have diaries, but when my mind is in turmoil, I pick up my brushes." She looked at him from uplifted eyes, "Would you want someone to read your diary? To weaponize your words against you?"

Holden swallowed, suddenly feeling like he was taking up too much space, inhaling too much sanctified air. "No…I'm sorry. Your work is private. I didn't mean to intrude."

She wiped her hands on a cloth as she turned away. "It's alright. Recently, I've come to grips with the idea of other people seeing them if I ever plan to sell any of my work. I imagine that they'll ask about the symbolism of the pieces and I'll have to get comfortable with such questions."

Holden scrutinized the large canvas as he turned over Eileen's words in his mind. He drew closer to the painting, inspecting the woman at the centre of it. Whatever was in her hands looked like it was wrapped in the blue and gold panels of the national flag. No matter what this painting was about, it was sure to be intriguing. He pointed at it. "May I ask about the symbolism?"

She smiled. "In time."

A horn beeped outside and she pulled back the curtain. "It's your taxi."

As usual, when it came to Eileen, time was playing yet another cruel trick on Holden. "Thanks for the juice and for giving me a chance to explain."

She nodded and extended a hand to him. Grateful, he clasped it in return and kissed her cheek before he walked out the door and closed it behind him. His heart skittered as he thought about her on the other side of the door alone without him, possibly going to shower and wash the paint off her skin.

The thought made him jog down the steps so he wouldn't be tempted to pay the taxi driver for his trouble and go back up the stairs to wile away the night with Eileen.

Holden glanced up at the apartment as he drove away, his mind roving over their discussion. Clifford talked ad nauseam about anything and everything, while Eileen seemed content to only disclose information when necessary. It might have been related to her being an orphan, but Holden sensed there was more to it.

Chapter 22
Whine and dine

Holden had made a good case for eliminating his brother as the perpetrator, but without a suspect, all Eileen had were a handful of mystifying clues: four victims, the sighting of a fancy black car, and newspaper ads.

So Eileen did the only thing she could: she whined to Holden.

"You gave Derricks the ads ages ago," Eileen groused the next morning. "Why haven't the police arrested someone?"

Holden sighed. "You can't just arrest people, Eileen. All they know is that someone is running ads for different jobs. It could be an employment agency."

She squinted at him. "With women going missing every time they run an ad and a drunk man answering the corresponding phone number at midnight?"

He raised an eyebrow. "I run ads too. I wouldn't want to be thrown in jail just because of it." He tapped his pen on the edge of the ledger and took his time framing his statement. "Look, this isn't easy for the country, the families or the authorities. The police have to investigate to make their case. Justice isn't linear."

"It shouldn't be crooked either," came Eileen's bitter retort.

"I'll tell you what." Holden dug into his pocket for a ten-dollar note. "How about you go to the bakery and get some pastries for everyone? I'll talk to Derricks by the time you get back."

By the time she returned with six soft turnovers, Holden was sitting at the lunchroom table with a cup of tea and his mouth pressed in a firm line. He muttered thanks when she placed the warm coconut pastry in front of him and looked down at the desk as he spoke. "Derricks said everything we gave him is circumstantial. The ad you got from home that Anna may have circled might carry a little more weight, but the one in the cane field is iffy."

"'Iffy'?" she repeated. "And what do you mean by a little more weight?"

"How can they be sure it was Anna who wrote the note and not someone else?"

Eileen was exasperated. "Anna lived alone! Who else could have written it?"

Holden sipped too quickly and recoiled as the tea burned his tongue. He was flustered and it showed on his face. "I get that. You get that. But it's not always so simple." He rubbed his singed lips. "You've got to realize that this crappy economy isn't only affecting us. The police had budget cuts too; it's impacted the manpower he can commit to following up on leads. Officers are already working overtime to patrol neighbourhoods as it is."

Eileen frowned. She had to admit that the situation was tough all around.

"Don't worry; he said he would look into it a bit further this afternoon."

But that afternoon was not to be. At 2:15 p.m. the wail of sirens issued from three different directions, growing louder and louder as they descended on the junction in front of Davis and Sons. Eileen ran to the plate glass door with a daisy wreath in her hand and watched as the traffic parted like the Red Sea as cars mounted sidewalks and a vendor blocked the funeral home's door with his boxed cart. The sirens reached a deafening din as motorcycle outriders, an ambulance, and the police commissioner's car met at the crossroads, converged into a convoy and raced down the street.

Eileen turned in alarm to Clifford who quirked an eyebrow at her and said, "Can't be nothing good." He twisted his mouth as though he'd sucked something sour and went back to reading the cricket scores. As the sirens faded, Eileen picked up the spray bottle and returned to the viewing room, her mind uneasy.

An hour later, she would ponder the inherent benefits and disadvantages of working at a funeral home. She had almost finished setting up the viewing room when the phone rang; Holden took the call. His face was solemn when he beckoned to her. Her heart plummeted. Had they been too late to stop the killer again?

"John just died."

"Who's John?"

He turned to Clifford and said, "Pick up Junior. We have to get to Illaro Court right now."

The next few days were unlike anything Eileen had ever seen. Burying a prime minister was like burying a regular person, except it wasn't. You met with the dean of the cathedral where other prime ministers and governor generals were buried, instead of the pastor of a rickety little church sandwiched between a rum shop and a mechanic's garage deep in the country. Flowers came from Queen Elizabeth II and prime ministers. The processional included the armed forces, government ministries and the deceased's mother whom Eileen had to refer to as 'Lady' since her husband had been knighted.

The whirlwind was a distraction during the day. Only at night when shadows came alive and the wind whistled through the leaves of the tamarind tree, rattling the fruit in their smooth brown shells, did the thoughts of the four dead women play on Eileen's mind. Only then would fear come rushing back as she raced up the apartment stairs and slammed the door behind her, her mind on high alert as she went quickly through the rooms, ensuring she was truly alone. In the end, Eileen took to leaving the lights on all day so she wouldn't have to enter a dark apartment. She vowed to eat less to accommodate the increase in electricity she knew would follow.

The following week, when the prime minister was safely interred, she went to Holden again, asking about the status of the commissioner's investigation into the serial murderers. "Derricks was busy with the prime minister's burial. He's a fellow who lives for that kind of pomp and pageantry. But, he said he would get to it today."

It never happened. Around 2:15 p.m. two prisoners jumped out of a van after their court date and escaped. The police commissioner declared the killers to be armed and dangerous and launched an islandwide manhunt. Later, Clifford looked at Holden and Eileen as the three of them gathered around the radio listening to the evening news, cocked his head to the side and said, "I'm seeing a pattern. Makes me wonder what's gonna happen next week at 2:15."

* * *

DONNA GREEN'S BODY WAS DELIVERED a few days later and it was all Holden could do not to blow out an exasperated breath as he surveyed Dr Thorpe's handiwork. Donna's hair was uncombed, her nails were dirty and there was dried blood on her fingertips. Holden comforted himself that Donna would be one of the last victims to cross Thorpe's table, which meant he'd soon be able to stop covering the good doctor's tracks. Clipboard in hand, Holden started making notes.

Eileen peered over his shoulder at the clipboard as she placed the tools they'd need on a tray. "Is it just me or are you taking a lot of notes these days?"

"Keeps the mind sharp," he replied, hoping that a vague answer would suffice. "Are you free this weekend? I was hoping to take you out for that date we had discussed."

She blushed. "I'd love to." But changing the subject wasn't enough to distract her. "Why do you need to keep your mind sharp?"

Holden sighed. "Well," he began in a low voice. "Since you think the police are a little slow, I thought we could keep our own notes. You never know; they may come in handy."

"Hmm, you're right." She perked up and then inspected the woman's grimy hand, her mouth puckering in disgust. "I guess it's a good thing that Dr Thorpe hasn't done a good job with the tidying up."

"Indeed," mumbled Holden.

"It's definitely the same L-shaped cut, isn't it?" Eileen said, jutting her chin at the victim as she squirted soap into her hand.

"Yes," Holden frowned as he looked at the young woman's neck. "What's odd is that a straight cut would do the same job." He tapped his scalpel on the metal tray, the sound echoing like tiny cymbals in the cold room.

He reached for a magnifying glass and peered closely at the girl's fingers. "There's pollen in the blood spatter on her hands."

"What are you thinking?" Eileen asked.

Holden chewed his lower lip and stared at the wound as though he hoped the truth would crawl out of it. Finding pollen on these women was more jarring than Holden was willing to verbalize. Something in the back of his mind told him that it was more significant than they had initially realized. "She's the second victim that we found pollen on."

"But where would pollen come from?" Eileen mused. "Sugar cane doesn't have pollen, does it?"

"It does actually, so the odds are it could come from the cane fields," Holden said as he straightened up.

Eileen frowned. Once again, they may have come up against a dead end.

Chapter 23
The Grand Plan

Eileen's anxiety rose as the week went on. With dangerous prisoners and a serial killer on the loose, she had switched from tea to coffee to help her stay awake and she cussed every day because of it. Bitter and acrid, the coffee tasted like burnt toast and she took to sweetening it with so much sugar that it tasted like burnt toast with marmalade. She was loath to have more conversations with Holden about falling asleep at work. She didn't want him to think that she was taking liberties with the situation just because they were dating.

It was Friday morning and Eileen was looking forward to her outing with Holden that weekend. Her feet were pulled up to her chest in a chair just outside her front door, as she absentmindedly flipped through the paper while she ate breakfast. Out of habit, she turned to the classified section and scoured the small blocky ads. She ran her finger up and down the columns, ignoring the wet ring that bloomed from the glass of juice she used as a paperweight. Finally, squeezed into the corner of page thirty-four was an ad seeking a cleaner with instructions to call a familiar phone number in the late afternoon. Her chest felt like it was on fire the way her heart started to beat. She ran inside the apartment, snatched up the receiver and spun the dial. Holden answered the phone on the second ring. "I just saw it," he said when he realized it was Eileen.

"We should call Derricks," she said, excitedly.

"I already tried calling him," Holden told her. "He wasn't home and his secretary said that he won't be reachable for the next two days."

"Two days!" Eileen exclaimed.

"I suspect Derricks is on some sort of sting operation to track down the escapees. He's gone from Rock Hall to Bush Hall and can't find the prisoners," Holden said.

"But we can just call the police. We don't need the commissioner."

"I'm afraid we do. How else will we justify calling to report an ad in the paper?"

She smacked her forehead. "I keep forgetting that you and I are the only ones who know what's going on."

"I'm sure finding this killer is important too, but the new prime minister has made finding those prisoners a top priority. I guess we'll have to wait to see how we can proceed."

"I'll reply to the ad."

"What?!"

"I'll call and arrange to meet the Slasher. You can follow me and we'll catch him in the act."

"Eileen, it makes no sense. Do you know how dangerous that is?"

"It's obvious that he's not afraid of the police, which is why he hasn't stopped. Do you think I like making up these girls? Painting foundation over stitches on their necks? What's stopping it from being me or somebody else?"

The tension on his end of the telephone was palpable. He always got quiet when he was uncomfortable, letting his brain go into overdrive as he calculated every angle.

"Holden..."

On the other end of the line, he hesitated. "Yes?"

"I know you won't let anything happen to me. But we have to do something."

He sighed. "Okay. You can call the number, but everything else we'll do my way."

* * *

By the time she pulled into the car park at work, Eileen was regretting her decision to ask Holden to play Tonto to her Lone Ranger. When she pushed open the door to the building, Holden was sitting at his desk, his brow furrowed as he watched her walk in.

"I tried reaching Derricks again," he said without preamble. His hunched shoulders told her that the commissioner was still out of office.

Eileen sighed. "It won't be that bad. I'll just go and see who turns up for the meeting. Then we'll leave and call the police. You'll be nearby so everything will be fine."

His eyes were pained as he stood and asked, "Do you really want to do this?"

"Yes."

"Alright," Holden pinched the bridge of his nose and said, "Then let's move up our date to tonight."

"Why?"

He scratched his chin, his reluctance clear in the way he said, "So that we can leave tomorrow open for us to see who turns up for the meeting. The ad says to call after 5 p.m.," Holden reminded her. "As soon as we do that, we'll lock up and go out."

A smile touched Eileen's lips. "That sounds fantastic."

He leaned over and kissed her then, a soft and sweet press of his lips against hers, heavy with promise for the night ahead.

* * *

NEVER BEFORE HAD ONE DAY DRAGGED ON as long as that day did. Every time the parliament building's clock tower gonged, Holden's heart accelerated to the point where he feared it would disconnect from its arteries and fall out of his chest. He'd been in high-pressure situations before, but never to the point where every single thing grated on his nerves and made his temples pound.

Across from Holden's desk, Eileen was working as though she hadn't a care in the world. She took calls, crafted schedules, made wreaths and generally appeared in good spirits. On the surface all was well, but Holden had come to realize that Eileen wasn't one to broadcast her discomfort. He suspected that she had purposely detached herself from the reality, trying her best not to become overwhelmed by the prospect of their plans. Clifford sauntered in the way he normally did, spouting his wacky theories and unfounded superstitions with unfettered glee. Today, he was particularly concerned about the possibility of a vast network of devices linked by wireless frequencies that communicated with each other at lightning speeds. Holden rolled his eyes. As usual, Eileen found Clifford's manic ravings charming, her profound delight evident in the tears that ran down her face. In recent times, Holden had been able to find humour in most of Clifford's inane babbling, but on days when he was stressed, his enthusiasm waned. And today, Holden's enthusiasm was at an all-time low.

When the clock finally struck five, Holden's mouth grew dry and his palms grew clammy, almost as though his saliva had gone down the wrong tube and ended up in his hands. Eileen cast him a quizzical look, but he said nothing as he picked up the phone and dialled the number. When it rang, Holden nodded at her, signalling that she could pick up her phone. He placed his hand over the receiver, worried that the killer would hear his anxious breathing. As the line kept ringing, it dawned on Holden that Eileen might be right. The only reason that the killer had carried on like normal, operating out in the open was that he wasn't fearful. The Slasher assumed his plan was ironclad. Holden gritted his teeth; he'd see to it that the Slasher's incarceration was iron clad too.

"Hello?" said a low voice.

"Hello," replied Eileen cheerfully. "I'm calling about the job."

"Very good, dear. What's your name?"

"It's Lisa."

"You sound very nice, Lisa. Pleasant and young. I'm looking for someone between sixteen and thirty and..." A car horn blared, and a metallic rattling drowned out the man's voice for a moment.

"Yes. I'm within that age range, but I'm so sorry, I barely heard you over the background noise. Do you mind speaking up?"

"Oh yes, my apologies. I was saying you should come to meet me at —"

“Boss, I thought you and Eileen was going out tonight,” said Clifford as he ambled into the office and slammed the door.

Holden and Eileen swung around, their eyes wide as they pressed their fingers to their lips. Had the killer heard Clifford?

Silence hung in the air. Holden held his breath and squeezed the receiver as he strained to hear something, anything, but the killer didn’t say another word before he ended the call.

Chapter 24
The Night that Changed Everything

Their attempt to catch the Slasher had been a disaster. Eileen was furious that they may have squandered their only chance to catch him, but Holden pointed out that a serial killer wouldn't be able to resist the compulsion to murder. All they could do was bide their time until The Slasher struck again. Eileen reflected that it was probably a good thing that they'd moved their dinner to that night; at least the day would end on a high note.

Holden hadn't said where they were going, but Eileen firmly believed that it was safer to be overdressed than underdressed. She chose a snug gold dress with a scooped back and flounced sleeves that her body filled out with reckless abandon and paired it with black heels and gold accessories on her wrists and fingers.

She picked up the phone to find out if he was ready but had only spun the rotary dial once when she heard a knock on the door. Peering through the wooden window, she was surprised to see Holden standing in the verandah clad in a smart shirt, a dinner jacket and formal slacks.

"I was just calling you," she laughed in surprise as she opened the door. "Did Clifford bring you?"

Holden grinned like a schoolboy with a secret. "I drove."

Eileen tried to contain her confusion, but couldn't. "The hearse?"

Holden held back a smile as he cocked an eyebrow. "I'm not a savage, Eileen. There's no way I could take a beautiful lady out for a night on the town and ask her to pick me up." He held up a narrow key on a silver ring and shook it until it tinkled like a cat's bell in the night air.

"You got a car?!" Eileen squealed as she stepped onto the verandah to look down. There, parked next to hers, was a sleek Hyundai Stellar Prima.

"I ordered it a few days ago and they delivered it this evening. Things have picked up quite a bit at the mortuary, thanks to you. I figured the least I can do is treat you like a queen."

His eyes twinkled as he held out his arm. "Are you ready to go?"

Eileen felt like she was floating on a cloud as Holden escorted her downstairs. Eileen sank into the buttery soft seat and savoured the feeling that coursed through her as Holden's eyes raked across her bare legs before he bit his lip and started the car.

They had reservations at a posh restaurant at the most exclusive hotel on the island. They ordered a meal of delicious crab cakes, sinfully creamy pasta and a fantastic bottle of white wine. Romantic piano music drifted across the dance floor as soft candlelight flickered at the tables around them. For a long while after they'd eaten, they looked into each other's eyes and held hands, thoughts of their harrowing day forgotten as they surrendered to the rhythm of the night.

"I'm not a ballet dancer like you, but if you'd like to dance, I'd be more than happy to take you for a whirl."

Goosebumps rose on her skin as he rested his hand on the small of her bare back and led her onto the dance floor.

She leaned her head against his chest as they slow danced, wishing she could melt into him right then and there.

"You're quite good...as I knew you would be."

Eileen grinned. "One of my many hidden talents."

He looked into her eyes with longing. "I've no doubt. How long did you study ballet?"

"About five years."

"Why did you stop?"

She shrugged. "I bounced from one hobby to another for years until I started painting. My life felt complete then, like I could finally express myself."

"Do you express all of yourself or just the parts you don't want anyone else to see?"

"What do you mean?"

He didn't break eye contact as he said, "I mean that I saw the way you stepped in front of that painting. There's a reason you didn't want me to see it. You're hiding something."

Her mouth grew dry and her feet felt leaden as she stumbled on his shoes. "It's not that simple."

"It's not that hard either." His face was pensive as he asked, "Will you ever tell me what you're keeping from me?"

With guarded eyes, she glanced up at him. "Yes. But, do I have to tell you right this instant?"

He quieted, his dark gaze penetrating as he responded. "Not now, but soon. I want you to be able to say every and anything that comes to your mind. It's been months and I don't even know your last name."

She raised an eyebrow. "This island is small and you've proven that you can search out any information you want. Why haven't you done that with me?"

"Because I want the truth to come from these lips," he said, kissing them lightly. "Because I want to have no secrets and only healthy boundaries with you. I'm not looking for someone to warm my bed. I'm looking for a life partner, a woman who can uplift me, a true better half. A woman that I can protect, even if she is a badass."

She wasn't quick to be impressed with words; they took little effort and weren't always followed by concrete actions. But his words were pure and burrowed deep. She was comfortable around him and he was the only person who didn't find her ideas too outrageous, who didn't say her painting was a waste of time and money.

Holden was encouraging and gave her free reign to try things. He'd helped to empower her, perhaps without realizing it. She'd pushed herself to limits she'd never known she had. Handling large sums of money, developing an eye for detail and facing her fears about death had all allowed her to grow by leaps and bounds in just a few months. Before, she'd hidden behind a brash attitude, overcompensating for what she lacked. Now, the idea of failure was almost laughable.

The two of them were so different that for a while she had wondered what had attracted her to him. Finally, she knew: their love for art, personal development and a good joke, even if sometimes Holden tried to pretend he wasn't amused. But above all else, their respect for each other and the truth was the lynchpin of their relationship. Eileen may have been a bit more colourful with her expressions, but Holden seldom sugar-coated anything either, no matter how discomfiting. The world was full of people who loved the safety net of a lie, as though they could weave a new reality with nothing more than saliva and artful imagination.

Should she tell him? He already knew about the night she'd spent with Paul. Maybe telling him everything else wouldn't be the worst thing she had ever done.

"We're done joking around," Holden said softly. "And we're done pretending that everything can stay the same. Because I don't want it to." He exhaled. "And I hope you don't either."

For a second she felt giddy and lightheaded as though she were in an airless bubble. Holden seemed so close, his eyes so endless and beautiful that she'd get lost in them, his words so deep and meaningful that she'd drown in them. Her heart beat so fast that her hand fluttered to her chest, the cold metal ring on her finger absorbing the warmth that flooded her body.

"I've never felt the way you've made me feel." She looked down at her feet, her mind trying to steady itself under the assault of her feelings for him.

"I'll tell you the truth, but I've stayed quiet for so long that I need time to be as open with you as I can. But, I promise that I won't evade your questions anymore."

He nodded, seemingly satisfied with her response.

Slowly, her heart started to beat again. "So, what's your first question?"

"I have only one." He leaned in and brought his mouth in line with her ear. "Will you share my bed tonight?"

Chapter 25
The Blissful Divine

The Stellar Prima sped across the highway, and less than twenty minutes later, Holden's car screeched to a stop in front of his house. Eileen made her way up the stairs backwards, kissing him deeply and tugging his shirt free of his pants as they went. Cool night air washed over their bodies as he pressed her against the door, his hands exploring her hips and exposed back as she hooked her fingers in his belt loops and pulled him to her. Dimly, she registered the lock clicking behind her as he slipped the key into the cylinder. The door gave way behind her and a square of moonlight fell across the living room's polished mahogany floor for a moment before he lifted her into his arms and kicked the door closed, dousing the room in darkness once again.

Her shoes clattered noisily as they flew across the room. She wrapped her legs around his waist and he cupped her body to his, their lips meeting in a champagne-tinged kiss as he carried her to the bedroom. A moan escaped her throat when his tongue brushed hers, a sensual caress that sent a tingle down her spine like a flame blazing across a forest floor. He tugged the sleeves of her dress to free her torso with his other hand. Eileen moved against him, her nipples tightening as his silk shirt glanced across her bare skin.

She grew light-headed when he reached the bed and laid her on the cool sheets. Moonlight glowed between the open slats of the louvred doors that led to the patio, gilding their bodies with silver light. She knew he was handsome, desirable — but when he shed his clothes, she realized just how much his sombre suits hid his perfect body. His shoulders were broad, his chest was chiselled and his dark skin glowed like polished river stones at midnight.

She squeezed her eyes shut as he pulled the dress down past her hips and kissed her again. She felt his hands travel slowly back up her body, touching her legs, hips and everything in between.

Their bodies grew damp as the heat between them rose. Her eyes fluttered open and met his as his hands caressed each breast. He snaked his tongue over her nipples, making them harden as she watched, her body trembling beneath him. The sheets rustled as he leaned back on his heels and positioned himself between her legs. Raw emotion unfurled inside her, ready to welcome this man into her body.

Eileen squeezed her eyes shut and parted her thighs, gripping his shoulders in giddy anticipation. Instead, something warm and moist flicked against her core. Surprised, she flinched, unaccustomed to such a delicious sensation. Holden held her legs in place as her restless hips mutinied. She sank her fingers into his hair, groaning breathlessly as she felt her climax build. She dug her nails into his shoulders, ground her hips against him and threw her head back as she felt it approaching. With a heavy gasp, she trembled and fell back against the mattress, wholly spent as Holden shifted and placed his weight over her. She had never known such intense pleasure, one that grew threefold when he pressed himself into her and sighed.

He was slow and deliberate at first, firm and full, as he looked into her eyes and kissed her neck softly. He panted, uttering her name, his tone that of a man begging to be set free from the bonds of lust that had built inside him.

His back was slick with sweat as he moved against her, his movements becoming insistent as his mouth found hers again, their lips and tongues moving in tandem as they yielded to each other. His thrusts gained strength, and his breathing became shallow as he tangled his fingers in her hair. She wrapped her arms around his neck, pulling him closer to her. With a guttural groan and a flex of his hips, he sank deep inside her. She gripped his back, felt the tremors that left his body and filled hers, leaving both of them sated and complete.

* * *

HOLDEN FOLDED HIS ARMS BEHIND HIS HEAD and exhaled. Moonlight bounced off the soft white walls and dusted the room with a faint glow, casting long strips of light on Eileen's face and making her look all the more beautiful as she slept with the sheets pooled around her naked hips. His heart swelled when he looked at her. Her curly hair was fluffed up against the pillow, her lips were slightly parted. He watched the gentle rise and fall of her breathing, and in that moment, he was at peace.

But, deep in his stomach, Holden knew his anxiety would build again. Their plan to find the Slasher had failed, and he wasn't sure if they'd have a chance like that again. They had made a critical mistake; he now knew that someone was on to him and he had heard Eileen's name. Holden rubbed his hands against his face. As much as he had initially disapproved of the plan, he could admit that discovering the man's identity would have been more worthwhile than lying in bed with a vexed spirit.

Holden had tried to brush away his new car under the guise of romance, but the truth was that he had bought it to keep Eileen safe. He didn't want her leaving home to collect him at ungodly hours anymore and neither did he feel comfortable with her living alone if it came down to it. It wouldn't affect her gas allowance, but he'd rather overcome his discomfort with driving than risk her safety. It had been excruciating the night when he'd driven her car from the cane field, holding his breath at every turn, trying to keep the flashbacks at bay. But last night had been easier. Over time, he hoped the fear would wane completely.

Until then, he would stay vigilant, biding his time until the killer exposed himself again so that Holden could finally put his anxiety to rest.

Eileen shifted in her sleep, nestling herself in the crook of his arm and pressing her warm behind against Holden's groin. Arousal flared inside him, but it could wait. He put his arm around her, his palm resting on her lower stomach. For now, his greatest desire was to go back to sleep, grateful that she was safe in his arms.

Chapter 26
The Tilt of the Scales

Eileen wasn't usually prone to fits of whimsy, but for a few moments, as the sunlight gilded their bodies like a golden statue of immortal lovers, she allowed herself to imagine a future with Holden. An honest future, not characterized by half-truths and false ideals of who they were. She bit her lip and stilled when Holden stirred, pressing his chest against her back. The gentle thudding of his heart against her shoulder blade resonated as a steady reassurance of the life they could have together.

She knew what it was to have her reality thrown into question, the truth of who she thought she was broken open and declared null. She had shed the lies of her old life, created a new identity from the vestiges that remained and given herself a new name: Eileen.

Now, as she lay next to Holden, she wondered how he would react if she told him the truth. Would he accept that she had hidden who she was for a chance at a better future? Her night on the street might pale in comparison if Holden knew what happened before that, if he found out her true identity.

Holden sighed in his sleep, cradling Eileen to his chest before he kissed her and mumbled, "Good morning." A nervous smile crossed her lips; she didn't want to give him up. Eileen gritted her teeth, the same way she had on the night they met. Losing Holden was not an option. She would tell him who she really was, maybe after work over a quiet home-cooked meal.

But little did she know that the night she'd planned would never come.

* * *

AN HOUR LATER, after Holden had taken Eileen home to collect her vehicle and get ready for work, they drove both cars to Buckworth Street. To her surprise, the parking lot behind the funeral home was almost full. Paul's corpse van was parked between his Camaro and a long green sedan. Directly across from Paul, Dorothy Greaves' brows were knit together in confusion as she got out of her car with her handbag dangling on her wrist. Clifford was also there, standing next to the white van, his jaw squared as though ready for battle.

Eileen parked and looked across at Holden. If his steering wheel was alive, it would have hollered for blue murder as his brutal grip left ten indentations pressed into its slim form. She got out of her car, wondering what fresh hell Paul had concocted so bright and early on that otherwise perfect morning.

"What do you want now?" Holden growled at his brother.

Paul merely nodded to the caucasian man next to him who stepped forward and said, "Mr Holden Davis, I'm representing your brother in the matter of the equitable distribution of property entrusted to Davis and Sons for preservative preparations."

Clifford squinted. "Christ, I hope you ain't paying him by the syllable."

Holden squeezed his bottom lip with his teeth. "That's what this shite is about? Some power ploy to get half of the bodies that your frightened ass can't even embalm?"

Paul bristled and glanced at the lawyer who went on, "Mr Davis, your father's will was explicit: the funeral home is one entity and, as such, there should be greater parity." He reached forward and offered Holden a stack of papers which Holden raised an eyebrow at before Clifford took them on his behalf.

Clifford read for a moment and then said, "We got five bodies inside…explain how you plan to share them *equitably*, as this overpaid thesaurus suggests."

Paul grunted. "Give me three and you keep the rest."

Holden looked fit to burst. "Paul, that's not how you share bodies, especially since you haven't done a single thing to solicit business or pay the bills."

Paul's eyes flicked toward Eileen and a smirk crossed his lips, "My brother, we've shared bodies before and you didn't seem to mind."

Eileen's handbag swung in a wide arc, landing on the left side of Paul's head with a crack that made everyone in the car park wince. Her fists weren't far behind, but Clifford grabbed onto her and whispered, "He deserved it, but be cool; too many witnesses."

The bag's buckle left a long bloody scrape on Paul's cheek that speckled his white shirt with crimson dots. He touched his face gingerly, his eyes looking daggers at her as he rasped, "Let's get the police and come back. I suspect Holden's little whore just made a much better case for me."

Eileen looked down at the blood that dappled her handbag. Somehow it didn't seem like enough. She'd had sex with him willingly, it was true, but she felt like he'd been raping her since then with his leering looks and nasty verbal barbs. Today had been the last straw. Paul's entourage drove away, leaving Eileen, Holden, Clifford and Dorothy standing in the morning sun as traffic eased its way along Buckworth Street.

"Boss, don't worry, we gonna deal with all of this."

"Deal with it how?" he fumed.

Dorothy cleared her throat, a sound like water over gravel, as she delicately injected herself into the conversation. "I hate to trouble you during this difficult time, but I'm a tad short on embalming supplies. Could I beg a boon of you so I could be on my way?"

Holden stomped to the door and threw it open. The others followed like creatures in the slipstream of an angry sea monster.

"Give her what she wants, Clifford," Holden directed as he slammed his attaché case on the desk. Dorothy and Clifford disappeared into the Prep Room and closed the door behind them. Eileen walked up to Holden's desk, unsure of how to manage him in such a mood.

He sank down in his chair and ground the knuckles of his hands against his eyes. "I'm so sick of him."

She sucked her bottom lip into her mouth and looked at him. Gently, she laid a hand on his shoulder. "I'm sure there's a way we can deal with this."

"How?"

She shrugged. "Maybe get your own lawyer. You know, fight fire with fire."

"Right…so pay a lawyer, figure a way out of this lawsuit he's dragged me into, pay all the bills and work like a dog so that no matter what happens, Paul benefits?

Eileen raised an eyebrow at his tone. "That's not what I'm saying. Maybe…" she heaved a breath, "…you could consider splitting the business in two as you mentioned before; give him his half and you keep yours. That's an option."

"So walk away and leave my only living relative?"

Eileen clasped her hands to steady her breathing. She sensed that he was growing irrational. "That's not what I'm saying. But the fact remains that Paul makes life difficult for you…difficult for us to be happy."

"The '*us*' I need to worry about is me and Paul." Holden's voice grated like a knife on ice.

Eileen's chest deflated as though he'd cuffed her. "Then what am I? Just a good way to end the weekend? What kind of relationship can we have with your brother saying I'm a whore while he drags down everything you're working so hard for?"

Holden rubbed his temples as he shook his head. "It's Paul's mortuary too."

She clamped her hand on her hips. "You said yourself that I've worked hard to help you save this business. I've done that because I love you, but also because I care about what happens to this place. Don't make it seem like I'm just here for a pay cheque."

Holden groaned, grabbing tufts of his hair as he shot up from his desk. "Eileen, stop! He's my brother. I can't just ignore that fact."

"Don't tell me about flesh and blood! You spilt yourself inside me last night," Eileen said, her voice rising by three octaves. "You don't think that connects us? Or should make us loyal to each other?"

The prep room's door creaked open. Clifford and Dorothy slid out sideways, trying to make themselves inconspicuous, an impossible task given the office's open-plan layout.

Holden fidgeted, nervous and embarrassed at being caught in an all-out brawl. He pulled out his chair and sat down again, straightening the books and pens on his desk. He didn't make eye contact as he said, "We'll talk about this later."

Eileen snatched her handbag off her desk. "No. Don't talk to me at all. I quit."

Chapter 27
A Change is Going to Come

"Excuse me, young lady. Eileen, is it?" Dorothy Greaves shouted as she hobbled across the car park. Despite Dorothy's sensible shoes, she could barely keep up with Eileen's high-heeled stomp as she called out to her.

Eileen dragged open the car door and tossed her belongings inside, cursing herself for romanticizing her relationship with Holden. She didn't care to hear Dorothy defending her sweet little Holden's love for his degenerate brother.

Dorothy's face was flushed and her gutsy wheezes sounded not unlike wind rushing past an uncovered Coke bottle. The bottles of embalming liquids inside the box clattered against each other as she finally caught up to Eileen and leaned against the car to catch her breath. *No wonder she sounds worse than my car*, Eileen realized with a start. The jaunt across the gravel lot had undone Dorothy, loosening her tightly tucked blouse from her skirt. Beneath the frilly pink top, Eileen saw a close-set row of eyelets and laces that ran straight up Dorothy's side. Her corset was pulled so taut that it was a miracle she could breathe in the first place.

Eileen reached over and took the box from Dorothy, then helped her to stand upright. "Can I help you?" Eileen said a bit more harshly than she intended. She wanted to get away from Buckworth Street, but it would be rude to leave the woman standing there.

"Y-yes," Dorothy rasped. "I wanted to talk to you about that unpleasantness back there…it's just unfortunate."

Eileen clenched her jaw. "It's also a private matter."

Dorothy looked away, focusing instead on the bottles inside the box. "You and I are the same, aren't we? The night of the party, Clifford went home with that skinny little thing, June Haynes, and it's troubled me since." Dorothy hesitated, her voice breaking as she fiddled with one of the bottles.

Shame crawled into Eileen's stomach. She bit her lip, unwilling to verbally classify herself as a rejected woman whose love was at a man's mercy. But dogged determination only had the power to deny the truth, not change it.

Her gritty voice cracked as she turned away. "You know that my brother recently passed — Lloyd. I haven't found any good hires since then, especially none with your talent for makeup and flowers."

Eileen exhaled. "I don't think I want to stay in this business, especially since —"

Dorothy held up her hand, making Eileen's words evaporate in her throat. "I'll double whatever Holden paid and you won't need to do prep or grief visits." She shrugged guiltily. "I shouldn't try to poach Holden's assistant — he's a good boy, and all — but you deserve better."

Dorothy's words struck a chord. For all the good that Holden represented, Eileen was now standing on the other side of his door. She'd grown a lot and gone through a gamut of emotions inside that peach building: fear, courage, pain, friendship, love and finally, distrust and confusion. Who was to say she hadn't outgrown the place?

Eileen straightened her shoulders and nodded. “When do you want me to start?”

* * *

HOLDEN FOUND NO SOLACE in balancing the books like he usually would. It was the day after Eileen left and he found it hard to focus on even the most mundane tasks. A ring of condensation formed around the glass on the pile of receipts, making the ink bleed and leaving a faint blue ring around the glass. Weak sunlight peaked through the faded blinds. His head was face down on the open ledger, his eyes squeezed shut as his mind tried to navigate the fuzzy edges the brandy had lent to his reality. In the background, the clock's incessant ticking was louder than usual; Holden felt sure it was trying to punish him for what he had done. Surprisingly, Clifford had strolled in two hours earlier than usual, toting brandy and a glass and left them on Holden’s desk without saying a word. As Holden poured, he reflected that as kooky as Clifford was, he was infinitely dependable, even if it meant that Holden's liver would pay the price later. Holden downed three shots in quick succession and then planted his head in the middle of the ledger, replaying the last twenty-four hours in his head.

His life had sank back into the pre-Eileen quagmire that he recognized but no longer wanted any part of, his mood vacillating between anger and despair since she'd quit. He cursed himself for making love to his employee and yanked his hair as he tried to find a way out of Paul’s latest snare trap. At first, Holden had been annoyed with Eileen’s lack of patience, although he was honest enough to admit that Paul had a way of pissing on anything that Holden held dear. Yes, it was his lot in life to look after the business, even if it meant tolerating his brother until both of them were cold in the grave, but that shouldn't be Eileen's cross to bear. A murderous impulse stole over Holden as he savoured the thought, but even he knew he didn't have it in him to kill.

By noon, he'd picked up the phone and put it back down four times. He wanted to call but he suspected that Eileen's steel-tipped tongue would eviscerate him no matter what he said. Holden knew he loved her, knew he wanted to give her everything, but all he could give her was lip service and not the good kind.

The bell tinkled as the front door opened and Derricks' hulking figure entered the room. Holden grumbled under his breath. He felt his inner old man coming alive, the version of himself who complained when the mail was late and pouted when his favourite TV show was cancelled. Derricks had gone missing for days on end and had never returned his calls. Now he showed up unannounced and expected Holden to comb through files to cover up the government's negligence. To say that Holden was not in the mood was an understatement.

Derricks spread the files on the table and poured himself a glass of brandy while Holden looked through them; luckily, there were only fifteen.

"How's Lynch faring in the new post?" asked Holden as he opened the first manila folder.

Derricks smacked his lips. "Not bad you know. Another pathologist was seconded to assist him so he'll be fine."

Holden eyed Donna Green's report. “I don’t see any mention of the pollen we found on her, so I’ll add that. It’s the second time I’ve come across pollen on these victims.”

Derricks nodded and sipped his brandy. “Make a note, young Davis, and I’ll investigate.”

Holden’s face sobered when he looked at the label on the next file: Lloyd Greaves. “It’s hard to believe he's gone. He wasn’t the nicest fellow, but it’s taking time for me to accept that he’s dead.”

The commissioner nodded and leaned back in the chair as he cradled his glass in his hands. “How come you’re taking so long to organize his funeral? He should have been buried by now.”

“Me?” Holden was surprised. “Dorothy said she was sending him overseas to be cremated since the island doesn’t have the facilities here to do it.”

Derricks nodded. “Oh yeah, you’re right.”

But Holden didn’t respond. He had reopened Donna Green’s folder and slid it next to Lloyd Greaves’. The handwriting on both was markedly different, even though they were both signed by V. Thorpe.

“Look at these. Which one is Thorpe’s handwriting?”

Derricks squinted at the files. “His penmanship is fairly scratchy. Looks more like this one." He tapped the one on the left.

“So who filled out this other report?”

Derricks rubbed his beard and shook his head slowly. “Young Davis, this is definitely a problem.”

Chapter 28
Happy Home

In theory, being at Happy Home was just like working at Davis and Sons. The commute was nearly the same since both businesses were less than five minutes drive apart. But while Davis and Sons was all business with its casket catalogues and polaroids of wreaths in a leather-bound album, Happy Home oozed cheerful charisma. It was housed in a well-kept grey building with a sign on the outside that didn't lose one of its peeling letters whenever it rained. The homey interior was modern with verdant potted ferns in every corner and flowering plants on almost every surface. Framed photos of the Greaves family lined the walls in the waiting area, most of them featuring the proud founders with their two children. Work finished at four sharp and in the three days Eileen had been away from Davis and Sons, Dorothy had only asked her to do make-up and administrative tasks. Months ago, Eileen would have ached for that job. Now that she had it, she was miserable.

Eileen missed Clifford's irreverence, driving to parts of the island she had never seen, and Holden's droll humour. Three days had passed since she'd left Davis and Sons. In that time, Holden hadn't sent flowers, called or even stopped by her apartment to talk. She knew because she had stayed up late waiting to see if he would visit. It hurt to think that she'd crossed the professional line with him, but it burned her to the core to know that she had almost bared her soul to him, possibly risking her life by exposing who she really was.

For the most part, Dorothy was an okay employer, but her shark-like disposition became apparent on the fourth day. Eileen didn't know if it was the adage of misery liking company that prompted Dorothy's declarations, but if the desired effect was to make Eileen unhappy, it worked.

Eileen was sitting at the reception desk mailing letters when she heard the heavy thud of thick soled shoes growing closer. Dorothy had been out and her echoing footfall announced her return through the back entrance. She placed a box of flowers on the reception desk and said, "I saw the work you did at the other parlour and thought we could start doing arrangements here. We'll need three wreaths for a funeral tomorrow; is this enough?"

Eileen nodded and took the box into the kitchen to fill a spray bottle with water and start creating the garlands. To her surprise, Dorothy followed.

"How do you like it here so far?"

"It's good," Eileen replied with a half-hearted smile.

A thoughtful look crossed Dorothy's face as she separated the baby's breath into small piles. "You miss Holden, they all do."

Dorothy's words short-circuited Eileen's brain; her hands stilled, her heart skipped a beat and her breath caught in her chest as she deliberated the implication of the four-letter word: *they*.

"I know what it is to be spurned, treated with indifference when people overlook you," Dorothy said with disdain as she made nosegays.

The white carnations in Eileen's hand trembled, but Dorothy didn't seem to notice. "You don't find it odd that two confirmed bachelors are content to just drive around collecting dead bodies? Or that they go through so many assistants?" She lifted a beefy shoulder as though even a blind man riding a horse in the middle of the night could see the obvious.

Dorothy picked up the shears and started clipping the stems on the baby's breath. "They make sure they get their money's worth out of the assistants, is all I'm saying. That's why Clifford never committed to any woman, not even his son's mother. As the old people would say 'you don't buy milk when cows are on the pasture.'"

Eileen felt sick but it didn't matter to Dorothy — she went in for the kill.

"Why do you think he didn't choose you over Paul? Because soon there will be another Eileen, another tight young body to amuse him — or him *and* Clifford. I certainly wouldn't put it past them."

Dorothy placed a meaty hand on Eileen's shoulder. "Oh no...I didn't mean to upset you. I just didn't want another innocent to fall prey to their trap. Don't worry, dear. It's better for you to be here with me than there with them." Her eyebrows knit together as she pulled a lacy white handkerchief from her bosom and dabbed Eileen's eyes. It smelled of flowers and sweat. Eileen pulled away and wiped her face with the back of her hands before she sniffed and said shortly, "I hope you don't think I'm rude, but I'd like to finish up here and then head home if you don't mind."

Dorothy clasped her hands and smiled benignly. "You need some time alone, don't you? I'm sorry to be the bearer of bad news, but trust me... soon they'll be a distant memory."

Eileen didn't want to believe what she said, but there was no denying that everything was drenched with possibility. Holden had never denied that the funeral home had a heavy staff turnover and Eileen had never thought to ask why. Was it true that she'd just been another conquest, the latest in a stream of willing assistants to bump groins with her boss? Eileen's hands trembled violently as she tried to arrange the flowers in front of her as Dorothy filled a water glass and headed back to her office. Alone at last, Eileen gave up on trying to appear nonchalant, her legs buckling beneath her as she fell forward onto the table.

Dorothy's heavy footsteps echoed down the long hall, keeping rhythm with Eileen's tears as they dripped onto the table.

* * *

"BOSS, EILEEN'S WORKING FOR DOROTHY."

Holden's head snapped up in surprise. "What? How do you know that?"

Clifford hadn't left the building all day because he'd been busy cleaning, so when Holden realized that Clifford had been hoarding this knowledge, it rankled his spirit in the worst possible way. He finally tried calling Eileen that morning, but the phone only rang and rang, leaving him to assume that she was avoiding his calls. Now he knew that she'd probably been at work.

"Seen her car there two days in a row." Clifford shrugged as he put two bulging garbage bags on the floor. "Only thing that makes sense at this rate."

Holden's nostrils flared. "And you're only telling me this now?"

Clifford propped his feet on Eileen's old desk and skimmed through the newspaper without looking at Holden. "And if I had told you before, what were you gonna do with that information?"

Holden frowned at Clifford. "If I knew Eileen was right around the corner, I wouldn't have sat here for days nursing a headache."

"And?"

"I'm going to talk to her so I can make this right."

Swinging his feet to the floor, Clifford folded the paper and looked at Holden. "Listen here, young Davis. Ain't no time like the present; you gotta squeeze the day by de balls to let it know you in charge."

Holden winced. "As colourful as your analogy is, I'll wait until she's home instead of going to her job right now."

"I hope Eileen comes back. You's fun to laugh at and all, but she really brightens up the joint."

"Indeed," said Holden dryly. He glanced at his watch; it was almost 3 p.m. He stood, tossing the papers his lawyer had delivered earlier into his attaché case and checking his pocket for his car key. "Did you finish the cleaning?"

"Yup."

"Excellent. Lock up for me, please."

"Going home already?"

"I need broken biscuits and something from my back garden for when I visit Eileen tonight, so I'm leaving now."

Clifford squinched his forehead as Holden went through the door. "I ain't know what madness you talking, but I'm on board." He shook his head and picked back up the paper. “I'm tired of being the only sane person in here.”

* * *

EVERYTHING HOLDEN needed to try to bring Eileen back in his life was within a one-kilometre radius: his house, the biscuit factory, a rum shop and a craft store. He spent another hour at the funeral parlour preparing part of his surprise for Eileen and by the time he left to go to her house, he was a little dusty, a little sweaty, but happy that he had done everything in his power to make things right.

The drive to Hampstead Village was nerve-racking, but to his consternation, Eileen wasn't at home. Her car wasn't in the usual spot at the side of the building and only the apartment beneath hers displayed any signs of life. A quick check with the downstairs neighbour confirmed that she hadn't been home all evening. Holden was practical if nothing else, but the irrational part of his brain didn't cooperate and immediately wondered if Eileen was out with a man. He had gone to her house braced for a possible argument, probably an emotional one that would devolve into him cajoling her to see reason. This anti-climactic outcome was too much to bear. His father's voice echoed in his head, propelling Holden as he took the box from the car, walked up the stairs and left it by Eileen's door. *A moment of discomfort or a lifetime of discontent*, he thought to himself as he stared down at the box. It glowed back at him in the dark, an apropos metaphor for the glimmer of hope he held on to. As he drove away, he had to hope it was enough.

Chapter 29
A Deadly Realization

As Eileen packed her things to leave work, she made up her mind that it would be her last day at Happy Home. It was hard enough working in the same industry and having to pass Holden's funeral home every day on her way to work, but listening to Dorothy drop tidbits about Holden's and Clifford's predilections was emotionally taxing. She had searched through the paper earlier and found two job options which she felt positive about. Tentative though she was, neither of the women who answered the phone numbers she called sounded like the Cane Slasher. She broke the news to Dorothy after she had put the wreaths away in the refrigerator and to her chagrin, Dorothy had insisted that they have tea together before Eileen left. Even though she was reluctant, Eileen didn't want to appear rude, especially since Dorothy hadn't paid her yet. After locking up for the day, Dorothy prepared a tray while Eileen sat at the front of the building in the enclosed gallery that overlooked the funeral home's roadside garden. Its exterior put Eileen in mind of a quiet country house, only marred by the modern addition of a payphone next to the hibiscus hedge.

It was much quieter than Buckworth Street and it's noisy stream of traffic, almost idyllic with the exception of the loose hydrant cover in the middle of the road that clattered every time a car drove over it.

Dorothy's sensible shoes thumped across the burnished floors, her chatelaine of keys jingling on her waist as she walked. She set down a tray of scones and two teacups in front of Eileen as she asked conversationally, "You didn't know my brother Lloyd very well, did you?"

"Uh...no," Eileen said as the parliament clock bonged. Her discomfort grew when she heard it. She hoped Dorothy wouldn't keep her too long.

Dorothy adjusted her wig as she sat down. "People often misunderstood Lloyd. They thought him grumpy and anti-social. But Lloyd possessed a far superior intellect to most other people," she said as she dusted a smattering of yellow dust off the sleeve of her black dress.

Probably pollen, thought Eileen. Since she'd been at Happy Home, she often found lots of it on her clothes whenever she brushed against the potted flowers that Dorothy kept throughout the building. Dorothy busied herself turning over the teacups as she chattered on about her brother. But Eileen wasn't paying attention.

She thought it was a trick of the light when Dorothy sat forward to pour the tea; the sleeve of her blouse shifted and Eileen caught a glimpse of waxen scars on her arm, scars that looked identical to the ones Eileen had seen on Lloyd's arm in the photos in the waiting room. The hair on the back of her neck stood up as Dorothy's eyes followed hers and realized Eileen was looking at her forearm.

"If you don't mind, I have to go," Eileen said as she stood up too quickly. Dorothy — Lloyd — stood up slowly, shaking his head.

It was hard to believe Eileen didn't see it before, but the person who walked around the chair and stood in front of her was very clearly a man with a cheap grey wig atop his head.

He took off the big spectacles, exposing the bottomless dark eyes behind them. Eileen's pulse hammered in her throat as she stared at him, trying to understand what she was seeing. "You're Lloyd."

He grabbed her shoulder, spinning her around until her back was pressed against his chest. "I should have known from the day I met you that you'd be a problem. I saw from the jump how fast those eyes of yours moved." He twisted her hand so hard that Eileen felt a small pop in her wrist; she whimpered in pain.

"What did you tell Holden about me?"

"Nothing," she gasped as she tried to straighten her arm. The pain in her wrist travelled up to her elbow and made her arm grow numb.

"Don't tell me lies!"

Eileen's eyes watered and her head started to pound as she struggled to catch her breath. "I didn't, I swear. I only realized it was you just now when I saw the scar."

Lloyd's chest heaved as he pulled the scarf off his neck and secured her wrists behind her back. She screamed at the top of her lungs hoping someone would hear, but Lloyd quickly clamped a hand over her mouth and dragged her toward the prep room.

Eileen knew all too well about the monstrous instruments and chemicals in that room. Was this how it was to end? With him killing her inside that room, washing her blood down the drain? He took a scalpel off the tray and turned to face her.

He lay beside her on the floor and smiled, exposing his teeth as he ran his free hand down her cheek and across her chest. His breath came in sharp bursts as he squeezed her breast, hefting them in his hand as she felt his excitement growing and pressing against her leg. She winced and looked away.

Lloyd licked his lips greedily as he touched the other breast.

She thought of the pollen on the victims and the dried yellow blossoms at the last crime scene and her stomach clenched.

Her mind went to the black Mustang GL at the side of the clean grey building; the sleek black car could easily be mistaken for Paul's. She had never pieced the clues together before, never suspected matronly Dorothy to be guilty. "You killed those girls," Eileen said through gritted teeth.

He waved the scalpel at her like a teacher chiding a student for a wrong answer."It was you that called the other day, wasn't it?"

She bit her lip. "Yes."

"Does Holden know?"

"No," lied Eileen. "I never told him that I figured out that the killer was finding his victims through the classifieds."

The shape of Lloyd's tongue traced a circle on the inside of his cheek as he studied her for a moment.

"That number in the ad," began Eileen slowly. "That's the payphone outside this building, isn't it?"

Lloyd didn't answer, but the tightening of his mouth told Eileen she was right. Suddenly restless, he got up and started to pace the floor, sweat beading his brow as he started muttering to himself.

"You don't know what it's like," he said as he pounded his head with clenched hands. "I never got a woman to do what I wanted unless I gave her money. That was okay at first, until Davis took the government contract from us. Money ran out...so did the women. One even told me that if a man wasn't giving a woman money, he'd better be giving her a job. That's where I got the idea. It's just... Dorothy never cared about a man other than Clifford. She had him and that was enough."

Eileen's mouth went dry. "Is that why you killed your sister?"

Lloyd looked at Eileen like a man begging a woman to understand. "I — I didn't want to, but..."

"She found out, didn't she?"

Lloyd nodded miserably. "Dorothy got suspicious because I kept waiting by the phone booth for calls, so I started using the unlisted number at the house. She answered one of the calls and said I had to be up to no good and she'd call the police." Lloyd's lip trembled. "She had no right to do that. I injected her neck with air and told Thorpe that I'd help him with the forms. Everybody knows Thorpe always takes a short cut if he can."

Eileen watched the way Lloyd paced, the way he shook his head irritably as he talked. Lloyd was not in his right mind and what made it worse was that he seemed completely comfortable with the fact. He'd kill Eileen too, she was sure of it. She wiggled her hands trying to loosen the knots as she said, "You didn't have to kill those girls. They belonged to people, they had families."

"I didn't mean to kill the first one. But it felt good, powerful — sweeter than sex ever made me feel." His voice changed; the lust rose up so powerfully in him that his entire body tensed. Lloyd gripped her shoulder like a lover would as he said pleadingly. "I just wanted to try one more time and see. You know?"

Eileen felt faint as she listened to him. He spoke fondly of murdering women, as though it were a rite of passage that he wished he had discovered sooner.

"Then I'd make love to them. When I was a boy, I'd play with the ones in the chiller before my father embalmed them." Eileen shuddered. "They would do the job but I wanted to try a warm one."

"I realized how perfect it was if I killed them myself. I could do whatever I wanted while they were almost lively." Bile rose in Eileen's throat. He spoke like a man with a proud legacy, a man ahead of his time. His eyes shone and he sometimes sighed as he spoke, reliving the visions that resided rent-free in his mind. "I branded them, you see, made them mine. They'll never be anyone else's."

He knelt on his haunches and looked into her eyes. "But you won't ever understand. You're a pretty girl; you can have anyone you want. And I can't let you leave."

Eileen's mind thought back to the red dots she'd marked on the map. It just occurred to her that they formed a perfect circle around...

"Your house..." Her eyes widened and her stomach churned. "You dumped all of those girls close to home."

Lloyd's shy grin was sickening. "Yes. I wanted them close to me."

She gritted her teeth. "Gonna leave me in a canefield with a big L on my neck too?"

Lloyd smiled as though Eileen had granted him a gift he'd yearned for. He knelt on his haunches, fluffing the skirt between his legs as he rested the scalpel's steel blade against her pulse. He traced the shape he wanted, as though trying to find the perfect orientation. A smile crossed his lips. “I’ve got something special planned for you."

Chapter 30
A Watery Grave

Holden's chest burned as though hot pepper sauce had been poured into an open wound as he drove through Hampstead Village and headed toward the city. Eileen's village sat on an elevation in the middle of the country, offering a bird's eye view of the island. At night, twinkling house lights spread across gently undulating hills like a smattering of fallen stars laid out on black satin, a romantic sight when seated on a windy hilltop with champagne and a loved one. But tonight, each light mocked Holden, signifying just one of the thousands of places where Eileen could be holed up with a man.

His mind was restless as he drove across the two-lane highway, his elbow resting on the window as he tapped his fingers irritably on the steering wheel. Returning home wasn't an option; surely he'd go mad as he lay in bed watching the shadows and trying not to imagine Eileen with someone else. Without realizing it, he had circled one roundabout three times, driving back and forth as he tried to figure out where to go. Eventually, he clicked on the left indicator and headed to town. Clifford usually spent his evenings at a dingy little rum shop not too far from the funeral home. If Holden showed up, a raised eyebrow and some verbal jabs were certain, but so was a drunken oblivion that would help Holden to sleep for most of the next day.

The car's engine hummed as he drove through the quiet streets. Although the rum shop was just around the corner from Davis and Sons, he purposely took the long way to avoid passing the business. It would be like rubbing salt in an open cavity to pass the spot where they'd met, the place where he'd grown to love her. But there was a crucial miscalculation to his plan since he'd have to bypass Eileen's new place of employment to reach the rum shop. He noticed Eileen's car parked outside Happy Home and his heart skipped a beat. Solace stole over him as he realized that blessedly, instead of being on a date Eileen was at work. No longer needing Clifford's company or alcohol, Holden briefly considered going home, but decided against it. Instead of letting his nerves get the better of him, he'd try to talk to her tonight.

Unlike Davis and Sons that was fashioned after traditional merchant buildings, Happy Home was a long one-storey residential conversion with a hipped roof so deep that it almost doubled the building's height. A single light bloomed from one of the rooms at the rear of the building, a sure sign that Dorothy and Eileen were still at work.

Holden was just about to flick on his indicator when the lights on Eileen's car came on and to his surprise, she pulled onto the road, turning right instead of left. *That's not the quickest way for her to get home*, Holden thought. Something inside his stomach squirmed as he spun the wheel and kept a distance behind her as he followed.

One of the Toyota Crown's brake lights glowed red when it reached the intersection by the Constitution River, turning right onto the winding road and heading into the city. It bypassed the bus terminal and drove straight across the street, leaving Trafalgar Square on the right and heading for the inner ledge of the murky careenage. The narrow arteries were hemmed in by tightly packed clusters of bond buildings.

Many of them were hundreds of years old, strategically placed next to the basin as warehouses. Small fishing boats and shipping vessels bobbed on the water, the moon's reflection mirrored on its inky surface.

Holden felt an uncomfortable sensation course through him. The area was adjacent to the screw dock, the last of its kind in the world and, as such, wasn't a place that saw much activity after nightfall. The only signs of life were the faint strains of music coming from a tiny cafe on the waterfront that glowed like a beacon against the darkness of the careenage. Eileen's headlights dimmed and then went dark as the car turned off the narrow road between the bank of buildings, heading away from the cafe and toward the screw dock.

Switching off his motor, Holden parked and got out of the car to walk through the dark alleyways to see what on earth Eileen was up to. His was the only car on the tiny road and the wind whistled eerily as it barrelled between the tall warehouses. He got to the end of the road and realized that Eileen hadn't parked when she had turned between the row of buildings; not a single car was to be seen. Holden looked around, suddenly uneasy. Eileen didn't like the dark, so why on earth would she come to a place like this at such a late hour to wander?

He turned at the end of the row, his footsteps quickening before he finally broke into a light jog, peering between buildings as he ran and looked for Eileen.

He had reached the end of the row of buildings when he saw the rusty Toyota Crown with its broken rear lights and leaky roof coursing smoothly toward the careenage. Holden stopped short, his mouth agape. The car gathered momentum, the rubber of its spinning wheels squeaking as it made its way to the edge. For a moment, it tottered like a thing intent on defying physics, rocking once, twice like a see-saw with two small children on either half.

Then finally, it gave in to gravity's demands, tipped further forward and with a gut-wrenching splash, fell into the murky water.

Chapter 31
Sink or Swim

Holden stood rooted to the spot. He knew the car had mechanical issues; had the slack handbrake made it roll away after Eileen parked? But the answer to his question became apparent when he saw none other than Dorothy Greaves emerge from a nook at the side of a building. She didn't seem to notice him as she hustled in his direction since Holden was hidden in the shadows of the building. But her nervous gait as she kept glancing back toward the water told Holden that something was wrong. It wasn't the urgent stride of someone hurrying for help but the impatient walk of someone who was trying to get away.

Holden stepped out of the darkness right in front of her and asked, "Where's Eileen?"

Startled, Dorothy staggered backwards, anxiously fixing the wig on her head as she said, "Oh, Holden... didn't know you were here."

"That's not what I asked you," he said impatiently.

Dorothy glanced over her shoulder. Her tone was urgent, sympathetic as though trying to make Holden see reason. "She's no good, you know. Always a million men calling for her at work, going to lunch with a different one every day. She finally got tired of her worthless existence."

Holden's eye twitched. "She's in the car?!" he thundered.

Dorothy pointed to the water. "Maybe you can still save her."

Holden grabbed hold of Dorothy and shook her. To his surprise, the wig fell off and a shiny bald head beneath glinted in the moonlight.

Holden stared at the person before him, his mind trying to reconcile what his eyes saw. "Lloyd...?"

He turned his wrists, tightening his grip on the frilly collar and yanking Lloyd toward him. "Don't play with me! I swear to God I'll take my time breaking each of your limbs."

A twisted sneer played on Lloyd's lips. "Your little girlfriend is drowning, star boy. Where are your priorities?"

Reluctantly, Holden released him and raced toward the edge of the wharf. His heart thudded in his throat as he ran to the spot where the car had fallen in. The careenage was the only stretch of water on the island that often looked dark and bottomless. Visibility was even worse after sunset. Behind him, Lloyd's chunky shoes beat a hasty retreat as he ran off into the night. Without a second thought, Holden dove in.

The water was still warm after a day of relentless sunshine, but there was nothing pleasurable about the way it swallowed him whole as he tried to find the car in its cloudy depths. He had only a trail of air bubbles to guide him; the hint of moonlight that broke the surface wasn't enough to illuminate the car's position. Holden kicked forward, stretching his hands out in front of him, feeling for anything large and solid and praying that Eileen stayed clam so he'd have enough time to locate her. He swam a few feet deeper, but again, all he felt were small fish circling him. His eyes stung, and his lungs strained until finally, he knew he had to go up for air and try again. He turned his head to the surface and kicked upward. A hollow clang echoed through the water when Holden flipped his feet, not unlike the sound of a shoe kicking a car door.

Holden spun around and opened his mouth in astonishment, swallowing a mouthful of the turbid water before he saw the faint outline of the car's roof beneath him. He hurried to the surface, his lungs pumping like bellows as he swallowed gulps of fresh air. Despite the pain in his chest, he dove down again, his lungs protesting as he thrust frantically toward the car. He found it quicker this time, but being more than ten feet beneath the surface made it impossible to see anything at all. His hands roamed over the metal body as it kept sinking, dragging Holden with it as it edged closer and closer to the bottom. He swam quickly, running his hands along the left side of the car, pulling door handles that wouldn't budge and hoping for an open window.

A heavy thud came from inside the car and Holden's heart skipped a beat: Eileen was alive. Relieved that she was still alive, he swam over the top of the car and went to the right side of the car and remembered her faulty rear window that never rolled right up and was always falling. Holden's chest wheezed painfully as he propelled himself downward and slipped his fingers between the edges of the window and its frame. With a shuddering heave, he forced the window down and reached inside. With a jolt of relief, his hands ran over Eileen's unconscious form on the back seat, her wrists bound tight with something that felt like silk. His pulse raced as he grabbed her, pulled her through the window and kicked frantically as he guided them to the surface. Beneath his hand, a weak heartbeat pulsed in her chest, but Holden knew he still had some way to go before he got her to the top. But under his relief, anger coursed through him.

There was no way Eileen could have bound her hands and feet in such a fashion, put the car in neutral, pushed it until it gained momentum and jumped into the backseat before it plunged into the water. Lloyd had lied to him.

Cool air washed over them as their heads broke the surface and oxygen flooded Holden's body. He lay on his back, clutching Eileen to him as he undertook a determined one-armed backstroke toward the embankment. The tide worked in their favour, ushering a tired Holden and unconscious Eileen toward a Moses boat that bobbed gently in the onyx waters. He pushed her into it and then hauled himself up, sputtering and gasping as he fell to the bottom of the tiny boat and got tangled in a damp fishing net. The odour of melts and seaweed filled his nostrils as the boat swayed beneath them.

Every muscle in his body ached as he reached over and puffed air into her mouth and pumped her chest to revive her. His formal training had never required him to keep anyone alive and he'd only become acutely aware of that after his father's accident. He'd asked Clifford to teach him mouth-to-mouth and other life-saving techniques, so determined was he to never feel so helpless again.

He thought back to the night he'd met Eileen, the conversations they'd had, the fear of losing her and he knew that he'd never forgive himself if she died. He wanted the arguments, the kisses, the drives through the country, the candlelit dinners and everything else they'd shared. Tears welled in Holden's eyes at the thought of living without her. He put his fingers against her pulse. A split second later, her back arched, her chest convulsed and Eileen coughed a mouthful of water onto the bottom of the boat. With a grateful shudder, Holden put his arms around her and sighed.

Chapter 32
The Message

Salt water chafed Eileen's throat like sandpaper as it forced its way from her lungs and out of her mouth and nose in a spate of raspy coughs. The first thing she saw when she opened her eyes was a bright sickle moon and a fishing net. A scarf held her hands in place and one of her wrists was bruised and tender.

"Thank goodness you're okay," Holden said as he pushed himself up on one elbow and looked at her. His eyes were bloodshot and his breathing was laboured and for a moment, Eileen's foggy brain tried to remember the bizarre circumstances that had led her here. Then she remembered it all: Lloyd dragging her into her car, driving her to the careenage, her cries when he'd let down the handbrake and pushed it toward the water. It had sunk quickly. She'd sworn she'd die until she'd seen someone floating through the cloudy waters trying to get into the car. The rear window never stayed rolled up and she knew she was taking a chance by kicking it; the force of the blow might have caused it to fall and let in water quicker, but if the person could prise it open, they might be able to get her out. The water had rushed in faster, dragging the car to the bottom, sucking in fishes and snake-like eels. Eileen had tried to hold on, tried to stay alert but she couldn't. The last thing she remembered was feeling someone pulling her out of the car before she lost consciousness.

Holden's eyes never left hers as he reached over and untied the scarf on her wrists. "How are you feeling?" he asked.

She blushed. She never imagined she would see Holden again given what had happened between them and she had never expected him to be her saviour. To know that he had saved her life was surreal. "I'm good. Why?"

"Feeling strong enough to go to the police station and get that demon Lloyd arrested?"

Eileen's eyes blazed with fury. "Yes."

* * *

DERRICKS LOCKED DOWN THE AIRPORT, deployed patrols at major docks and dispatched almost every police car to hunt down Lloyd Greaves. He had looked Eileen and Holden up and down when they'd first walked into Central Station sopping wet and smelling like day old fish. His mouth had fallen open when he'd heard their story and he wasted no time in setting things in motion to apprehend Lloyd. Less than an hour into giving their statements to the officers, a voice crackled over the police radio announcing that Lloyd had been stopped on his way to the airport with a box containing clumps of hair and four bloody scalpels. Derricks clapped Holden on the back and shook Eileen's hand, thanking them for their assistance before he got into a waiting police car, plopped the red siren on the roof and blazed through the night to claim the glory for bringing the Cane Slasher to justice.

Holden lifted an eyebrow and asked, "Ready to go home?" The tone of his voice was unmistakable. To him, a single night had wiped out everything, the bad memories and deal breakers scratched from the record with one act of contrition. But she knew that it wouldn't be enough, it couldn't erase the truth nor fix the cracks that had broken them.

"Yes," she bit her lip nervously. "They said they'd take me home since my car is —well you know. You were there."

Holden grinned and waved a hand dismissively. "I'll take you home."

"Actually..." Eileen took a deep breath "...I'd rather if they took me home." She bit her lip as she lowered her voice and said, "Look, I'm truly grateful that you saved me. And I'll forever be in your debt for that reason, but I'd rather if we didn't try to salvage something just because someone tried to kill me."

Holden tilted his head as though he hadn't heard her properly. "But Eileen..."

She held up a trembling hand and looked down at her feet. "I don't want us to be one of those couples who're on, then off, always tipping the scales trying to find a balance between happiness and misery."

"That's never going to be us."

In the back of her mind, she heard Lloyd's voice: "They get their money's worth out of the assistants."

Eileen shook her head as a tear slipped down her cheek. "Two confirmed bachelors would never be content with driving around collecting bodies. He told me about you and Clifford."

Confusion marred Holden's handsome face. "What about me and Clifford?"

“That you ‘share’ the assistants,” she said making rabbit ears with her two forefingers and pumping them twice when she said the word “share”.

“What?!” He stared at her for a moment before he sank down on the wooden bench behind him and asked, “And you believed him? The man who tied you up and tried to kill you?”

Eileen’s mouth tightened. “You’re not saying it’s a lie so why *shouldn’t* I believe him?”

“Lloyd has always been a chronic asshole, plain and simple. We tolerated the family because of Dorothy but he’s always been a liar. I have *never* once been inappropriate with a single assistant and you should know this.”

She stepped back. “I’m tired and they’re saying I have to go to the hospital for a report —“

“I’ll come with you.”

“No,” she said loudly. “Just stop.” Eileen shook her head irritably. “Thanks for saving me, but I have to go.”

Holden folded his lips, but said nothing as she walked toward the officer waiting for her. He stood on the steps of the station and watched as the policeman opened the back door of a police car and let her in.

When she drove away in the police car clutching a blanket around her, Holden was still there.

* * *

EILEEN SPENT MOST OF THE NIGHT under observation at the hospital. Lloyd had damaged the ligaments in her left wrist, resulting in her leaving the A&E with a bandaged hand and painkillers. Luckily, that was the worst of it. The doctors proclaimed that she hadn't suffered any brain damage from being submerged for so long and they believed she'd made a full recovery. But Eileen knew that she wouldn't feel very lucky once she got home. How could she forget what had happened, the trauma she'd experienced at Lloyd's hands, knowing how close she'd come to death. She sighed when she got into the police car just after sunrise. She'd made it through the ordeal and now, she could only hope to get better.

She'd dozed for a few hours in the hospital so she wasn't overly tired when the constables deposited her at her door. She sorely regretted the loss of her handbag and house keys; they were probably waterlogged and drifting out to sea with the tide. Eileen trudged up the stairs and reached under the mat for the spare key. She was just about to unlock the door when she noticed something glowing in a cardboard box next to the mat. She leaned over and lifted out a jar of fireflies and smiled. Nostalgia stole over her as she watched them fluttering around in their glass enclosure; they reminded her so much of her childhood. As she'd always done in the past, Eileen opened the jar and let them fly into the predawn light like golden confetti adrift on a zephyr. It would never do to keep them captive for a whole day.

There was also a large see-through bag filled with broken chocolate biscuits, two beers and a bulky envelope with a foreign object that slid back and forth inside its paper prison. "Oh, Holden," Eileen said softly to herself. Only he could have left this box at her door: the fireflies she said she loved, the beer and biscuits they ate the first time they had a proper conversation. A tear slipped down her cheek as the memories came flooding back. She thought she could just move on from him, but she couldn't. In a few months, they had clicked into place like two broken halves wanting to be whole. Eileen heaved a deep breath as she looked at the envelope. Did she really want to know what was in it?

She used her house key to slit it open, its jagged edges revealing a thick sheath of papers, a key and a small note written in Holden's neat handwriting. The papers were legal documents with a lot of jargon that Eileen barely understood, but the gist of it was that Holden had submitted a petition to dissolve Davis and Sons, transforming the funeral home into two businesses. Eileen clutched her hand to her chest. She suddenly felt weak; had she been the reason that Holden gave up on his father's dream? It wasn't her intention to break up their family. Eileen pressed her hip against the door jamb and rubbed her temples slowly.

The sun peaked over the balustrade, shining softly on the key and the note in her hand. To her surprise, it was the same one she'd used to access the funeral home when she had to lock up. The note was only a few lines, but it was enough to shake Eileen to the core:

Eileen,

My father used to say sacrifice has no short cuts. It's the only saying he had that I never understood until now. We can't expect any kind of growth without stepping back and taking a chance that what we give up today will make way for a bountiful yield tomorrow. I love Paul, but I trust that throwing him out of the nest will make him a better man in the end. I've enabled him for too long and his antics are not only stressful for me, but everyone else too.

There's room for you in my life, literally and figuratively. Your key is enclosed and everything is upstairs. I hope that you'll take a chance on me too.

Holden.

Chapter 33
A Room for Two

Eileen leaned her head against the door and tried to hold back tears. Adrenaline took over as she rushed inside the apartment, changed her clothes and raced down the stairs to catch the first bus. She cursed Lloyd as she hurried down the uneven road; thanks to him, she had no car and probably wouldn't again for a long time. She sniffed hungrily as she ran. The aroma of bakes, oats and sago hung over the village like a swarm of locusts. Eileen arrived at the bus stop, panting and bent double as she propped herself on the pole and waited. It didn't take long before Debra sauntered past with a bucket of water. "Mornin', where part the car?"

"Good morning. I'm well, thanks for asking. My car got wet."

"Wet?" Debra wrinkled her nose. "Hmph, you talk so pretty, but ain't know you got to roll up the windows to keep out the rain?" Debra shook her head. "You going to town?"

Eileen bit her lip. "Yes."

Debra looked her up and down. "Well, I ain't got time for gossip because I going and get ready for work. But when you come back you could tell me why the tall dark fella with the sexy lips was by your house last night."

* * *

VERY SELDOM HAD EILEEN seen Buckworth Street rendered in its catatonic early morning state. The vendors who lined the road with wooden crates of golden starfruit, bumpy sour sops and spindly cassavas weren't there. Businesses were shuttered, traffic was sparse and not a single pedestrian trod the weather-beaten sidewalk as she slipped the key into the lock and entered the funeral home.

The building felt like a comfortable old T-shirt the way it welcomed her back. The aroma of tea mingled with the woody scent of coconut frond spines and orange oil. The mottled pattern of old grey tiles mixed with new hadn't changed. A crudely sharpened pencil with neat indentations left by her front teeth and a stack of catalogues were exactly where she had left them on her desk. But on top of the catalogues was one thing that wasn't familiar. Eileen picked up the small slip of paper and read the three words written in Holden's neat hand.

Please go upstairs.

Upstairs? thought Eileen. In all the time she'd been there, she had never known there to *be* an upstairs to Davis and Sons, but it suddenly dawned on her that there had to be. The building had two stories, but it had never crossed her mind to ask how to access the second floor. She went inside the viewing room, looked around and noticed for the first time that the wood-panelled walls that ran the full length of the room were unbroken except for the far corner where a waist-high brass handle stared back at her. Surprisingly, the door didn't creak when she pulled it; the smell of grease told her that it had been recently lubricated.

At the top of the narrow steps was an area with a layout similar to that of a living room except that it looked more like an abandoned art gallery. Thin slats of light from the bi-fold doors streamed across the room, landing on two easels and a stack of palettes and brushes. Eileen raised her eyebrows. She wasn't entirely sure what she was supposed to be looking for but before she could search any further, she heard footsteps behind her.

She turned to see Holden standing in the middle of the staircase, his eyes wary as he watched her watching him. He took a step back as though trying to decide if he should leave. She took a step forward.

"Good morning."

"Good morning." He jutted his chin at her bandaged hand. "I didn't know you would have been released from the hospital so soon, but I'm glad you're well for the most part."

"Yeah..." she jutted a thumb toward the floor. "You left me a note telling me to go upstairs."

He shook his head and made to retreat. "No, it's nothing. I just came to pack up...some things."

Silence descended, dwarfing both of them as they stood less than five feet apart. They'd reached an impasse, an awkward moment in which neither of them was sure what to do or what to say. Eileen felt something stir inside her, not lust nor longing, but the sensation she got whenever she was near him. At first she had interpreted it as mutual respect, but as time went on and she noticed the little things about him, became enthralled by them, she knew it was something else.

She took her time broaching the distance between them until she stood two steps above him on the staircase — even then they were barely eye-level in the dimly lit space.

"Why did you tell me to go upstairs?" she asked softly.

"Why does it matter? You said it would never work."

"I don't want to come between you and Paul."

"Hasn't it occurred to you that he's done that himself?" Holden snorted. "I'm not a masochist, you know." He smacked his thighs with his hands. "And frankly, if someone is going to torment me, I'd rather it be you."

Eileen laughed. "I'm not that bad."

He stepped up and held her by the waist as he placed his feet on either side of hers on the landing. "Yes, you are," he said earnestly. He was so close now that his jagged breaths tickled her forehead. "Since you practically hired yourself, I've felt different, almost like I was a robot without batteries until you jump-started me. And you've bloomed here too. You're an incredible business woman and I know we can take over this whole country, and even the region, if we want to."

She glanced behind her at the wide open space and smiled. "So I can paint up here during lunch?"

He beamed and took her right hand, leading her up the stairs until they were standing in front of the easels. "You can paint during lunch if you want to. But I was thinking that we should turn this space into an art gallery for your pieces. I'll build stairs at the side of the building so people don't have to come through the parlour." His excitement was palpable as he let go of her hand and unbolted the bifold doors, throwing them open and flooding the room with light. "Look...imagine how amazing your art will look on the walls when the doors are open."

Eileen's eyes shone. She looked around dumbstruck as she tried to absorb what Holden was saying. She reached out and touched the colourful tubes, fanned her fingertips across the paintbrushes' soft bristles. "M-my own gallery?"

He nodded earnestly. "Yup. I'll hire a new assistant — Clifford's son is interested in the post — so you'll have all the time in the world to paint."

She wrapped her arms around his waist and kissed the tip of his chin. "I can't believe you're willing to do this for me."

He leaned down and kissed her softly, his eyes burning with intensity as he looked at her. "My wife deserves the best."

She pulled away and gazed into his eyes, unsure as to whether she'd heard correctly.

Eileen blushed. "Really?"

"Really."

Holden pressed his lips against hers and for a fleeting moment, in the space where she'd set up her new gallery, in the arms of the man she loved, Eileen's mind flashed back to the dark night they'd met. It dawned on her then that if they were to spend the rest of their lives together that there was no time to lose before she told him her secret.

Chapter 34
The Truth and Nothing but the Truth

Lloyd Greaves' arrest sent shockwaves across the island. The idea of a well-to-do businessman committing murders was enough to set tongues wagging about what other nefarious deeds he might have gotten up to. Commissioner Derricks held a press conference declaring the police force's operation to be a roaring success as he thanked members of the public for their help in apprehending the culprit.

"Well," said Holden as he closed the newspaper the next morning. "I guess Greaves will be going away for a good long time. Derricks provided the prosecutor with enough evidence to see to that."

"Derricks sat on his chunky ass for months and never once listened to anything we told him until it was time to collect the credit," Eileen fumed as she rolled her eyes. "And up to now he can't even find the last escaped prisoner."

Clifford sat on the edge of Holden's desk looking across at her as she grumbled. He chuckled. "At this rate, that fellow is gonna be on the run for the next twenty years."

"Nah..." Eileen waved her hand. "On the run for twenty years on this little two by four island? Impossible."

"Meh," replied Clifford. "Stranger things have happened." He sauntered outside, whistling the cheery tune he always did when he felt sure that his prophesies would come to fruition.

Eileen grinned. She had never come across anyone with such outlandish convictions as Clifford. Holden shook his head wryly. “The day he dies, his brain will be sold to the highest bidder.”

“I’d pay good money to read their findings,” said Eileen with a giggle.

Holden smiled. “So...” his heart caught in his chest as he contemplated her for a moment. “I was hoping we could finish our conversation if you don’t mind.”

She bit her lip and said, “Yes, we can.”

He pushed his chair over to her desk and sat next to her. His mouth grew dry as he tried to recall what he had practiced in the mirror as he had gotten dressed that morning. He studied his fingers for a moment, willing himself not to lose his nerve before he dropped to one knee and pulled a small box from his jacket pocket. “You’re spunky, creative, you make me laugh and if I had to be marooned on a desert island with you, I suspect we’d turn it into a lifelong holiday. I love you.”

The tiny hinge on the velvet box creaked softly as Holden opened it. Inside was an elegant gold band, topped with a glimmering stone.

Eileen rested her hand against her chest and tears formed in her eyes. “I love you too.”

He slipped the band on her finger and kissed her softly. She put her arms around his neck and returned his kiss with such tenderness that Holden thought he would melt in her arms. They pulled apart and rested their foreheads together, they sighed in unison.

“So,” Eileen said. She caressed her fiancé’s cheek. “Should we seek Clifford’s blessing before we run off to get married?”

Holden's deep laugh echoed through the office. "He likes you more than he likes me anyway, so I doubt that will be a problem." He grinned. "I'm glad you two get along so well. Clifford is cordial with everyone, but he never clicked with the other assistants the way he did with you."

Eileen smiled. "He's like the father I never had."

He pursed his lips. "I know it won't make up for the fact that you didn't know your parents, but we'll have a beautiful family of our own some day." His chest grew warm at the thought of having children with the woman in front of him.

Eileen cleared her throat. "I haven't been entirely honest with you about my parents." She tore her eyes away from his and fixed her stare on her fingers as she twisted them together. "I know who they are."

Holden was confused. "Then why say you didn't know them?"

Eileen got up and started pacing, her breath coming in sharp gusts as she spoke. "I didn't lie; I never *met* them. But I *know* who they are."

Holden stood up slowly. Something uncomfortable wormed its way into the pit of his stomach. "Eileen…what are you telling me?"

She took his hands between hers and looked at him with pleading eyes. "I don't want to keep this from you if we'll spend our lives together. But…I didn't want you —or anyone else — to judge me for what my parents did."

She sank down into a chair, a deep frown on her pretty face. "I've heard the rumours," she said bitterly. "I knew how I'd be treated if anyone found out the truth about who I really am."

Loving Eileen was easy, but Holden was suddenly worried for his future wife's safety. Never before had he seen her so agitated. His palms grew sweaty. He wiped them on his pants, knelt in front of her and asked, "Who are you?"

Her eyes met his and for a fleeting moment, Holden feared she would refuse to tell him. That she would run away and he'd be left nursing a broken heart.

"My mother is the woman they call Pretty-Eyed Susan."

He tried to but couldn't stop himself when his mouth fell open. The corners of his mind summoned childhood memories of the biggest political scandal the island had ever seen. Pretty-Eyed Susan's tell-all book had practically forced the country to its knees. For years, no-one knew what had happened to her. Youthful indifference had caused him to forget most of the details, but Holden remembered the merciless taunts that accompanied the infamous nickname that all Caribbean people assigned to traitors.

"You're Susan Taylor's daughter?"

She nodded numbly.

Holden stared at her, his mind pulling together the pieces of everything that had happened since he met Eileen. Everything now made since, coloured with the clarity of Eileen's confession. "Well…it certainly explains why you didn't tell me your name before."

She bit her lip. "My real name is Cordelia Taylor. I go by Eileen because I just never wanted to be affiliated to my mother in any way."

Holden felt faint.

She reached for his hands, her eyes pleading as she said, "I wanted to tell you before. But I didn't want that stigma clinging to me and making life harder than it already is."

She looked him in the eye. "Would you have hired me if you knew?"

In spite of himself, Holden took a moment too long to respond. "Well… I guess that maybe I still might have."

The young woman raised a brow. "There wasn't a single affirming word in that sentence." She sighed. "If you don't want to marry me anymore, I understand."

Colour rose in his cheeks as he looked away. "Eileen — Cordelia — good heavens, what am I supposed to call you?"

"I still like being called Eileen."

"Fine…Eileen. This doesn't change how I feel about you. I've seen you for the woman you really are. You're kind, smart and thoughtful." Holden shrugged. "Truth be told, I was too young to know a lot about what happened, but I do remember my father saying that he couldn't understand why your mother was castigated for telling the truth."

"Really?" her eyes were hopeful.

"'Son, it's a dark day in hell when the truth doesn't light the way.' My father thought it was shameful how the country turned her out on her ear.

"When Watergate happened, my father was quick to point out the parallels. He said the problem was that both Susan Taylor and Martha Mitchell knew too much." Holden shook his head and looked pityingly at Susan's daughter. "Sometimes people just need someone to focus their hatred on. I believe that's all that happened to your mother."

"I guess so," was all she could say. She glanced at him, her eyes hopeful. "And you're sure it doesn't bother you?"

In his heart, Holden knew that nothing about their relationship was conventional. Everything from the way they'd met, to the work they did, to the serial killer they'd hunted down belied a unique connection that wouldn't be easily broken by something as trivial as a parent who was spurned by society.

"No," he said firmly. "All that matters is that you love me."

"I do." She said with a smile.

Holden's heart fluttered. Without a doubt, he believed her.

EPILOGUE

"Hurry, Clifford," Holden said as the two of them raced through traffic. The empty stretcher in the back of the funeral van bumped and rattled against the sides of the vehicle as they sped through the narrow city streets.

"Boss, no offence, but I ain't accustomed to driving passengers that in a rush. You got me nervous," Clifford replied as they turned into the hospital's car park.

Holden's nerves were on edge and he threw open the door and jumped out of the van before Clifford could press the brakes in front of the Accident and Emergency bay. He hastened to the nurse at the front desk who stared back at him with disinterest as she chewed gum. "Nurse…it's an urgent matter. My wife called and said she'd been admitted and I need to see her immediately."

The woman blinked at him. "Did she tell you which ward she was on?"

"Yes…T8."

"Take the stairs to the fourth floor and then turn right. The ward will be three doors down."

Holden took the stairs two at a time, his heart pounding unsteadily as his mind whirred.

He was just about to push the double doors when they burst open. Two nurses ran past him pushing a gurney with his wife's bloated form covered in blankets. "Holden," she gasped in pain as she snatched at his hand. Her palms and forehead glistened with sweat, as she writhed in agony. Holden's heart dropped. He couldn't bear to see his wife in this much pain. He broke into a run, clutching his wife's sweaty palm as he raced in tandem with the nurses down the corridor to the hospital theatre.

"Sir, you'll have to wait out here."

"But I..."

"Sir," the nurse said pointedly. "It's policy. You can either go home or wait here."

Holden sank down on the long bench across from the theatre door. In his mind, he saw his father die again, lying next to him in the mangled car wreck. Reflexively, he yearned for his accounts ledgers, longed for a productive distraction that would help him to pass the time. He closed his eyes and imagined the smell of ink, summoned the feel of crisp pages beneath his fingers and heard the clacking of calculator keys as he reconciled the accounts. Holden exhaled and opened his eyes. His chest felt tight as he kept clasping and unclasping his hands.

"Boss?" Clifford said ten minutes later when he sat next to him. "Babies does born every day. They're gonna be alright."

Holden nodded numbly.

Clifford nudged Holden's foot. "I remember when my son was on the way. So many thoughts in my head but I couldn't grab onto a single one." He grinned and clapped Holden on the shoulder.

Holden wasn't sure why he could never admit it, but Clifford was always a steadying presence in his life and it was times like now when he felt certain that Clifford knew it too. "Yeah...it's just that when you know how fragile we really are that it's hard to automatically assume that everything will be okay."

"Pashaw!" Clifford exclaimed with a surprisingly elegant flick of his wrist. "Young Davis, you does always be reading something or the other. You know we got a low mortality rate for mothers in Barbados."

"Yes, but..."

"Then the odds are in your favour," interrupted Clifford. "Besides, that baby got a sturdy mother. You know full well you can't knock down Eileen just so."

In spite of himself, Holden grinned. "You're right about that."

"Baby looks like her too."

"How do you..." Holden glanced up, his eyes widening as he saw the nurse walking toward him with a swaddled bundle in her arms.

Holden shot up out of his seat and held out his arms when the nurse offered the baby to him. The smallness of the personage in his hands was jarring. It's face mirrored Eileen's with its delicate oval shape, but Holden recognized the cupid's bow lips as his own. His heart fluttered. Seeing a hint of himself in the child stirred warmth in his chest, filling him with the most pride he had ever known. His and Eileen's world had shifted in the past nine months to prioritize the life of someone neither of them had met, but had developed an unconditional love for.

"Boy or girl?" asked Clifford, his face aglow as he stared in awe at the baby.

"A girl," beamed the nurse.

"She's a pretty little thing, ain't she?" said Clifford.

The nurse nodded as though personally responsible for the child's good looks, fussing with the blanket's embroidered hem and stroking the child's covered head.

The baby's eyes had been closed up until that point. As though sensing she were the centre of attention, her little eyelids opened slowly, her sensitive eyes testing the light before she finally fixed her gaze upon her father.

Clifford peered at the child again. "What's wrong with the eyes?"

"Hmm..." the nurse glanced at the little girl. "Oh, they will settle in the first year, but when their eyes start off with that swampy colour, they might end up with green eyes."

"Green eyes?" asked Clifford quizzically.

"Uh huh." The nurse nodded and then shrugged. "Or that kinda mixed-up gold colour that they call hazel."

Holden nodded, a knowing smile on his face. "They'll probably be hazel...just like her grandmother's eyes."

Behind-the-scenes details

This novel is loosely based on the still unsolved murders of five young women that rocked Barbados from 1973 to 1982. This spate of deaths became known as the Canefield Murders because most of the victims were found in cane fields. I invoked creative license, shifted the timeline and condensed that timeframe into a year, setting it in 1985.

I've always found the 1980s to be fascinating in terms of Barbados' culture and history. For that reason, I decided to move the dates of the murder timelines to coincide with other moments in Barbados. The names and circumstances of all of the victims have been changed since they don't accurately represent the events. Only two facts have been maintained: the young women were found primarily in cane fields and the clue that cracked the case was a newspaper vacancy ad.

Don't forget to leave an Amazon review.

Hi there,

I hope you enjoyed 'The Vanishing Girls", the follow up to my first novel "The Girl with the Hazel Eyes'. I loved, loved, **loved** writing this book and I hope you enjoyed reading it.

A huge part of the reason why I relished this experience so much is because all three of the main characters (Eileen, Holden and Clifford) resemble me so much in their own way. I'm somewhat rough around the edges like Eileen, I'm definitely that uppity friend who wouldn't want to play scrabble without vowels like Holden and I'm snarky like Clifford. It's been so much fun sharing bits of my personality with you in this way and I look forward to hearing what you think about "The Vanishing Girls"

As a self-published author, nothing is more valuable to me than feedback and I hope you'll be kind enough to leave an honest review on Amazon and Goodreads. Leaving feedback helps me to become better at writing and publishing so that I may enhance your reader experience. It also helps other readers make informed decisions about if they may enjoy this book.

Scan below to leave a review.

X,

Callie

Muse Magazine

Visit **www.calliebrowning.com** to
sign up for my literary magazine, Muse!

(because, seriously, who wants another boring newsletter?)

Free short stories
New books
Sales & promotions
Exclusive Giveaways
Behind-the-scenes photos

About the Author

Callie Browning was born and raised in Barbados. She is an avid reader and has been writing since 2009. She has won awards for her short stories and her first full length novel, The Girl with the Hazel Eyes, was a finalist in the JAAWP Caribbean Emerging Writer's Prize. She lives in Barbados with her family.

Follow Callie on Instagram, Facebook and Twitter
@BajanCallie

Credits

Cover design by Ebook Launch. Special thanks to Author Annabella for her assistance with information on the preservative preparation of human remains in the Caribbean.

Made in the USA
Middletown, DE
28 September 2021